P9-DWV-376

LORI COPELAND

The Bride of Johnny McAllister

An Avon Romantic Treasure

AVON BOOKS ◆ NEW YORK

AVON BOOKS, INC.
1350 Avenue of the Americas
New York, New York 10019

Copyright © 1999 by Lori Copeland
Inside cover author photo by Mary-Lou Gilbert/Sothern Studio, Inc.
Published by arrangement with the author
Library of Congress Catalog Card Number: 99-94797
ISBN: 0-380-80248-1
www.avonbooks.com/romance

First Avon Books Printing: September 1999

AVON TRADEMARK REG. U.S. PAT. OFF. AND IN OTHER COUNTRIES, MARCA REGIS-TRADA, HECHO EN U.S.A.

Printed in the U.S.A.

WCD   10 9 8 7 6 5 4 3 2 1

REVENGE WAS ALL
HE WANTED ...

Accused of a crime he didn't commit, rough and rugged Johnny McAllister wants vengeance, pure and simple—and a release from his year-long sentence to remain in the dusty, one-horse town of Barren Flats. But suddenly nothing is simple when he gazes into Ragan Ramsey's beautiful, guileless eyes.

UNTIL HE MET HER

Entrusted into Ragan's company, Johnny finds himself sitting down to dinner with the smartest, prettiest, most kissable lady in town—and thinking about all sorts of crazy things, like having a permanent place to hang his hat and a family of his own. These are certainly not the thoughts any self-respecting drifter should be having—but the wary Miss Ramsey is a temptation no red-blooded male could resist. And although the innocent beauty will have no part of him, is it possible she'll succeed where all others have failed, and make an honest man of Johnny McAllister?

"Readers will surely delight in another scrumptious treat from Lori Copeland."

Romantic Times

Prologue

~~~⌒∽○○⌒~~~

California
July, 1876

Trouble's like an ill-fitting shoe: you pay a high price for a poor choice, and can't wait to get out of it.

Johnny McAllister stood before Judge Robert Leonard and waited for the axe to fall. He'd been tried for a crime he didn't commit, in front of a jury that found him guilty with no way to prove his innocence. The judge raised his gavel, and Johnny braced himself.

"Johnny McAllister, you stand accused of robbery of the First Territorial Bank of California." The judge peered solemnly over the rims of his spectacles. "And for kidnapping my daughter, Mary Beth, and scaring the holy pea waddin' right out of her. Please restate your plea."

Johnny glanced at the girl. "Not guilty, your honor."

The judge pointed his gavel at the accused. "You plead not guilty. However, in this court of law the jury finds you guilty, and requests you be hanged by your neck until dead."

Hanged. The word echoed in Johnny's ears. He'd never find Bledso, never avenge his family's death. That gave him more pain than the sentence.

Judge Leonard focused on him. The old man's shock of snow-white hair made him look like an insightful old owl. "You present quite a problem for me, Mr. McAllister. To be honest, I don't know what to do with you. For the life of me, I can't find any way in which you resemble any of the gang of brothers you're accused of associating with. The Puet bunch is as mean as they come and they've ridden together for some time. It doesn't stand to reason that they'd accept a drifter like you in their ranks. You don't fit their profile."

He studied Johnny. "But, I have my duty. Therefore, it is the decision of this court that you, Johnny McAllister, be remanded to the custody of Judge Proctor McMann in Paradise, California, for a period of no less than one year, and no longer than two years. The exact amount of time served will be determined by Judge McMann and the manner in which you serve your sentence."

Johnny's knees threatened to buckle in relief. He wasn't going to hang! One or two years—he could do anything for a couple of years. Hell, he could do three if he had to, and still keep an eye out for Bledso.

Johnny waited as the judge gathered his thoughts.

Peering over the rim of his spectacles again, the magistrate said quietly, "You're wondering why I'm going so easy on you."

"Yes, sir, I am."

"Well—I'm not necessarily convinced that you did rob the bank, if that's any comfort. Of course, you could be pulling one over on me, I'll allow for that. But you saved my daughter from certain harm, and I owe you a debt of gratitude."

His features softened. "Judge McMann is an old friend and trusted colleague. He and I have been working together for the past two years on a program that I will permit him to explain. But foremost, I sense something in you that I don't find in most men who stand before this court."

Johnny couldn't imagine what that would be, but he wasn't going to argue.

"I may never be certain whether you did or did not rob the bank—and we're talking about my money, too. You understand that, don't you, young man?"

"Yes, sir."

"I'm giving you a second chance. Do you know what it means to get a second chance from the law, Mr. McAllister?"

"I do, Judge."

"Good, because not everyone gets a reprieve. I hope to God that you make the best of yours. It isn't likely you'll get another."

Johnny nodded. No one had to explain that the judge had given him a break.

"At the time of your arrest, you carried a handgun." The judge motioned to the bailiff, who laid the pistol in front of him. "It's a fine firearm."

"It belonged to my grandfather."

"Then it must hold a great deal of sentimental value to you."

"Yes, sir, it does." Gazing at the old gun, he could feel Grandpa's arms tighten around him and steady his hands as he sighted the pistol for the first time. The old man's gentle voice brushed his cheek and quieted his turmoil. He'd give up almost anything he owned before parting with that gun.

It was Grandpa who took him in after his parents died, and quieted his nightmares when he woke screaming during the night. The old man had instilled in him a deep respect of right versus wrong. Grandpa was the only one he had after the murders. He felt his presence now as surely as if he stood beside him.

"Your gun will be returned to you at the successful completion of your time with Judge McMann. At that time, you will also receive a just and fair price, along with accrued interest, for the sale of your horse, which will be sold immediately at auction."

He paused, then said quietly, "If a year or two in the custody of Proctor McMann doesn't mold you into a God-fearing, productive citizen, then may God rest your soul, because money or firearms won't do you any good. In the event you fail to serve your sentence, proceeds from the sale of your pistol and horse will go to compensate bank patrons for money lost during the robbery. Do you have any questions, Mr. McAllister?"

"No, sir."

"Are the terms of the sentence clear?"

Johnny nodded. Serve the sentence without incident, and he'd go free. Violate the rules, and he'd spend twenty years in prison at hard labor, or worse.

"Crystal clear."

Chapter 1

Paradise—aka Barren Flats

Ragan Ramsey parted the judge's parlor curtains, her eyes widening as she got her first glimpse of the prisoner. He came into town handcuffed inside a buckboard, dressed in black, looking meaner than sin and three times as evil.

The buckboard rattled to a halt in front of the house. Two men with badges, rifles, and holstered firearms climbed down, knocking dust off their clothing. One moved to the back of the wagon and unlocked the prisoner's shackles, then nudged him out of the wagon bed with the barrel of his rifle.

Ragan stepped onto the porch, wiping her hands on her apron.

The man in back got out slowly, his dark gaze fixed on the officer. Motioning toward the house, the lawman shoved the prisoner through the gate and followed him up the walk.

Resentment burned hot in the bound man's gaze. Ragan's pulse quickened. His scruffy appearance couldn't hide the pride and defiance of his stance. He looked as if he hadn't slept in days; purplish-blue circles ringed his dark eyes, eyes that suddenly raised to meet hers without apology or shame.

She swallowed against the sudden dryness crowding her throat. The man's raw masculinity nearly stole her breath, and she shivered against a sudden premonition that he was going to be more—much more—than she'd bargained for.

Thick road grime layered his clothes, and his hair hung limp and dirty beneath a black hat. She would have to be sightless to ignore the broad set of his shoulders, the muscular, unyielding stance, the square chin that jutted defiantly upward.

A cold chill raced down her back. This man was not only the most handsome man she had ever seen, but also the most dangerous looking. She swallowed.

One guard paused in front of the steps and touched the brim of his hat. "Afternoon, ma'am."

Ragan's gaze focused on the prisoner's foot shackles. It took a moment for her to force her eyes up. "Would you care to come in for a cool drink?" The men were dusty and obviously trail worn.

The officer shook his head curtly. "Much obliged, but we'll be movin' along as soon as our business here is completed."

She stepped aside, allowing room for them on the porch. Digging the barrel of the rifle into the man's side, the lawman moved the prisoner slowly up the stairs. The iron shackles clanked against the wood.

Ragan's gaze took in the criminal's soiled boots. Old, scuffed—in bad need of new heels. He'd be visiting Jerald Hubbard's shop first thing, if she had any say in the matter. Her eyes raised to the prisoner's face, and she shivered again. It would take a lot more than a new pair of boots to improve this man's spirits.

For some crazy, unfathomable reason, she felt his humiliation. He and others like him had ruined her town: she should feel nothing but revulsion. Instead, she felt pity. Pity that the young, incredibly virile man hidden beneath all that grime would throw his life away for a few moments of excitement and a bag of bank money. Maybe Procky was right to agree to take him.

He looked her way, and she stepped back. Then again, maybe Procky wasn't.

The guards paused before the screen door. "Where would you like him, ma'am?" one asked.

The judge suddenly appeared in the doorway in his wheelchair, his face flushed from an afternoon nap. His thatch of gray hair stood on end. "Bring him into the parlor, officer." He opened the screen, and the aroma of frying chicken penetrated the air. Judge McMann smiled. "Come in, son. It's hot out there."

The men stepped inside, and one officer knelt to unlock the ankle manacles. Straightening, he tipped his hat. "I'd watch this one, Judge. He's a hardhead."

Judge McMann nodded. "Thank you, gentlemen. Sure you won't stay to supper?"

As he chatted with the sheriff's men, Ragan stepped into the foyer with the prisoner, flicking at imaginary dust on the hall table. She supposed she was uncomfortable because the prisoner was near her own age. Or was it because, criminal or not, he was the most attractive man ever to come to Paradise? She felt flushed again, unusually heated for this time of day. Patting her warm cheeks, she avoided his eyes.

The man stood quietly, hands folded in

front of him. His stance made it clear he wasn't inviting conversation, so she didn't have to worry about entertaining him. She smoothed her dress, aware she must look a sight. She'd been cleaning all day—maybe she would put on a clean apron before supper. . . . She slid another sidelong glance at the prisoner, feeling heat spread through her.

Well, this is plain silly, she told herself when she felt perspiration begin to dampen her back. They couldn't stand in this strained silence all day! The judge was a talker, and her chicken would need turning.

"You must be thirsty. Would you like a glass of tea?"

The man shook his head, his dark eyes avoiding hers.

"Well, Procky does tend to go on at times. I'll show you to your room."

Judge Leonard had said the prisoner wasn't considered unduly dangerous. He wasn't to be locked behind bars, but his whereabouts were to be known by Ragan or Judge McMann at all times until they felt comfortable giving him more freedom. Ragan didn't care for the idea of trusting a prisoner with any freedom, especially since the last two adult prisoners had proved Judge Leonard's judgment wrong.

She climbed the stairs leading to the second landing, motioning for the prisoner to follow. He carried a small brown satchel. Pity that a man's whole life could be carried in such an insignificant bag.

Opening the door to the east bedroom, Ragan smiled. "I think you'll be comfortable here." The room was her favorite of the guestrooms. Sunny in the morning, shaded during the hot afternoons. Maddy McMann had stitched together the pretty wedding-ring bedspread the year she died. The walls were wallpapered blue, and the old lilac bush beneath the open window perfumed the room with its heavenly scent.

The prisoner's gaze traveled the room dispassionately, and she couldn't tell if he liked it or not. She supposed it didn't matter; he had no choice. It would be his home for the next twelve to twenty-four months.

"You'll be needing a pitcher of water for the wash bowl," she said softly. "I'll get you one."

He nodded, setting the valise on the floor, and she hurried to the door.

"Is that it?" His voice was deep. Deep, and disturbingly masculine. Heat suffused her cheeks again, and she wondered if she was coming down with something.

She turned. "Oh—sorry. Breakfast is at six, dinner at noon, and supper at five o'clock sharp. Please try to be prompt—Procky gets cranky if he doesn't eat on time."

He lifted a questioning brow.

"Procky—Judge Proctor McMann. His friends call him Procky." She supposed he wouldn't find that information all that useful. "And one other thing: no profane language. Ever."

His gaze roamed the room again, coming to rest on the open window. "Are you the judge's daughter?"

"No, his housekeeper. I leave after the supper dishes are done and return to fix breakfast."

His eyes came back to meet hers briefly. Goose bumps rose on her arms as his dark gaze boldly assessed her. "That's all that's expected of me? Show up for meals on time?"

"And don't curse."

He gave her a hard look.

"You rest up from your trip and eat your supper. The judge will let you know what's expected of you later."

He turned and walked to the window. Pushing the curtain aside, he looked out. "I'm not hungry."

"Oh . . . well, you'll have to sit at the table anyway." Prisoners attended meals, hungry or not.

He slowly turned to face her, his dark eyes locking with hers.

"I'll get that water for you," she said.

"Don't bother. I can wait on myself."

Kitty shot through the door, darting between the man's legs. He looked down as the cat purred, rubbing her whiskers against his boot.

"That's Kitty, the judge's pride and joy. If she bothers you tonight, just push her off the bed. She'll likely end up trying to sleep with you."

The man's expression said she wouldn't be sleeping with him.

Not tonight.

Not ever.

"Well—if you'll excuse me," Ragan murmured. It was this insufferably hot weather making her feel faint. "My chicken needs turning."

She left the room, pulling the door closed behind her. Leaning against the doorframe, she released her breath, rapidly fanning her hands in front of her face. She always hated this part—laying the basic ground rules. The judge left that to her, and the prisoners almost never took to the restrictions. She thought about the dark, dangerous man behind the door and fanned harder. This one troubled her.

Her legs felt a bit shaky as she descended the stairs, thinking about the coming months. How would she ever manage this man? Judge Leonard expected Procky and her to set his scuffed boots on a righteous path, but at the moment, that seemed highly unlikely.

She couldn't even be sure she'd convinced him to come downstairs for supper.

Well, the judge couldn't fault her. She'd warned him this prisoner would be trouble. From the moment Everett delivered the wire from Judge Leonard, she'd been against it.

"Want me to get that?" the judge asked when the knock had sounded at the door.

"No, stay where you are." Ragan wiped her hands on her apron and went to answer it. When she opened the door, she found Everett Pidgin trying to catch his breath. The lanky telegraph operator panted as though he had run all the way from the telegraph station. His breath came in ragged jerks. He eyed Ragan, flushing four shades of red before he could state his purpose. "Afternoon, Miss . . . Miss Ragan."

"Hello, Everett."

"Tele . . . telegraph just came in for the judge. I came as soon as I could."

He looked for the entire world like a puppy that wanted his owner's approval for retrieving a thrown stick. Ragan had to squelch the urge to say, "Good boy."

"Telegraph for me?" The judge made his way to the door to join them. "Now who could be sending me a telegraph?"

Everett grinned, his eyes fixed on Ragan. "Robert Leonard in Barrow County."

"Robert?" Judge McMann quickly scanned the missive.

Ragan returned Everett's smile. "It's warm out there today. Would you like to come in for a glass of lemonade?"

The besotted young man took a step backwards, and promptly dropped off the front of the porch. He landed in the rosebush at the side of the steps, spindly legs floundering in the air.

Ragan hurried down the steps to assist him. "Everett, are you hurt?"

The embarrassed messenger thwarted her efforts. Arms flailing, he rolled to his feet, red-faced. "Not hurt, thank you, just a misstep. Could happen to anybody."

She reached to brush off a clump of leaves, but he backed away.

Jerking his suit jacket into place, he stalked off, opened the whitewashed gate, and then latched it carefully. Striding toward the telegraph office, he kept his chin held high. She probably should have told him about the rose branch dangling from the *back of his jacket, but it would only embarrass him further.*

"Poor man's got it bad," the judge chuckled when Ragan came back into the house.

"I know, and I wish he wouldn't think of me in a romantic vein. He's had his share of rejection, and I don't want to hurt him further."

Everett was a wonderfully kind young man, but Ragan had no fanciful feelings for him. His infatuation with her made him the laughing stock of Barren Flats. He had been in love with her since he was in the first grade, and she was in the fifth. He refused to accept the fact that she didn't love him back. She'd tried, desperately tried, to center his interests elsewhere, but he only had eyes for her.

After Sunday services, he followed her around like a lovesick fool. During the week, he waited outside the mercantile to carry her parcels.

If the sun was too hot, Everett was there with a parasol to shade her. If it rained, he held an umbrella over her head.

He laid his coat across puddles to spare her shoes.

When it snowed, he shoveled a path in front of her.

It was a wonder he found time to run the telegraph office! He smothered her, yet she couldn't and wouldn't hurt his feelings.

"Well, well." The judge had refolded the message, following Ragan into the kitchen. "Seems we're about to have company again."

She whirled to face him. "Procky, not again! You said we had enough material." The last case had left just a few weeks earlier. She'd hoped for a few weeks of peace and quiet.

"It is a little soon, but we'll manage."

Who was Judge Leonard sending now? Hopefully it wasn't another fifteen-year-old. Last year, Joey Wester almost did them both in.

"This particular fellow is a little older than you," the judge mused. "Says here he's twenty-seven."

Ragan's heart dropped. "Robert promised no more adults, Judge." The last one had put the program in serious jeopardy: Ed Harris had walked away before the first week was out.

"I know, but Robert must feel this case is an exception. We do need the documentation, you know."

"Wire Robert back and tell him we can't accept another adult, and make it stick this time, Procky. We agreed we could limit the experiment to youngsters."

"Not much we can do about it now," the judge said. "The prisoner is already on his way."

Ragan groaned.

"One last try," the judge soothed. "If this one doesn't work out, then you have my promise, we will quit the adult aspect of the program and complete the book as is." The old man chuckled. "If Robert knew about all the trouble we're having with gangs here he'd never send us another case." The judge dumped cream into a saucer and set it on the floor for Kitty. "He'd insist that I move."

Ragan cracked an egg into the bowl. "If we had the sense God gave a goose, we'd all move."

"And where would we go, missy?"

"I don't know, anywhere but Barren Flats." Ragan added more salt, then began to knead the dough.

"I'm not going anywhere. This is my home." The judge's faded eyes roamed the kitchen, pausing on the cracked floor covering, walls begging for paint, and cabinets needing repair. The old house was falling down around his ears, but that obviously wasn't important to him.

"This is where I brought Maddy the day I married her. This is where my three children were born, where two died of smallpox. Maddy drew her last breath there on the parlor sofa." His tone wavered as it always did when he reminisced about Maddy and the twins, and he blinked to clear the mist from his eyes.

"I'm an old man. I'm not leaving the only home I've ever known. Paradise is where I was born, and it's where I'll die. No matter how bad it gets, I'll stay right here. They'll bury me right out there next to Maddy. No-good hoodlums aren't going to run me off."

Covering the bowl with a cloth, Ragan set the dough on the counter to rise. The judge was lonely. His only living relative was his son, Blake, who lived in Colorado. They were seldom able to see each other, and the judge had never made the trip to Denver.

She sighed. "When will the prisoner be arriving?"

"The wire didn't say. I'd guess soon, if I know Robert. He insists on swift justice. He'll either hang a man or dole out suitable punishment. He won't keep a man guessing."

Ragan yelped when she walked back into the kitchen and smelled the chicken burning. Jerking off the skillet lid, she turned the scorched pieces, her mind still on the dangerous man who now occupied the east bedroom. She'd bet her last dollar that Procky was making a mistake by agreeing to take this one.

And she was rarely wrong about these things.

Chapter 2

So *this is Paradise*, Johnny thought.

Someone needed to buy Judge Leonard a dictionary.

Main Street stretched north to south and appeared to have the necessities. He'd noticed a livery and blacksmith shop as they came into town. Then they'd passed a general store, a mercantile, telegraph office, bank, the sheriff's office, saloon, surveyor's office, and title office. Didn't look like a place where there'd be much buying and selling going on, though. As near as Johnny could tell, there wasn't a whole lot else to the town.

Houses were strung along McMann's street, and at the south end there was a steepled white building that looked to be in bad shape. Various stretches of land supported cattle a few miles out.

Johnny let the curtain drop back into place,

his mind going back to that ill-fated day two weeks earlier.

Stepping down from his saddle, Johnny climbed the three wooden steps to the First Territorial Bank of California and scanned the row of weathered wanted posters flapping in the hot breeze for information on the outlaw Dirk Bledso. Two smiling women emerged from the land title office, and he touched the brim of his hat.

"Morning, ladies."

They eyed his trail-worn appearance and the dark, ragged shoulder-length hair. Chins tilting upward, they pointedly looked in the opposite direction. One raised a dainty lace handkerchief to her nose and sniffed as she passed.

And a good-morning to you, mister. He wasn't surprised by their lack of civility. A lot of folks didn't cotton to drifters.

His gaze shifted back to the posters. No telling how old these things were. He smoothed a torn fragment, holding it down with his palm. Outlaw Jack Brooks, wanted for thieving horses. He'd been hanged two years back, in seventy-four, for his crimes.

A gust of hot wind ruffled the tattered flyers and Johnny reached to steady one. Nothing posted about the Bledso brothers, in particular Dirk— the yellow-bellied coward who had consumed Johnny's life since the day he shot and killed the

McAllister family. Bledso, known in some circles as the Viper, always seemed to be one county ahead of him. Then about two years ago, all news of the Bledso brothers had dried up. They seemed to have vanished from the face of the earth.

The slaughter drilled through Johnny's mind as it had hundreds of times in the past fifteen years— Mama's screams, her pleas that the children be spared. Baby Elly's frightened whimpers while little Lara slept, never knowing the danger she faced. Johnny's hand tightened into a fist. Pa's angry shouts, in his struggle to save his family, rang in his ears. The images cut through his soul like a knife.

Memories tightened Johnny's stomach, and the acrid taste of sun-dried hay choked him. Sweat rolled down his temples into his shirt collar as he huddled in the barn loft, terrified for his own life. No twelve-year-old should have to witness such carnage. Hell, no one of any age should be subjected to that.

A ruckus inside the bank jerked Johnny back to the present. Raised voices barked orders, getting persistently louder. He stepped toward the open door just as three masked men burst through in a hail of bullets. Two aimed their pistols over their shoulders, returning the fire.

A big man with a bushy red beard encircled the waist of a young, screaming girl with one arm *while he shot with the other. Fighting to break free, the girl kicked and struggled.*

Johnny stepped out of the way, dodging another round of bullets. Instinctively, his hand flew to his holster. Before he could pull his pistol, the frantic girl latched onto his hand. His fingers reflexively clamped around her arm and he pulled, trying to break her assailant's grip.

The outlaw held on.

"Let go of her!" Johnny shouted.

The bearded man tightened his hold, trying to drag his hostage toward a waiting horse.

Diving in headfirst, Johnny knocked the man to the ground. They scuffled, each trying to gain control of the hysterical girl.

The young woman kicked and clawed. Her skirt flipped over her bonneted head and Johnny found himself blindly grappling with a sea of frilly petticoats. Bystanders stood glued to their spots, eyes wide and mouths agape.

A fourth man backed out of the bank, guns blazing. Two doors away, the sheriff and a deputy spilled from their office, weapons drawn. Bullets zinged and ricocheted in rapid-fire volleys.

Johnny finally gained control of the female. He tucked her close, and in a split-second decision, he made a break for his horse, shielding her with his body. The girl fought like a wildcat, flailing and squealing, pounding his chest as he forced her across the porch, keeping low.

She dug her toes into the boards. "Let go of me this instant!"

Clamping his arm tighter around her waist, he grasped the saddle horn, and his foot found the stirrup. Something heavy suddenly slammed into his chest and wedged itself between him and the girl. Teetering in the stirrup, he strained to balance, then swung into the saddle, positioning her protectively in front of him. His spurs dug into the horse's sides.

The four bank robbers disappeared in a hail of bullets, hightailing it out of town.

Dust rose in red plumes as the sheriff and his deputy returned fire toward the disappearing cloud.

"Put me down! Let me go!" The girl twisted and gave Johnny a hard uppercut to the jaw. His teeth rattled, and stars floated overhead. He fought to stay astride, biting back the metallic taste spreading through his mouth. She could have knocked out his teeth with that blow! He did an inventory—uppers, then lowers—all there. The only casualty was his tongue.

Tightening his grip on her, he warned, "Don't do that again, young lady." He grasped her wrists, pinning them against the saddle horn. The big sorrel galloped headlong down the road.

"You put me down this minute!" She thrashed, striking out until her heel connected with his shin.

"I'll be only too glad to do that—as soon as the sheriff catches up and has the robbers in sight." He glanced over his shoulder, spurring the horse harder.

Lawmen pounded behind them, firing their weapons. Whipping the sorrel faster, he kept the retreating bank outlaws in sight. Far ahead, the four gunmen cut off the road, and ducked into a creosote thicket.

The girl twisted in the saddle and looked back at Johnny, her face contorted. Johnny swore under his breath and hitched her tighter. "Now, don't you start crying on me. You're all right."

"Are you going to hurt me?" she whimpered. Her body quaked against his chest.

"Hurt you? Why would I hurt you?" He was trying to save her from harm. "Just calm down, this will be over in a few minutes."

He slowed enough to trail the robbers but stay out of their range. With the girl in front, he couldn't take a chance of her taking a bullet. The sheriff and his posse were closing in. Soon the thieves would be apprehended, and the girl could be safely returned. He cut the horse through the thicket, and up a steep embankment.

A bullet zipped by his ear. He bent lower in the saddle, glaring back at the posse. Why didn't they hold their fire? The robbers were out of range. "My daddy's going to be very unhappy," *the girl promised, her voice jolting with each hoof beat.*

Her daddy would be unhappy? What about him? One minute he was minding his own business reading the wanted posters, and the next he was in the middle of a bank robbery, trying to save her hide. And she was complaining? He ducked another round of fire.

She started sobbing, great, anguished wails, and Johnny finally had enough. To hell with the robbers; let the lawmen do their jobs without his help. Slowing the horse, he awkwardly patted the young woman's heaving back. "Okay, okay. it's over. I'm not going after them. Dry your tears— you're safe."

She shook her head, sobbing louder. "You're horrible—and—and you're mean! You robbed our bank, and kidnapped me. You are in so much trouble!" She glared at him, then her lip quivered, and the corners of her mouth dipped downwards.

"Robbed your bank? Do you think I was a part of that?" The irony of the situation hit him. Hell yes, that's what she thought—why wouldn't she? He did a quick take at the fast-approaching posse. Did they think he was part of the gang? "Lady, I didn't rob that bank."

"Oh, yes you did, too." She sniffed. "I saw you."

Damn! Shifting her to the side, he eased her to the ground. He was getting out of here. "Stay right there. The posse will take you home. I'm out of this. They don't need me anymore."

She gazed up at him, tears spilling from her big brown eyes.

Johnny glanced at the dust raised by the disappearing gang, then at her. "Look, I know what you think, but I'm not one of them."

She sniffed again. "Well, if you're not a bank robber, what do you have in that bank bag?"

He glanced down, and his stomach pitched. A bank bag lay in his lap. He recalled the feel of it being slammed against his chest when he mounted back at the bank. He swore and quickly tucked the bag into his saddlebag, fumbling with the strap. He'd have a devil of a time explaining this.

A shot whizzed by his ear, and his mount lunged forward. He let the horse have his rein. They hanged bank robbers in this state. He turned for a final glance at the girl who stood, hands on her hips, in the middle of the road.

"You can't just leave me here!" she wailed, stomping her foot. She hopped up and down, stamping and yelling.

Whipping his horse, Johnny flew down a ravine. The sorrel's hooves pounded the brush, then slid on loose rock. The posse was on his heels now. Damn—he just should have stayed at the bank and let the law handle it. How had he gotten himself into this mess?

* * *

Johnny grimaced, coming back to the present. He turned, his eyes roaming the small bedroom. It was cheerful enough: papered walls, a homey spread on the bed. A lot of time and love had gone into the handwork. He touched the pattern, running his fingers along the intricate stitching.

Grandma had made quilts. On summer evenings she sat on the front porch, a basket of outgrown clothing by her side. She cut and sewed for hours, patiently explaining the history behind each scrap of fabric, weaving stories and spinning tales as she sewed.

Elly especially loved the pink remnant of her baby blanket, and Lara always pointed a chubby, dimpled finger at the flower print of Ma's work dress. Winters, Grandma sat by the fireplace, her needle flashing as she tackled her piecework with a vengeance. That seemed a lifetime ago. He turned from the window. It *was* a lifetime ago.

He moved to the side of the bed and sat down, careful not to muss anything. Sitting up straighter, he bounced once, testing the old mattress. It had been a long time since he'd slept in a real bed. Months, maybe a year.

He lifted a pillow and smelled the soap, sunshine, and fresh air. A far cry from his sleeping bag. Arranging the pillow carefully back in place, he glanced around him. What was he doing here? Instead of searching for Dirk Bledso, he was stuck in a blue-flowered prison with a quilt made from scraps of a shirt an old man wore fifty years ago.

A light tap sounded at the door, and he waited. A few seconds later the knock sounded again, followed by a woman's voice. "I have your water."

Lord, she was stubborn. He'd told her he'd get it himself. It had been a long time since he'd had a pitcher of water in his bedroom. It had been a long time since he'd had a bedroom. "Leave it in the hall."

The bowl clanked as she set it down. "Mr. McAllister?"

He ignored the effect that her warm voice had on him—stirring things best left unstirred. "Yes?"

"I cannot overly emphasize how the judge likes his meals on time. Supper is at five." Johnny glanced at the clock over the bedstead. It was ten of five.

When he didn't answer, she rapped softly. "Did you hear me?"

"I heard. I'm not hungry." Or deaf. Or in the mood to think about how long it had been since he'd enjoyed a woman's company. Too long, according to his body. Was this part of Judge Leonard's sentence? Make him think he was getting off easy, then entrusting him to a jailer who wore her dress like a weapon? Was that his punishment?

"Are you coming?"

"Pretty soon."

He wasn't about to go sit at a stranger's table and make polite conversation. He had nothing to say. Well, he did, but she wouldn't want to hear it.

"Oh," she said from the other side. "That is a problem. Judge McMann hates cold food. Well, go ahead and unpack your clothes. Supper won't be on the table for another few minutes." Her footsteps were barely audible as she went back downstairs.

Johnny got up and walked to the dresser. How long would it take to unpack an extra pair of pants, a shirt, and a change of longjohns? There were three large drawers in the chest. Great. One for pants, one for shirts, and one for underwear. He found that the bottom drawer already held an extra blanket. He'd need an extra blanket in this desert town about as much as he needed Miss Blue Eyes coming on to him.

Grinning, he stretched, moving to the north window. That thought was considerably more pleasant than any he'd had lately. Leaning out the sill, he watched the lazy activity below. It was strange—everything looked shot to pieces.

Scents drifted up the stairway, and he turned and stared at the closed door. Something smelled mighty good. His stomach growled. Maybe he would go down to supper. No, he was a prisoner: if they wanted him to eat, they could bring his meals to him.

He sat back down on the side of the bed. He'd be so docile they'd think they were baby-sitting the archangel Gabriel himself. He'd keep his nose clean and his eyes open for word of Dirk Bledso. Maybe he'd get lucky, and Bledso and his no-good cutthroat, yellow-bellied, baby-murdering brothers would save him the trouble of tracking them down. Lying back on his pillow, he closed his eyes. Maybe, with a little luck, they'd pay him a visit right here in "Paradise."

And when they did, he would kill them. One by one, he'd put a hole through each of their black hearts, then kick dust in their faces before he walked away.

His stomach rumbled again.

That chicken smelled good.

The sun sank lower. Johnny lay across the bed, careful not to muss the quilt. The hands on the clock crept past five, then five-thirty. Six. Quarter to seven. He could hear the judge's voice, and what did she say her name was? Ragan. Ragan, with the long, blond hair and smiling blue eyes.

Seven o'clock, and not a hint of a breeze came through the open window. His eyes fell on the slop jar. There was no way he was using one of those, so he opened the door and quietly descended the staircase, heading for the outhouse. Muffled voices floated up from the first floor.

Pausing on the landing, he glanced toward the dining room and did a double take when he saw the woman and the judge sitting at the table. Their plates were clean, napkins folded carefully at the side, the silverware untouched on each napkin. A third place was set opposite the woman.

The judge spotted him and smiled. "There you are. Take your seat, Mr. McAllister, supper is getting cold."

Ragan rose to pour him a glass of tea. Platters of food that had been hot two hours ago sat stone cold in the middle of the table. She motioned to the chair. "I'll get the biscuits out of the oven."

Johnny edged through the doorway and sat down, his eyes trained on the judge. What was this? Some sort of joke?

When Ragan returned, Judge McMann waited until she sat down, then bowed his head. "Dear Lord, bless this food to the nourishment of our bodies. Thank you for blessing us with the presence of yet another of your children at our table. Let us be a light unto his path and a lamp unto his feet. Amen."

He looked up pleasantly. "Mr. McAllister, I hope you like fried chicken and biscuits—please, help yourself."

Johnny shook his head. A loony bin. He'd been sentenced to a damned loony bin. "I'm not hungry."

"Nonsense. A man has to eat." The judge picked up a bowl of greens and dished up a healthy serving onto his plate. "We've found if we keep our meals on time, the day runs more smoothly. Breakfast is at six, dinner at noon, and we prefer supper to begin at five." He handed Johnny the bowl of greens. "And we do appreciate our guests being on time. Try to remember that."

Johnny was about to pass the greens along untouched, but Ragan calmly ladled a serving onto his plate. "Do you like sorghum with your biscuits, Mr. McAllister? Or do you prefer butter?"

Two fat biscuits plopped onto his plate before he could protest.

"Butter . . . I guess."

The chicken was cold and so was the

gravy, but it was the best cold gravy and chicken he'd ever eaten. Before he realized it, he was putting food away like a half-starved animal. When apple pie was served, he downed two pieces, feeling ashamed of himself. He hadn't tasted food this good since Grandma died.

Judge McMann rolled his wheelchair back from the table, a merry twinkle in his eyes. "I like to see a man with a healthy appetite. Another slice of pie, Mr. McAllister?"

"No. Like I said, I wasn't hungry." Johnny pushed his empty plate aside. He met Ragan's laughing eyes—Lord, they were blue—then looked away.

The judge chuckled. "My dear old mother used to say she'd rather feed a hungry man than one who wasn't hungry any day of the week—saved on food. Better reconsider that other piece of pie: you'll need your strength. You're doing the dishes tonight. Supper's run late, and Ragan needs to be getting on home."

Dishes! He'd rinsed out his own coffee cup for years, and washed a skillet in a stream occasionally. He'd never washed a whole pan of dishes.

Judge pulled a pipe out of his pocket. "We all take our turn at the sink."

Ragan picked up their plates and the food

bowls, disappeared into the kitchen, and came back in a few moments untying her apron.

"I'll just gather my things." She moved aside as the judge wheeled by her and into the parlor.

"Be careful walking home."

"Thank you, I always am." She turned back to Johnny, who still sat at the table, uncertain what he should do. She seemed to read his thoughts, and he didn't like it. His thoughts were his own; the law couldn't take those away from him. She smiled, and he fought the unwelcome stirring inside. It had been a long time since a woman's look affected him this way.

"You'll find hot water on the stove. Clean dish cloths and towels are in the top drawer, on the right side of the sink."

They were serious—they wanted him to wash dishes! He'd expected to do men's work while he was here; since when did a man wash dishes?

"Any questions?"

"What's the chance of an early parole?"

"None yet," she said softly. "Be sure to rinse the dishes twice with scalding water."

Johnny doused the soap off the last dish and laid it on a clean towel to drain. He glanced up when the judge wheeled into the kitchen.

"Looks like you found what you needed."

Johnny nodded and hoped his sentence didn't include keeping the old man company.

"Hmmm," Judge McMann pulled on his pipe, sending a plume of smoke towards the ceiling. "Not much of a talker, are you?"

"No. Don't have a lot to say."

The judge chuckled. "The world might be a better place if more folks thought that way. Well, no matter. We have plenty of time to get acquainted."

Johnny picked up a dish and dried it. That was an understatement. Two years in this tea parlor wasn't going to be easy.

Judge McMann drew on his pipe thoughtfully. "Tasty chicken—Ragan's a good cook. She's a fine woman: all the Ramsey girls are. It's surprising Ragan's not been snatched up by some young man, but the girls have their hands full with their father."

"Yes, sir." Johnny wasn't sure what he was expected to say, but he was sure the judge spoke the truth. Ragan was a fine-looking woman. The way her hair caught the sunlight, the ready smile. A man could get used to a woman like that.

"Fulton Ramsey's well thought of in this

town, and we don't make light of his problems." Judge McMann leaned forward, knocking the ashes out of his pipe onto a plate. He repacked the pipe bowl and lit it. "He's led many a man to God in his day. Now that his mind's taken leave of his body, folks look after him. He spends his time whittling and telling Bible stories to the children. I feel real sorry for the Ramsey girls. Lost their mama early on; now they have a hard row to hoe."

Johnny dried a skillet and set it aside. Ragan Ramsey's problems weren't his concern. Getting involved with other people's problems had landed him here, and he wasn't about to repeat the mistake.

Ragan came into the kitchen carrying a wicker basket. "I'll be running along now, Judge."

"Hold on a minute, missy. I want to talk to the two of you while I've got you both in one place."

Johnny mentally groaned, hoping that a lecture wasn't coming. He'd had about all of this cockamamie sentence he could take today.

Judge motioned him toward a chair. "Sit down, son."

Glancing at Ragan, Johnny lay the dishcloth aside and took a seat. Ragan sat across the table from him, looking uneasy.

"Mr. McAllister, I guess you're wondering what's expected of you," the judge began.

Johnny's eyes shifted to Ragan. "She told me."

"She did?"

Ragan's eyes widened. "I told him no profane language and that you like your meals on time, nothing more."

"I understand the rules," Johnny snapped. "I'm a prisoner; not a moron."

The air in the room suddenly charged as the young couple faced off.

Sitting up straighter, Ragan met his stare. "Mr. McAllister, I'm getting a little weary of your attitude. I have been trying my best to be nice to you. I offered hot water and invited you to supper, and you refused both courtesies."

"I don't like fried chicken."

"You ate *four* pieces."

His eyes narrowed. "I was *hungry*."

She glared back at him. "You said you weren't."

"Get off my back, lady. I don't need a mother hen clucking over me; I can take care of myself." He looked out the window.

"Obviously, you haven't," she muttered.

He snapped back to confront her. "Where do *you* get off telling me how to run my life?"

"Where do you get off talking to me like a—"

"Children!" The judge threw up his hands. "We're having a simple conversation. Let's not turn this into an all-out war."

Crossing his arms, Johnny refused to meet Ragan's eyes. He had one nerve left and she was stepping on it.

Judge McMann cleared his throat. "I'm sure Judge Leonard explained our program—"

"He didn't."

"Well, then permit me. Robert and I have been working hand-in-hand on a plan designed to rehabilitate prisoners who seem worthy of a second chance. Obviously Robert's seen something in you that he feels is worth saving. Ragan and I are writing a book on the project, and you will be one of our subjects, maybe the last one. Now, we're not hard to get along with, Mr. McAllister. You're at liberty to move about on your own, but you're not to be out of our sight without permission. Once you prove that you can be trusted you will be permitted more freedom. I ask very little: my meals on time, Ragan treated with the utmost respect, and that you keep yourself out of trouble."

Johnny sent a sour glance in Ragan's direction. Her fiery stare returned the sentiment.

"Are there any questions?"

"She's in charge of me?"

"No one's in 'charge' of you, Mr. McAllister. You'll be judged on how you take responsibility for yourself while helping others, but Ragan will be supervising your efforts. My condition keeps me close to my chair and the couch, I'm afraid."

Johnny wanted to tell him what he thought of the so-called plan, but he didn't. All he had to do was survive for two years.

"So, do we understand each other?"

Johnny nodded and kept his eyes trained on the wall opposite the table.

"Good." The judge gave a wide yawn. "Well, it's this old man's bedtime. If you'll turn the lamp out when you're finished, I'd appreciate it." He rolled to the doorway, then turned to look back over his shoulder. "Ragan has breakfast on the table at six."

And dinner at noon and supper at five. Like he said, he wasn't a fool. "Yes, sir."

Ragan got up from the table, looping the basket over her arm. Brushing past him on her way out she said, "You can make this as hard or as easy as you want. I'm willing to make this arrangement amicable, but it's entirely up to you."

"Don't press your luck, lady."

Lifting her chin, she proceeded to the back

door and left. He winced when the slamming door rattled the kitchen window.

He might have to be under her wing for the next couple of years, but he didn't have to like it.

Chapter 3

The next morning, Johnny woke at daylight to the sound of a rooster crowing. The smell of frying sausage drifted up to him as he shaved.

Suddenly shots broke out. He jumped, muttering an expletive when his shaving mug crashed to the floor and his razor dropped into the water. Whirling, he went to the window. Chickens squawked, dogs barked, and a bullet hit the side of the house. Yells and whoops and the sound of galloping horses jolted the morning silence.

He saw two riders hightailing it northward, firing toward one house, then another. The riders paused to reload, then spurred their horses on down Main Street.

A movement in the side yard caught Johnny's eye. Ragan ducked, hurrying across the grass and onto the back porch. He heard the screen door flap shut as she let herself in.

Turning from the window, he walked back to the shaving bowl and picked up the pieces of broken glass. Breakfast at six, he reminded himself.

Raids weren't his problem. Dishes were his problem.

Judge McMann took his seat at the breakfast table, smiling. "Good morning, Mr. McAllister. Did you sleep well?"

"Yes, sir."

"Raid bother you?"

"No, sir."

Ragan sailed through the kitchen door, carrying a plate of eggs and biscuits. Johnny's eyes followed her movements, his gut tightening when she met his gaze and smiled. The judge was right; some man should have claimed her by now.

Her freshness disarmed him and made him feel like a man, not a criminal.

"Well, they certainly scared the wits out of me. I almost broke the eggs I'd just gathered." She turned to address Johnny. "Alvin Lutz, our town sheriff, is getting up in years—deaf as a fence post. He needs a successor but no one will take the job. Nobody, including Alvin, will stand up to those thugs."

The judge nodded, buttering a stack of flapjacks. "We have to do something. We won't have any dishes to eat off of if it doesn't stop soon. Maddy's entire cherry blossom pattern is almost gone. Bounced right off the shelves with all the commotion and noise. She loved those plates."

"It's not safe for little ones to be out on the street," Ragan agreed.

Images flashed through Johnny's mind. Elly's screams, little Lara's terrified cries.

Sweat beaded his forehead, and he set his knife aside, his appetite suddenly gone. Would he never be rid of the nightmare? Could he ever see a little girl again without feeling the pain?

Ragan leaned on his shoulder as she reached to pour his coffee. A shock coursed through him as her rosewater scent wafted over him, and his breathing quickened. "Holly and Jo have learned to evade the raiders," she said. "We all avoid the main road."

Johnny was still aware of the spot she'd touched after she moved on. He shifted slightly, uncomfortable with the sensation, but the warm pressure remained.

"Holly, Jo, and Rebecca are my sisters, Mr. McAllister. Holly's engaged to Tom Winters, and they plan to marry in the fall, if finances work out. I don't know what I'll do without her when she leaves. Jo, who's fourteen, and

Becca, who's nine, help with the housework and cooking, but much of the responsibility falls on Holly's shoulders. More biscuits?"

"No."

"Jo's a dear girl, but she's still young in many ways. It's not easy to grow up in such difficult times, with Papa and all."

Done serving breakfast to both men, she sat down to fill her own plate.

He didn't care, he reminded himself. He didn't care about this town, about these people. Or about her. Being here only kept him from tracking down his family's murderers, and he resented the hell out of that.

"There you are!"

Johnny stiffened when he heard Ragan call his name the following afternoon. She marched toward him like a woman with a purpose.

If she was looking for him, it meant one thing: she wanted him to do more demeaning housework. What was it today: mattress beating? Polishing the stair railing? He had it shining like a diamond in a goat's fanny as it was.

He pretended to be interested in the porch step he was repairing. "Need something?"

"Actually, I do."

It figured. "What?"

"I need your help in the kitchen. The Ladies' Auxiliary is having their annual library bake sale and I've promised to contribute nine dozen sugar cookies."

"So?"

"So, I need your help."

He turned to stare at her. "Baking *cookies*?" She wasn't serious, was she? He could barely boil water without burning it.

"It won't take very long—if you'll just roll out the dough and cut them out, I'll get them in the oven." She smiled when he gave her a cool look. "Oh, come on, it will be fun."

Fun my foot. It was just one more thing to harass him. Tossing the hammer aside, he stood up.

"You'll do it?"

"Do I have a choice?" On some distant level, he realized he might enjoy spending an afternoon alone in a kitchen with her. On another level, he knew the more he was around her, the more he'd want to be.

"Of course you have a choice. We're not ogres, Mr. McAllister—and I could sure use your help."

He trailed her into the kitchen and spotted a large bowl of cookie dough sitting on the table. A rolling pin, flour, and several odd-shaped cutters littered the top.

"The Ladies' Auxiliary is small; just Minnie, Pearl, and Roberta—when Roberta's not busy at the millinery. But they manage to have a lovely bake sale every year." She stopped and grinned when she saw the face he was making. "I assume you've never baked cookies before?"

"No, ma'am."

"Please, call me Ragan. I have not been sent to torture you, Mr. McAllister." Tying an apron around her waist, she said softly, "We'll make this as painless as possible. Do you need an apron?"

He stiffened. "Hell, no—I don't need an *apron.*"

Stepping around him, she admonished, "We'll need to watch our language, Mr. McAllister. The judge is a real stickler about his rules." She picked up the sifter and dusted a generous amount of flour onto a large, white cloth. "What's your favorite cookie?"

Images of Ma making oatmeal cookies surfaced in his mind. She'd blend rich yellow butter, sugar, eggs, oatmeal and flour, allowing him to lick the spoon when she'd finished. By the time the hot treat came out of the oven, he'd eaten more batter than cookie. The memory curled around his heart as warm and sweet as the treat itself.

"Pie's more to my liking."

She glanced up, her face flushed from the

kitchen heat. For a moment it was hard for him to take his eyes off of her. "That's a shame. Personally, I favor molasses cookies."

Molasses gave him a belly ache.

Reaching for a mound of dough, she laid it on the floured cloth, then picked up the rolling pin. "Roll the dough very thin, then cut it into any shape you like."

She rolled the dough smooth as a baby's bottom and a second later she laid a perfect image of a bell on the cookie sheet.

Johnny studied the row of cookie cutters. An animal of sorts—maybe a dog—awaited a steady hand. Stars, bells, and a symmetrical shaped object looked easier to handle.

"Now, let's put you to work rolling out more dough. Do you want to stand or sit?"

"Stand."

She brushed by him, trailing her flowery scent. What was it? Lemon? One of those womanly scents designed to drive a man out of his mind?

Handing him the rolling pin, she smiled. "Let's see what you can do."

His first attempt was pathetic, even to his untrained eye. The dough wadded into a sticky ball and clung to the rolling pin. Lifting the tool, he looked at her helplessly. "What's the problem here?"

"Inexperience." She took the pin away

from him and cleaned it. "You need lots of flour, but not too much or the cookie will be dry."

Lots, but not too much. What was that supposed to mean? A bushel or a teaspoon?

Moving around him, she looped her hands around his waist and steadied the pin, rolling the dough to a delicate consistency. His fingers moved over the wood to capture hers.

The pin paused, and she eyed his hand.

"Mr. McAllister."

"Yes?" Running his fingers lightly over the satiny texture of her skin, he deliberately invited a response. He was going to be here a long time; he might as well make it interesting.

"You're touching my fingers."

He looked down. "So I am."

"Are you . . . trying to get my attention?"

"Could be."

Moving her hand, she patiently cut out a wreath and laid it on the sheet.

After watching her do a few more, Johnny captured her hand again. Her gaze shot up, and he smiled.

Eyes narrowing, she said softly, "Why aren't you cutting out cookies?"

"I don't know how to cut out cookies. And, I don't want to cut out cookies."

"I'm can't do anything about you not

wanting to cut them out, but I'm trying to show you how."

His eyes slid over her suggestively. "Come now, Miss Ramsey. Can't you think of a better way to spend the afternoon?"

Leaning closer, she whispered, "Such as?" Their mouths were close now, nearly touching. This was going easier than he thought. What would she do if he kissed her?

"Such as," he drawled, "we could go for a walk, look for a little privacy." He reached over, touching a dot of flour on her cute little nose. She was a looker, all right. Maybe the next few months weren't going to be so bad, after all.

"Privacy?"

"Sure, darlin.' " He brought her hand to his chest and pressed it there. "See how my heart beats for you?"

"Infinitely—and such a strong, masculine heart it is," she said throatily. "I'm touched, truly. But I do feel compelled to point out that you're my prisoner, and I'm responsible for you."

His smile faded. "I know that."

"Then you must also know there can't be any hanky-panky in this relationship."

He grinned, slow and lazy-like. "Says who?"

Leaning closer, she pressed her mouth to

his ear and whispered, "Says me." Picking up the sifter, she calmly dumped it over his head. Flour covered the front of his shirt, and he choked.

"We have nine dozen cookies to bake, mister. You'd best get started."

Johnny was in the kitchen two days later washing the breakfast dishes when raiders came through again. He paid them no mind until he heard footsteps rushing up the back porch steps. Ragan slammed inside with a choked, "My God!"

Johnny dropped the cup he was washing and whirled to face her.

"What's wrong?"

"The . . . the . . ."

She was so upset she couldn't get the words out. Had a snake bitten her? A rabid dog? Had one of those perverts accosted her?

He wiped his soapy hands on his jeans and crossed to the screen door to look out. "Does the judge need the gun?"

She shook her head, biting her lower lip between small, even white teeth. "They shot all the chickens!"

He frowned. "They shot what?"

"The *chickens*." She wrung her hands, tears spilling from her eyes. "They shot the judge's *chickens!*" Unexpectedly she threw herself into his arms and burst into tears.

Stunned, he awkwardly patted her back. The scents of sunshine and woman enveloped him and he automatically drew her closer. Hell, what were a few chickens? It just meant sixteen fewer beaks to feed.

His hand came up to gently stroke her hair. "It's not the end of the world. You can get more chickens."

Hell, he'd *buy* her more chickens if she'd just stay where she was for a few more minutes.

She lifted her head, sniffling. Her huge blue eyes, wet with tears, made him want to go after the men who'd put her in this state.

"You don't understand. What am I going to do with *sixteen* dead hens?"

His smile waned and he groaned. Hell, he hadn't thought about that. They sure were going to get tired of eating chicken.

That afternoon, the Honorable Proctor McMann dropped his tea cup and dove under the dining room table as bullets ricocheted through the front parlor. "The cat, Ragan! Get the cat!"

Johnny dropped out of his chair, dodging the hail of gunfire.

"Here Kitty, here, Kitty, Kitty." Ragan

crawled along in front of the sofa, groping underneath for the missing pet. Her eyes focused on a tuft of black fur quaking beneath the round lamp table. "There you are."

Reaching for the feline, she tugged. The cat dug into the wool rug, refusing to budge.

"Kitty!" Judge McMann yelled, concern tinging his voice.

"She's all right, Procky." Ragan ducked as shots whizzed over her head.

"Don't be ... obstinate, Kitty," she muttered as she carefully dislodged the claws one by one. She shook her head in resignation as a down pillow on the sofa exploded. The picture of a young Maddy McMann, which had been hanging over the mantel, spun across the floor like a toy top.

Ragan tucked the yowling animal safely under her arm and crawled under the table to join the judge. Motioning for Johnny to join them, she made room for him in the cramped shelter.

"Oh, my." Judge McMann reached for his pet, tenderness shining in his eyes. "Young lady, you scared me to death. You know that when the shooting starts, you're to come running."

Kitty nuzzled the judge's chest, purring loudly.

Ping!

Another bullet bounced off the porch.

The judge sat back and made himself comfortable, stroking Kitty as a crystal chandelier swung overhead, the dangling bangles tinkling and sending tiny flashes of light bouncing from wall to wall. He removed his pipe from his mouth, frowning. "The bowl's gone cold. Can you reach my tobacco, Mr. McAllister?"

Johnny fumbled blindly beside the judge's wingback chair until he located the round red tin, then quickly drew it beneath the table.

Judge McMann smiled serenely. "Thank you. Nasty habit, but I'm too old to stop now."

"More tea, anyone?" Ragan asked.

The judge beamed. "Why yes, tea *is* in order, thank you."

Horsemen galloped down the block, then turned to make another pass by the judge's house.

Crawling from the table's shelter long enough to reach the serving tray, Ragan carefully scooted the silver service along the pine floor. Rattling cups and saucers joined the sound of pounding hooves as the gang thundered back by.

Ragan saw Johnny's disbelieving stare as she poured, but he'd soon get used to it.

Gangs were a common occurrence around here. Adding two lumps of sugar, she stirred the tea, then handed him a cup.

He stared at her as if she'd lost her mind. "Cookie?"

"I'll sure have one," the judge said. He selected a lemon round and settled back against the table leg as hoof beats pounded by. The three sat sipping tea as bullets flew.

Johnny flinched as a bullet took a hunk out of the table leg. "*Why* do you people put up with this?"

"Well, I suppose because we don't know how to stop it," the judge said.

"We've tried," Ragan added.

"Tried real hard, but to no avail. It's hard to believe the town was once called Paradise," the judge said.

"Yes." Ragan glanced at Johnny, who was clearly uncomfortable with their tea habits. "Last year the citizens voted to call the town Barren Flats." She sighed again as hot lead shattered a windowpane. "If only we could do something to stop this."

"Well, your father tried." The judge tapped tobacco into the pipe bowl.

"Yes, and look where it got him."

Fulton Ramsey was once a community leader. He'd pastored Paradise's only church, and cared deeply about his flock. Fulton had tried to stand up to the gangs and was burned out, his cattle shot, and the church torched and burned to the ground. The death of his son, Jacob, was the final straw.

Ragan still hurt when she thought about her young brother. The boy had died racing his horse home to warn them that raiders were coming from the north. He was thrown in the lane leading to the Ramsey house, and died where he fell.

Papa had finally succumbed to despair over his losses. His anguish was so deep, so irreversible, that he'd retreated into a world that no one, not even his daughters, was able to penetrate.

He now sat silently for hours whittling toy animal figures, staring into space, a broken man. Once Fulton Ramsey had been looked upon as a charismatic man of God; now the townsfolk merely looked upon him with pity.

If Ragan could just hold the family together until Jo and Becca were raised, she'd be grateful.

Procky was getting on in years, and Papa— well, there was no telling how long Papa would live. His body was healthy, even though his mind was not.

Once her responsibilities were fulfilled, Ragan wanted to leave this hellacious town and attend school; perhaps, if Procky had his way, study for the bar. There would be sacrifices if she decided to do that. She'd have to move far away from the girls since it was mostly midwestern schools that admitted women for law degrees. Then she'd have to fight to prove that as a lawyer, she could handle cases as well as a man. Most women took over practices begun by their fathers or husbands, but she would have to prove herself on her own.

The judge had already told her he would provide money for her tuition, and she could go anytime that she wanted. But right now that was impossible—she had too many people in Barren Flats depending on her.

Meanwhile, the project she and Procky were working on kept her occupied. Rehabilitation for criminals instead of punishment was an interesting theory, and she enjoyed researching the cases. So far, they had been rewarded with a good measure of success with Judge Leonard's controversial program.

She and Procky were working hard to see the plan completed, and the book they were writing on the subject published. With the notable exception of results on adult prisoners, the program had proved favorable and should be completed within the year.

Personally, it couldn't come soon enough for Ragan.

She glanced at Johnny, lifting the teapot expectantly. "More tea, Mr. McAllister?"

After supper that evening, Judge McMann pushed back from the table, patting his full belly. Sighing, he looked at Johnny. "It's been a difficult day. We'll leave the dishes, and have our coffee on the porch tonight."

Ragan nodded. "I'll bring dessert."

They settled on the open porch, where a cool breeze relieved the day's heat. Ragan handed the men huge bowls of blackberry cobbler with a generous portion of thick cream over the top. The judge sat back, obviously enjoying the evening. "These raids are getting more and more violent. It's time to call a town meeting." He focused on Johnny. "Now son, I'm curious. What would you do about this problem?"

A muscle tightened in Johnny's jaw. "It's none of my concern."

Disappointment lined the judge's features. "Any suggestion would be welcomed at this point. Being new to the problem, you'd have a fresh outlook on it."

Pouring coffee, Ragan said softly, "We

don't want to impose, Mr. McAllister, but if you have any ideas—"

"I don't."

Ragan glanced at the judge. They both shook their heads.

She finished pouring coffee and set the pot aside, then sat in a wicker chair beside the judge. "Shooting the chickens is really the last straw. I'm glad you suggested the town meeting, Procky. Surely someone can come up with a plan this time."

Judge McMann stirred sugar into his coffee. "Yes, you'd think so."

"I'll make posters tonight and hang them in the morning." Ragan smiled at Johnny. "You can help, Mr. McAllister."

Johnny spooned a bite of cobbler in his mouth. Of course. He would have bet on it.

The next day Ragan and Johnny tacked up posters about the town meeting that night. Curious crowds gathered around trees and storefronts to read the circulars.

"Count on the Southerns being there," Frankie called to Ragan. His wife, Kensil, nodded.

"See you tonight," Timothy Seeden promised as he left the bank.

"We'll be there with bells on," Minnie Rayles said. "I'm sick to death of all this violence!

Shooting chickens, the very idea!"

"I'll shore nuff be there," Rudolf Miller called, laying his hammer aside his anvil and waving.

Handing Johnny the last notice, Ragan stepped back to watch him post it. "Isn't this exciting?"

"Thrilling." He missed the nail and walloped his thumb instead. "Damn!"

"No profanity, Mr. McAllister." She picked up her skirt and moved on.

The Oasis Saloon cleared out for the town meeting. The proprietors, Florence and Hubie Banks, took orders for lemonade and coffee as people made their way into the saloon a little after five. By five-thirty all the seats were filled, with people lining the walls. Judge McMann left the group he was chatting with and rolled to the front of the room. He raised his hand for attention and gradually a hush fell over the crowd.

"Folks, I'm glad to see you here. Appreciate your concern. Now, we've called this meeting to make some decisions. This raid problem is out of hand and we can't ignore it any longer. But first, Reverend Pillton has something to say." He waved toward the black-frocked minister sitting near the back of the room. "Reverend."

Samuel Pillton stood and a hush fell over the crowd. "Folks, it's time we repair our place of worship. I don't think it makes a lot of difference to God where we say our prayers, but we need to take a stand and show these hooligans what's important in our lives. You folks decide." His voice was soft, but like his sermons, everyone understood his message.

There was silence, then a mounting buzz. They decided to begin restoring the church on the following Saturday, and work assignments were made.

"Now, let's decide the best way to deal with the main problem at hand," the judge said above the noisy clatter.

"The chicken killers!" Rudolph shouted. "Any man who'd shoot our chickens is just plain mean. We got to do somethin'!"

"What are you goin' to do about 'em, Judge?" someone called.

"That's what we're here to decide. What are we going to do about them?"

Johnny looked at Ragan, who was sitting in the second row. Three younger girls sat with her. They were undoubtedly the sisters she talked about; the girls bore a marked resemblance to each other. His eyes effortlessly slid over Ragan's slender frame, the swell of her breasts, the way her nose tilted slightly—

just enough to be interesting. What was she thinking? Was she interested in any man in this room? His eyes searched the crowd, wondering what sort of man attracted the comely Miss Ramsey. Did she know what a real man was—a man who could fan that spark in her into a fire?

"We gotta do something, Procky! There's not going to be anything left of the town if we don't!"

The judge lifted his hand again for quiet. "We've been burned to the ground twice. It seems to me we're going to have to take action soon or face the risk of getting burned out a third time."

"I think we should move the entire town," Maggie Anglo volunteered. "Get farther from the border. These hoodlums ride through, go into Mexico and wait a few days, then they come riding back and shooting up again. Barren Flats is right in their path."

A man in the back stood up. "Maggie's right. If we move twenty miles further north, we wouldn't be in their way."

The old sheriff held his hand to his ear. "You going to pack that big, two-story house of yours onto the back of a horse and move it?"

"Yeah, and how about the bank, the sheriff's office, the stores, and all the other buildings? You going to give 'em all to the gangs?" Rudolph Miller called out. "We can't run away from our trouble. We have to face it, and face it now!"

Alvin Lutz got to his feet. "As sheriff of this town, I'm doin' the best I can. There are at least a dozen different gangs that I've counted riding through here. Some have as many as fifteen riders."

Jewell Scott twisted a lace handkerchief and seemed on the verge of tears. "Oh, my . . . Alvin's right. I've counted at least that many. It's very disturbing. I'm thinking about moving clean away from here. I just don't feel safe in my own home anymore."

Several women, some openly crying, spoke fervently of their fear for their children and their frustration with having to clean up after every raid.

"Plaster sifts down from the ceiling when they ride through. There are so many bullet holes, Clifford can't even get them repaired." Sylvia Kincaid shot her husband a frustrated look. "The mister was taking a nap in the parlor yesterday when they passed through. When he woke up, he had so much plaster on his face he looked like a ghost." When her neighbors laughed, she blushed. "Well, he did!"

A man stood up near the back. "I say we

build a new road around the town. Make 'em change their course!"

Heads bobbed at the suggestion.

"Oh, I don't know, Frank. That could be bad for business." Shorty frowned. "Real bad. I get a lot of drifters coming through here for groceries, and there's always a few with horses that need reshoeing."

"Dad burn it, Shorty, neither you nor Rudy do business with the gangs. What business would you lose?"

"Well there could be *some* lost with a new road."

"Be a lot of trouble to build a new road, wouldn't it?"

"Yes, it would. We'd have to put it a mile or so to the west—"

Austin Plummer jumped to his feet. "Now, hold on there. That'd cut up *my* land. I just got my fence back up from that cattle stampede a week or two back." The farmer's face flushed and his fists balled. "We'd have to make that new road to the east of town."

A second man stood and appeared ready to fight anyone who agreed with Austin. "Wait just a blamed minute! I can't split up my farmstead—I don't want those bandits riding through my property. Don't be planning any road through *my* land."

Fans waved in front of faces and handkerchiefs mopped foreheads.

"Listen to yourselves: can't no one agree on a blasted thing? We got to do something, people. And now!"

Johnny sat quietly, listening to the exclamations and declarations break out around him. It was amazing how far grown men would go to avoid trouble.

Minnie Rayles shot to her feet. "I say we hire a shootist!"

A hush fell over the room. The citizens of Barren Flats looked at one another, then murmured back and forth. A shootist? What shootist?

"What are you talking about, Minnie?" The banker's wife turned around in her seat to stare at her.

"A shootist." Minnie leaned back in her chair and straightened her hat.

"Good Lord, Minnie." Her husband, Carl, filled the stunned silence. "Where are we gonna get a shootist?"

"Well, right here, that's where." Minnie fished in her purse and came up with an article from a journal. "Says here, Sulphur Springs, up north by San Francisco, was having the same trouble as us. They hired them a shootist: Dead Eye Mercer. He cleaned that town up, slick as a whistle. He could do the same thing here."

Johnny sat up straighter. Dead Eye Mercer? The legendary gunslinger?

Carl took the piece of paper from his wife, his eyes scanning the article.

"A shootist?" Alvin Lutz got slowly to his feet, his hand cupped to his ear. "How much would something like that cost?"

Minnie frowned. "Don't rightly know—but we could wire Mercer and find out."

Everett lifted his hand. "I could send the wire off first thing tomorrow morning."

"Anyone know where the shootist is?"

"I can find out!" Minnie volunteered.

A buzz went up as the crowd warmed to the idea. Johnny couldn't believe what he was hearing. They were willing to hire a shootist to do their dirty work? He shook his head. Dead Eye Mercer was lethal, but why didn't these people just clean up their own town?

Judge McMann cleared his throat. "It seems to me, we should be able to confront this problem without outside interference." He eyed the audience. "We have plenty of able-bodied men right here in Barren Flats."

"Who can't do a blessed thing to stop these gangs," Lillian Hubbard said. She looked at her daughters. "When will our children be safe again? I say hire this shootist! Pay him anything he wants! We want our town back!"

An outcry went up. "Get the shootist!"

"Get our town back!"

"Pass the hat. I'll put in five dollars."

"*Five* dollars—now hold on here."

"Money isn't the issue. Getting our town back is, and you can't put a price on that! It's worth whatever the cost," someone else shouted.

Ragan's eyes met Johnny's as the uproar continued. It wasn't hard to read her silent plea. *What would he do?* He calmly looked away. What he'd like to do was take her somewhere secluded and kiss that soft, sweet mouth until she pleaded for mercy. His eyes slid back to her.

But that didn't solve the immediate problem.

Judge McMann rapped the bar for order. "All right! We'll take a vote. Those in favor of sending for a shootist, raise your hand."

Fifty hands shot up.

"Those opposed?"

Johnny counted forty-six.

"The yea's have it." The judge banged his gavel. "Everett, send a wire inviting Mercer to come in and clean up the town."

Everett turned to look at Minnie. "You'll have to tell me where to send it."

Minnie nodded. "I'll have it there when you open tomorrow, Everett."

As everyone got up to leave, Johnny shook his head in disgust. These people had shi— spit for brains. Mercer wouldn't stay forever, and then the gangs would return. But stupid plan or not, Johnny supposed they went home thinking they'd solved their problem.

Chapter 4

⌒～◯◯～⌒

"**S**tick the needle through the hole, and pull the thread tight."

Tongue wedged between his teeth, Johnny concentrated on spearing the eyes of the button.

"That's it, nice and easy. You're quite good at sewing buttons."

"I'd rather chop wood."

"Judge McMann believes sewing builds character." That wasn't exactly true. Actually, Procky said the busier a man was, the more likely he was to stay out of trouble. But Ragan was running out of things to keep Mr. McAllister busy. He'd beaten rugs, and hoed the garden, whitewashed the fence, and helped old Mrs. Curbow with her garden. The afternoon loomed ahead when Ragan spotted the basket of sewing.

"Damn!" Johnny swore as the tip of the

needle pricked him for the third time.

"Mr. McAllister..." Ragan gently reminded.

"Shoot!"

"Gently," Ragan instructed. "You sew as if you're branding cattle. Think: lightly, carefully." She selected a button and effortlessly attached it to a shirt. Johnny seemed to eye the exhibition with cool detachment, but his jaw tightened and she heard his teeth grind.

Demoralizing him wasn't her intention. Indeed, she was starting to enjoy his company more than she should. Though he didn't talk a lot, she did glimpse an occasional smile, tempting her to think that he was warming.

Lately, her thoughts wandered where they shouldn't. Like noticing how nice his hair looked after a bath, all soft and touchable in long, brown waves. Or when he nicked himself on the chin while shaving. She found herself wanting to wet a cloth and wipe the tiny flecks of dried blood away. She glanced at him, then back at her handwork. They both needed to stay busy—when she was supervising, it was much easier to keep her mind on her business.

But he had finished most of the repairs on the house, and now she simply did not have the resources to keep him busy during the day. It had been easy enough to send Joey

Wester outside to play stickball when his work was finished. He'd spent many idle hours honing his batting skill. She even played catch with the boy a few times.

She eyed the ridge of muscles in Johnny's forearms. He most certainly was not a boy. Her gaze followed the line of muscles up his arms, across his broad shoulders. It took little imagination to know how they would feel if she ran her hands over his back, down the sides of his ribs . . . Heavens, it was uncomfortably warm again. The judge needed more windows in his kitchen.

She held the repaired shirt up for inspection. "See? Good as new."

Johnny glanced at her, then the shirt. "Sewing's woman's work."

Ragan set a pile of mending in front of him. No matter how attractive he was, it would be nice if he would cooperate with a more willing spirit. For now, they were stuck with each another.

"By the time you've worked your way through that pile of mending, you'll be able to sew on buttons as well as, or better than, any woman." She smiled sweetly, "In case you ever wish to take up tailoring."

He grunted something, and kept on sewing.

Untying her apron, she slipped it over her

head. Sewing wasn't her favorite chore either. "I'll be back to check with you in a few minutes."

"Damn!" he whispered under his breath. The needle drew blood again. He gave her a look black enough to sour milk.

"Carefully," she repeated over her shoulder. As she closed the door behind her, she released a sigh. If he thought sewing was trying, he should try overseeing a man who shamefully overheated her senses and was hell bent on making her job more difficult.

Soon she was bent over the woodpile, chopping kindling. The axe bit into the fine wood, chips flying. The sun was warm, but she didn't mind. She enjoyed outdoor chores far more than indoor ones. She picked out a few chips for her father and laid them aside. He was prone to leave the house to search for wood when his basket was empty.

Absorbed in her work, she didn't hear the approaching footsteps. A shadow fell over the woodpile as she raised the axe above her head to swing. A hand shot out to clasp her wrist. Startled, she stared into John McAllister's face, as dark as a thundercloud. Her heart flew to her throat, and her hand automatically tightened around the axe handle.

His eyes darkened even more at her response. "Afraid of me, Miss Ramsey?"

If she were, he would never know it. Her gaze met his steadily. "Are you through with the mending?" He couldn't be. There were enough missing buttons in that pile to keep him busy all afternoon.

His eyes shifted back to the woodpile. "I'll swap chores with you."

Shaking off his hand, she raised the axe and swung it. Kindling flew. "No thank you. I'd just as soon chop wood." She'd just as soon do about anything other than mend. Or stand here getting weak in the knees over him!

He took a step back to avoid being hit. "Women sew. *Men* chop wood."

She took another mighty swing, splitting a log in half. He stared at the two pieces, then at her.

"Not in this household." They'd had the same argument this morning when he wanted to paint the shed instead of beat rugs. She refused to humor him. He would never learn discipline if she caved in every time he argued with her.

Reaching for another log, she jerked back when a green garter snake slithered from under the pile. Dropping the axe, she hopped aside. Try as she would, she couldn't overcome her snake jitters. The little reptile darted her way, and she whirled, colliding with a wall of solid chest muscle. Her eyes locked with McAllister's, and goose bumps broke out on her arms. She'd never been this close to a man—and the feelings he aroused in her could be straight from one of Papa's "sinful thinking" sermons.

Swallowing hard, she tried to keep her voice even. "Would you please pick it up and carry it to the garden?"

Johnny cocked his head and frowned. "It? You mean the kindling?" He bent to pick up the wood she had just split.

She gritted her teeth. "No, Mr. McAllister. It, the snake."

A slow smile started at the corners of his mouth and spread across his face. Her cheeks grew hot and her heart sank. This was his moment of triumph. That snake could dart straight up her skirt, and he wouldn't lift a hand to prevent it.

"Ohhhhhhhhh, it, the snake." His innocent eyes held hers. "Sorry. I have buttons to sew on." He turned and sauntered back to the house.

She glared at his retreating back. Where was a rock when you needed one? Well, all *right*! The battle lines were drawn. By cracker, she was through being pleasant to this impossible man!

Keeping one eye on the snake and the

other on McAllister's retreating back, she picked up the axe and prodded the slithering garter toward the garden with the handle. Just let him ask her for help with the dishes—or mending—or rug beating—or anything!

The screen door slammed shut.

She fanned her face.

Rogue.

When she returned to the kitchen a short while later, the judge was up from his nap. The two men sat at the table, sorting buttons. Kitty perched in the middle of the activity, batting at strays. Dumping an armload of wood into the kindling box, Ragan gave Johnny a dark look as she reached for a match. "Up from your nap so early, Procky?"

The judge frowned, placing a blue button on a pile. "I couldn't sleep. Came to the kitchen for a glass of buttermilk and John, here, looked like he could use my help."

Ragan closed her eyes. Procky was too soft-hearted to deal with prisoners. If only he would realize that his sympathy made her job that much harder.

Her eyes touched briefly on Johnny's hands. They looked like raw meat where he'd pricked himself with the needle. A pile of messy-looking mending was piled in front of him, and her heart turned over.

Johnny avoided meeting her eyes.

The judge frowned, reaching for another button. "Are all those potatoes for us? Are we feeding an army this evening?"

"No, I fixed extra so I could take some home to Papa tonight."

"Your sisters don't know how to mash potatoes?"

"Of course they do, but Papa seems to think mine are special."

"Well, I'd have to agree with Fulton on that one." He smiled at Johnny. "Guess you've noticed she's a dandy cook."

"She's okay."

Ragan struck a match and threw it in the stove. *Okay!* He sure ate her apple pies without any problem. The kindling caught, and she shoved the iron lid into place. Shooing Kitty off the table, she moved to the cabinet.

The judge dropped another button on the pile. "You know, John, you've been mighty quiet since you got here. Tell us a little about yourself."

Ragan pretended interest in what she was doing, but her ear was tuned to the conversation. She'd like to know something about him: where he came from, how he came to be in his present situation. What sort of woman he found desirable . . .

Johnny kept his eyes on his task. "There's nothing of interest to tell, Judge."

Cutting through the underbrush, Johnny rode a dry riverbed through a canyon. The horse was winded, but he pushed the animal harder, up and down ravines, in and out of thickets. He turned up a steep incline. When they burst out of the brush, the sorrel's head jerked up, and the animal shied nervously.

Johnny found himself staring down the barrels of a half-dozen rifles.

Crows circled and cawed overhead. Heat bore down as the six men rode leisurely forward, forming a circle around him, their rifles centered on the middle of his chest.

"Throw down your gun," the sheriff ordered.

Johnny shifted in the saddle. "Look. I know how this seems—"

"Throw it down, boy!"

Johnny's hands were already in the air. He gingerly lifted the pistol from its holster and let it drop into the dirt.

The sheriff swung off his horse and walked toward him. The man was big and stocky, and had thirty pounds on Johnny. There was no way to take him, and even if there was, he couldn't take on the others.

"Where's the money?"

"Left saddlebag."

"Get off your horse."

Johnny dismounted and stood beside his horse, hands above his head.

The sheriff rummaged through the bag. "Ain't here. Where is it, boy?"

Johnny took a step toward the horse to search. A gun clicked.

"Stay where you are, mister," one of the men said. "I don't relish dragging a corpse back to town."

Johnny lifted his hands higher. "I don't relish that either."

The sheriff wasn't amused. "Where's the money?"

"I'm telling you, I put it in the saddle pouch."

"Ain't no money here." The leather saddlebag landed at Johnny's feet.

He grabbed it and shook it upside down. His heart sank as the contents spilled to the ground. The bank pouch wasn't there. He studied the men. Not an eye blinked as they stonily returned his look.

"I must have lost it on the trail."

Heads swiveled to stare back at the way they'd come.

Straightening his shoulders, the sheriff had leveled the barrel of his rifle at Johnny. "Get off your horse, son."

*   *   *

Smiling, Judge McMann assembled a pile of red buttons. "I find that hard to believe. Every man has something interesting to tell about himself. How did you come to be involved in a bank robbery?"

"I didn't." Another button hit the pile.

"So you've said." The judge continued sorting. "Well, there must be something you'd like to tell us about yourself."

"No—nothing."

"You have parents, don't you?"

"No, sir."

"Family—brothers? Sisters?"

"No. No brothers or sisters. No parents."

His tone was guarded now, evasive. What was he hiding? Ragan wondered. He didn't just materialize out of thin air. Was he being stubborn? Was he ashamed of his behavior and trying to protect his parents' identity? Somehow Ragan doubted it, and she was seldom wrong about these things. Ask anyone: her premonitions were usually right on.

She studied the prisoner's dark good looks as she started to pour flour into a bowl. What set a man like him on the path of self-destruction? He made it plain that he was a loner, a man with a chip on his shoulder, daring her or anyone else to befriend him. She longed to befriend him, to kiss that solemn look off his tight features . . . . She gasped as the flour spilled over.

"Been on your own for some time, huh?"

"A long time, Judge."

Ragan swallowed the sudden lump in her throat. Vulnerability in his voice was the last thing she'd expected to hear. *He's a criminal*, she reminded herself, shoving sentimentality aside.

He was as uncaring as the men who terrorized Barren Flats. She detested them all for the misery they caused innocent people, and Johnny McAllister was no better than any of them. At least that's what the law said. If Judge Leonard hadn't shown this particular hoodlum leniency, he'd be hanged by now.

Judge McMann changed the subject. "Tell me, John, you attended the meeting yesterday. Think hiring Mercer's a smart move?"

Annoyance flooded Ragan. The town didn't need a shootist, or advice from the likes of Johnny McAllister. What they *needed* was less talk and more action.

"Well?" The judge prompted when Johnny didn't answer.

"Perhaps Mr. McAllister doesn't *want* to offer his advice." Ragan set a stack of plates on the table. The prisoner had made that clear when Procky broached the subject earlier.

Judge McMann glanced up. "Is that true, Mr. McAllister? I don't want to bother you; just thought that now you'd had a spell to think about the problem, you might want to offer some advice."

Johnny reached for another button. "No bother, Judge. I just don't have any advice for you."

The judge cleared his throat and shifted in his chair. "I understand the circumstances of your involvement in the bank robbery are questionable."

Silence dominated the room.

Judge McMann glanced at Ragan and continued. "You have nothing to fear from us. We're all in this situation together, and you might as well reconcile yourself to the fact that you're going to be here a while, sure as the sun comes up in the east. Now Ragan and I, we're bound to this project by years of research and writing. We have great hopes the program will work and will be of benefit to future generations. I'd say it's best if you lower your guard and make the most of your situation."

It was as close to a lecture as Ragan had ever heard from Procky.

The judge leaned forward and patted

Kitty. "Isn't that what you'd say, old girl?" He looked back at Johnny and watched as Kitty jumped down to walk over and rub against Johnny's leg. Back and forth she moved, gracefully arching her back and purring loudly. Johnny moved his foot to the side, and the cat followed to continue rubbing against his boot.

McAllister met his gaze evenly. "Judge Leonard has my grandfather's pistol. I intend to get that pistol back."

"And you will, as long as you serve your sentence with no trouble. Break your word, and the matter is out of my hands. We're not going to ride shotgun on you. You'll have access to tools of destruction—such as the axe for chopping wood. What you choose to do is your responsibility. The idea of the program is to allow a convicted man to prove his worth."

Johnny reached for another shirt. "I won't give you any trouble." He gave the cat a slight push with his boot. She moved back to the judge.

"I'm glad to hear it. We should get along fine." Judge McMann wheeled his chair from the table. Patting his knee, he invited Kitty to join him. She landed gracefully on his lap and he chuckled when her nose nudged his ruddy cheek. "Yes, old girl, I love you too."

His eyes met Johnny's over the cat's head.

Ragan reached for the shirt, taking it out of his hand. "I'll finish the mending. There's another pile of wood to be split." She could afford to be generous; the sewing was almost done.

Johnny was on his feet before she finished her sentence. The judge reached to steady the table.

"Supper's in a half hour," Ragan called as he disappeared out the screen door. She slid a pan of cornbread into the oven, avoiding the judge's gaze. "I believe he'd rather do men's work than sew on buttons."

Judge chuckled. "That's the impression I get."

"I'm not sure about the wisdom of handing an axe to a prisoner."

"In some cases I'd say no, but I don't believe McAllister's a threat. I'm surprised you've kept him inside as much as you have."

She brushed a wisp of hair out of her eyes. "He's just not responding. He has a chip on his shoulder and refuses to warm to anyone."

"Now missy." She always knew Judge disagreed when he called her "missy." "All of our guests have begun their time with a chip on their shoulders. That's a part of the process. Our success is measured by the wearing down of that chip. Sometimes it wears away fast, but others . . . well others have to be whittled away a little at a time. Depends, to a degree, on how the chip was formed in the first place. Did it form a little at a time through years of abuse, or did it fall across his shoulders like a tree felled in the forest?"

He pulled a folded paper from his shirt pocket. "I think there's more to John McAllister than meets the eye. There's something about this boy." He smoothed the paper and pushed it toward Ragan. "Here's the message I received from Robert this morning. He contends his suspicions at the time of the trial were strongly in favor of Johnny's innocence. There's no concrete proof that McAllister is a member of the Puet gang; none at all."

Ragan stood at the window and watched the mystifying man chop wood. Powerful muscles played across his back as he swung the axe with a vengeance. She sighed. Whoever he was, he didn't intend to let anyone—most of all her—near him.

After supper, Ragan packed a large crock of mashed potatoes and a pot roast into a basket, and closed the lid. She handed a bowl of green beans to Johnny and picked up the basket herself. Then she stepped to the parlor doorway. "Goodnight, Procky. Mr. McAllister is helping me carry the food home tonight. He won't be gone long."

The judge waved back from his spot in front of the window where he was reading. "See you in the morning."

She held the screen open for Johnny. Carrying the bowl of green beans, he preceded her to the porch.

They reached the gate just as the sound of galloping horses caught their attention, and riders came into sight. Banditos, holding liquor bottles in the air, shouted drunken obscenities and spurred their mounts faster, heading straight for the house.

Grabbing Ragan's hand, Johnny pulled her the few steps back to the house and dove for the porch floor, shielding her body with his. Her heart slammed against her ribs as he curled around her, putting himself between her and the riders.

Glass shattered, and green beans spilled down the wooden steps. The judge's petunia patch exploded in a barrage of gunfire. Bullets ricocheted off rooftops, accompanied by derisive shouts and ribald laughter.

He gave her a push and Ragan scrambled

under the porch swing, ducking as gunfire riddled the house.

"Keep down," Johnny warned, crawling on his belly across the porch toward the screen door. "Judge?" he shouted.

Judge McMann's muffled voice came back. "I'm all right. Kitty and I are in the hall closet."

The riders fired into the air, their horses toppling a section of picket fence. Weaving back and forth, they shot out windows, and bullets pinged against the weather vane on top of the judge's house.

Trampling the lawn, they fired into the night, their merriment filling the once-peaceful evening.

Then as suddenly as they appeared, they galloped off. Johnny crawled from behind a wicker settee and helped Ragan to her feet. Green beans and bits of purple and white petunias littered the porch floor.

Ragan surveyed the damage, outraged. "The hoodlums!"

She was about to thank Johnny for protecting her when she noticed how his dark eyes followed the riders' trail of disappearing dust. She frowned when she saw his features harden.

"Mr. McAllister?"

His eyes remained on the disappearing riders.

"There . . . is there something you'd like to say?" Perhaps now that he'd almost been killed, he would drop his guard and offer a solution to this horrendous problem.

His gaze dropped to the littered porch floor. "Green beans are getting cold."

The feel of Johnny's body curled protectively around her lingered with Ragan as they set off again. The evening was calm, the sinking sun a fiery glow in the west.

"I meant to put salve on your hands," she apologized as they walked to the Ramsey homestead. "Those fingers will be sore by morning."

"I don't need any salve."

She glanced at him impatiently. He never thought he needed anything, much less attention. He was being stubborn again and for no reason. If he didn't need medicine for the nicks, then why had he winced each time she passed him a bowl during supper? You'd think a man could accept a little concern without feeling threatened.

"These raids. How long have they been going on?"

Ragan was so surprised he'd started a conversation, it took her a moment to organize her thoughts. "For years. Actually, they had stopped recently, but all of a sudden they're back."

"Why doesn't the town do something to stop it?"

Ragan shook her head. "We've tried, but there are too many different raiders and people just plain don't want to move. Barren Flats is home, no matter how rowdy it is. The town's been burned out a couple of times, and people have lost their will to fight. We're all a little afraid, actually. Most of us have to live and work here, and we can't afford to lose everything again."

"A shootist isn't going to solve your problem.

She glanced at him. "Do you have a better idea?"

"It's not my place to have an idea."

"Saying a shootist isn't going to help is having an opinion."

"Having an opinion is not the same as having an answer."

Conversation ceased, and they walked in silence until they turned the bend in the lane leading to the Ramsey home.

"What you said about having no family—is that true?" The smell of honeysuckle was sweet along the path in the fading twilight.

He was quiet for so long she wondered if he would even answer.

Finally, he said, "Does it matter? I'm the one serving time, not my family."

"No, it doesn't matter—I just wondered who you are. Family's important to me. Is your family in California?"

"You could say that."

She could say that and still know nothing about him, and it wasn't likely she ever would. Still, she knew she had no right to pry. Even a man serving time was entitled to his privacy.

"Papa pastored the church here in town until a couple of years ago." He didn't respond, but she went on anyway. "The gangs burned his church, then our house and barns. We were able to build the house back, but they just torched it again. Then my brother died, and after seeing everything go up in smoke a third time, Papa broke, just couldn't take any more."

She didn't know why she was telling him about her problems; he clearly wasn't interested. But talking made her feel better. She didn't even want Johnny McAllister to *say* anything, just listen.

"Mama died ten years ago, so with Jacob gone, it's just me and my sisters. The money I earn isn't much, but it's enough to keep food on the table and clothes on our backs. Holly and Jo take in sewing, and I put up a large garden every year. We get by."

"The town ought to save its money—stop doing foolish things like hiring a shootist."

She turned to look at him. He hadn't listened to a word she said. "We have to do something."

A young man on horseback stopped at the end of the lane and waved at Ragan.

She returned the wave. "Everett Pidgin," she said under her breath. She realized she made the name sound like a curse. Thank goodness he headed on, and didn't approach to talk as he usually did.

Johnny glanced in Everett's direction, but he didn't offer a response. They turned at the fork, and proceeded up the rutted path leading to the Ramsey house. The lid on the green bean bowl rattled as they covered the uneven ground.

"Everett lives on the farm south of the water tower." She gestured toward the direction the young man was headed. "Papa owns the town's only deep well. Folks pay us what they can afford for water, but mostly they catch the rains when they come, and store the water in the old tower. You've seen the water tower setting out near Muriel Davidson's place?"

He shook his head.

"It's back behind the rise, southeast of the church. Water's a precious commodity around here. It doesn't rain that often."

As they approached the simple frame house, a young girl ran out to meet them. Racing down the lane, her long blond hair flew out behind her, a smile lighting up her face.

Ragan caught her sister, laughing. "Hello!"

Jo hugged her neck, holding on tightly. "I've been watching for you." Her eyes traveled to Johnny, her smile wavering.

"Jo, this is Mr. McAllister."

Jo nodded solemnly. "The bank robber. I saw him at the town meeting yesterday."

"Jo!" Ragan reprimanded softly.

The girl graciously extended her hand. "Good evening, Mr. McAllister. My name is Jo—short for Josephina. I hate Josephina, so please call me Jo." She paused, her blue eyes sparkling with mischief. "What's your given name?"

"John."

She cocked her head. "John or Johnny?"

Ragan was surprised to see a smile soften the corners of his mouth. "I answer to either one."

"I will call you Johnny."

Jo was young and sometimes talked too

much. Ragan said, "Run along, and tell Papa I'm bringing mashed potatoes."

"Mashed potatoes—he'll be dee-lighted." Giving Johnny a smile, she skipped off, calling ahead, "Papa, Ragan's here, and she's bringing mashed potatoes!"

"I guess I could have yelled to him, myself."

They climbed the back steps and Ragan stepped into the kitchen. Closing her eyes, she drew a deep breath. "Mmm—cinnamon cookies."

A dark-haired girl close to Ragan's age stepped away from the stove, smiling.

"I knew you'd appreciate them. Where have you been? I was beginning to worry about you." Her eyes moved to the stranger.

"Holly, this is John McAllister. John, my sister, Holly."

"Nice to finally meet you, Mr. McAllister."

Setting the beans on the table, Johnny nodded. "Holly." He shook the hand she extended to him.

Holly turned back to the stove. "I thought you and the judge might be working late on the book."

Ragan bit into a warm cookie and offered the plate to Johnny. He shook his head.

"No, but we finished chapter seven this morning."

"Seven? You're coming right along."

"Yes, we are. I'm sorry I worried you. We were delayed a few minutes."

"We heard the shooting."

Ragan nodded. "Another gang."

"Well, the shootist will be here any day now. I talked with Minnie at the mercantile this morning. She said Everett sent the wire, and Mr. Mercer has already replied."

"Thank goodness. It can't be soon enough. I thought you'd be with Tom this evening." She lifted the basket to the cabinet.

"No, Tom's cutting hay. I don't expect to see him all week."

Ragan gave her sister a quick hug. "How's Papa tonight?"

Holly sobered, shaking her head. "He's been very quiet all day."

Ragan stepped to the parlor door and peeked in. A thin, stooped man sat in a rocking chair before the open window. Although the night was warm, a heavy blanket rested around his shoulders. Nine-year-old Rebecca read from the Twenty-first Psalm. She looked up, smiling when she saw the visitors.

Closing the door, Ragan said quietly, "I'll ask Marta to stop by tomorrow."

Sighing, Holly stepped to the stove and removed another batch of cookies from the oven. "Wish the town could afford a real doctor."

"Marta's as smart as any doctor; you know that." She turned toward Johnny to explain. "She's an old Cherokee woman who's nursed the whole town at one time or the other."

Holly frowned. "Is there enough money—"

"Marta will settle for canned goods. We can spare a few jars of peaches, can't we?" She absently handed a cookie to Johnny before biting into another one. What man didn't like hot cookies? Unless he was being stubborn.

"If necessary," Holly murmured.

Johnny handed the cookie back to Ragan. "If you're through with me, Miss Ramsey, I'll be going."

Becca burst through the kitchen doorway, almost bowling Johnny over. "Papa refuses to eat, says he isn't the least bit hungry. I've been reading to him." She took a moment to catch her breath. "Oh. Hello. You must be Mr. McAllister."

Johnny nodded.

"I'm Becca. It's very nice to meet you."

Ragan reached in the cabinet and took out a plate. "I'll see if I can tempt Papa with my mashed potatoes."

"Shall I walk Mr. McAllister to the end of the lane?" Jo asked.

Ragan set the plate down with a bang. "No!" She carefully tempered her voice at Johnny's quick look. Although he had so far proved himself trustworthy, she could not allow Jo to be alone with him. "No, Jo, it's dark. It isn't safe—not with the renewed gang activity."

Jo's face fell.

Johnny stoically met Ragan's gaze. "Your sister's right. A young lady shouldn't be out after dark."

The girl left the kitchen with an unhappy sideways glance at Ragan. Smiling her apology, Holly excused herself and followed her sister.

One look at Johnny's dark features and Ragan felt compelled to explain her refusal. Resentment burned deep in his eyes. "Mr. McAllister—"

He cut her off coldly, brushing past her. "Judge McMann is expecting me back."

Ragan trailed him outside and watched as he stepped off the porch and started back down the lane. She kept an eye on his tall frame until it faded into the darkness. Leaning against the porch column, she wondered if she'd hurt his feelings. Of course she had; she couldn't miss the resentment in his eyes.

Resting her head against the post, she gazed at the darkened sky. It was a beautiful night: millions of stars shining overhead, fireflies flickering in the field. She didn't want to cause anyone unhappiness. With the exception of a sour disposition, Mr. McAllister had stayed in line. Yet it was better to hurt feelings than endanger Jo.

She made a mental note to speak to her sisters, to warn them to stay away from Johnny McAllister. He was young, good-looking, and brash. Her heartbeat quickened at the memory of his body pressing into hers.

But he was also a convicted felon.

She even had to remind herself of that from time to time, and Jo was much more impressionable. Johnny McAllister could easily steal a young woman's heart.

Best she remember that fact, and often.

Chapter 5

The sounds of hammers and saws filled the air on Saturday morning. The town had assembled in full force to work on restoring the church. Johnny, Ragan, and Judge McMann arrived a little before nine o'clock.

"It will be nice to have Sunday services there again." Ragan shaded her eyes from the sun to watch the activity. Men crawled around on the rooftop, assessing the damage.

"Indeed it will. Before the day's over, the church will be a place of worship again." The judge twisted in his wheelchair to address Johnny. "Don't you agree, son?"

Johnny shrugged. Ragan smothered a spark of irritation. She'd like to shake the indifference out of him. But it *wasn't* his town, and it really wasn't his problem. She grudgingly conceded that point. If circumstances were reversed, and she were the detained

97

and he the keeper, she would be feeling a bit constricted herself.

"We could use a hand over here!" Austin Plummer called from the roof. He and two of his older boys were already soaked with perspiration.

"I'll be glad to help!" Judge McMann called back.

Plummer grinned good-naturedly. "Come on up!"

Proctor swiveled his chair to join the effort, but a large, iron hand reached out to block him.

Johnny shook his head solemnly. "Maybe you ought to hand up nails."

The judge's face fell. "Oh, fiddle faddle."

He feigned disappointment, but still, Ragan thought Proctor seemed downright smug over what he'd just accomplished: he'd gotten Johnny McAllister to respond in a positive manner.

The judge sighed. "Well, I suppose you're right."

Johnny rolled the chair to rest in the shade of the building. As he handed the judge a fistful of nails, Ragan overheard him say, "Your Miss Ramsey gets upset easily. Let's not ruffle her feathers by having you climb up and down those ladders."

Judge McMann chuckled. "You've noticed

she flies off the handle once in a while, have you?"

The very idea! Ragan felt her cheeks grow hot. Procky would be climbing up and down ladders and all over the roof if he had his way. Then she'd have to listen to him moan and groan for a week about his joints.

"Hey, McAllister!"

Johnny straightened to look up when Austin shouted his name.

The sun-browned Swede with twinkling blue eyes grinned. "Got enough work for everyone!"

Ragan joined the other women setting up the long rows of food tables, but her eyes refused to leave McAllister as he scaled the ladder. The slight breeze ruffled his hair and made him look boyish. Her gaze fastened to the back of his sweat-soaked shirt, stretched over powerful shoulders, and she swallowed hard. A slow, agonizing warmth spread through her mid-section, and her mind played tricks on her, making her imagine things she'd not ordinarily imagine. How many women had he held in those arms, those wonderfully muscle-corded arms, and whispered words that made her blush to even think about them? How many women had he needed, really needed, to hold him? Had Johnny McAllister ever needed anyone?

When she realized others were watching her shamelessly gawk, she quickly averted her gaze, surprised at how giddy the sun was making her feel. She should have worn her bonnet, as the judge suggested.

On top of the roof the men gathered, hands on hips, and took stock of the damage. It was a mess, all right, they agreed. It would take more than a day to repair this kind of destruction.

"The last fire took most of the old roof," Rudolf Miller said. "The gangs have about finished it off." He tested a section with his foot, kicking aside some broken shingles.

Miller's fourteen-year-old son, Clayton, frowned. "Not much sense fixin' the old thing if it's only gonna be shot up again, Pa."

"Well, the reverend thinks it bears fixin', son, so we'll repair it. Could be it'll hold until we can afford a new one. Besides, Mercer's going to rid us of the problem." He glanced at Johnny. "Ever hear of Dead Eye Mercer, McAllister?"

"I've heard of him."

"What do you think? Can he do the job?"

"His reputation says he can."

"Yes," Rudolf agreed with a solemn nod. "Hiring Mercer's the smartest thing we could do. Bound to signal better days for Barren

Flats. With the gangs gone, this town can get back to normal."

A tall, thin, intense-looking man joined the conversation. "Roberta's all the time talkin' about calling the town Paradise again. That sure would be nice. It would do us a world of good to take back our rightful name."

The men readily agreed. Johnny McAllister contributed nothing except another nail.

Ragan could hear the men's banter as she set dishes of food on the long, cloth-covered tables. Crisp fried chicken and biscuits, jars of pickles, corn relish, and spiced peaches scented the thick air. Most every able-bodied soul in Barren Flats had turned out to help with the reconstruction.

The workers set upon the repairs as if with personal vendettas. Children worked diligently grooming the grounds. They piled debris to be burned later, and even the smallest tikes picked up tinder and hauled it away.

The clock hands inched toward noon. Mazilea Lynch reached for the dinner bell and swung it in a wide arch, and the workers laid down their hammers and saws and migrated toward the food area. Children scrambled toward the tables and were quickly taken in tow by their parents.

Ragan poured lemonade and watched Johnny, who was helping the judge fill his plate. Procky seemed to be unusually picky about his food today, and she realized with a sinking feeling that he was actually enjoying Johnny's attention.

For a moment she struggled with a disturbing thought. Procky's only son lived hundreds of miles from Barren Flats, and rarely got home for a visit. The judge missed him terribly, and she prayed Procky wasn't beginning to see Johnny as a substitute for Blake. That would only complicate things and end up hurting Procky. She stole another glance at Johnny—whose thick, soft-looking hair gleamed in the sun—and realized she was the one in danger of being hurt, not the judge.

When Johnny's time was up, he'd be gone, and neither she nor the judge would ever hear from him again.

Remember that, Ragan.

And don't let me have to keep reminding you.

Johnny finished the last of his potato salad and leaned back against the tree trunk. Tipping his hat over his eyes, he enjoyed the temporary respite. The sun was hot, and his belly was full. His mind wandered back to the day of his trial.

*   *   *

The crowd was tight outside the courtroom and they booed when Johnny came through the doorway.

"Clear the way," the sheriff yelled, pushing bystanders aside.

A burly onlooker pressed closer as Johnny was led from the courtroom.

"McAllister."

Johnny turned at the harsh whisper, and the man stepped in closer. His eyes narrowed, and a set of rotting teeth flashed beneath a bushy red beard. The evil smile widened on the man's ruddy features.

"You're a dead man, McAllister."

The bank outlaw! Johnny halted and turned to say something to the deputy but the officer shoved him ahead.

"Get on," he ordered.

Johnny stumbled and righted himself. Turning to look over his shoulder, he searched the spectators for the outlaw.

There wasn't a person who looked remotely like him in the crowd.

Johnny shook his head. If Puet wanted him, he'd have to come to Paradise to get him.

"More lemonade, Mr. McAllister?" Johnny cracked an eye to find Jo Ramsey standing over him, a pitcher of lemonade in her hand.

He checked a smile. He didn't know what it was about Jo, but Ragan's younger sister reminded him of his own sister Lara. She'd have been close to Jo's age now. And like Jo, Lara'd be so darn pretty, she'd steal every boy's heart that looked her way. Pain twisted his gut, and he looked away. "I've had enough, thank you, Jo."

She set the pitcher aside and smiled shyly. "Mind if I join you?"

Johnny glanced in Ragan's direction. That probably wasn't a good idea; he didn't want her mad at him today. He'd rather have her smiles than those looks she could give him. "I'll be going back to work shortly."

The young girl's face fell. "But not for a while."

She looked so disappointed, he didn't have the heart to refuse her. What could a few minutes hurt? He nodded.

Flashing a quick smile, she sat down beside him. "Did you enjoy your dinner?"

"Too much," he conceded. It would be real easy to get used to this lifestyle. Good food, clean sheets, a woman looking after him. Sweet-smelling Ragan, serving him breakfast every morning. Lovely, soft Ragan in his bed at night. He clamped down on that thought, hard.

His mind wandered to the one time he'd

seriously thought about marrying. Her folks owned a spread next to Grandpa's. She was young, pretty, and mad as hell when he rode away without asking for her hand. At the time, he knew it was the right thing to do. He might have loved her. He'd at least been mighty attracted to her for a boy of seventeen. Maybe he should have married her, started a family .... But there was always Dirk Bledso.

"Don't you think, Mr. McAllister?" Jo's question brought him back to the present. He lifted his head to meet her questioning eyes.

"Sorry, did you say something?"

"Don't you think that a girl has the right to tell a boy that she likes him?" Morningglory blue eyes gazed adoringly at him. "Ragan says—"

"Jo!"

A flushed Ragan stood over them, her eyes snapping, a wooden spoon clutched tightly in her hand. Jo looked up at her sister expectantly. "Yes?"

"Roberta needs your help cutting desserts."

"Yes, ma'am." The girl obediently got up, brushing dried grass off the back of her dress. She turned and gave Johnny a smile that would melt the devil's heart. "Thank you, Mr. McAllister. It's been nice visiting with you."

Ragan's left foot tapped impatiently. "Hurry along, Jo."

Johnny waited until the girl joined Roberta at the dessert table and was out of earshot before he turned to confront Ragan, his features taut. "I'm not going to hurt your sister."

Flushing a deeper red, she thrust a plate toward him. "I brought you a piece of pecan pie."

"No thanks." He thrust it back, his earlier good mood gone. She sure knew how to take the fun out of a picnic.

Expelling a deep breath, she extended the pie, insistent that he take it. "Minnie's real proud of her pies. Just because you don't like me doesn't mean you need to hurt Minnie's feelings." She motioned toward the row of tables. "She's watching to see if you eat it."

Johnny mentally groaned when he saw the mayor's wife wave at him. Hell, he didn't have to appease Minnie Rayles by eating her pie; he was sentenced to a year of monotony, not gluttony. He half-heartedly waved back, then turned back to face Ragan. "Who said I didn't like you?"

"You." She sat down, setting the pie plate on his chest. She was still upset, but she never stayed mad long, just long enough to pin his ears back. A grin played at the corners of his mouth. A little fire at the right time never hurt any woman. And he bet this particular little spitfire had all the heat he could handle.

The smell of pecan pie drifted to him, and he sat up. Hell, he'd eat the damned pie. He didn't want accusing female eyes on him all day.

"Exactly when did I say I didn't like you?" He bit into the tender crust. How could a woman take flour and lard and nuts and come up with something that tasted so good?

"You haven't ever specifically said it, but I know you don't." Ragan pushed a damp strand of hair out of her eyes, and he forgot the pie.

Clearly she believed what she was saying, and why wouldn't she? He'd given her a hard time from the moment he got here. He supposed he was blaming her for his troubles, troubles she had no part in.

She sighed, her tone softer now. "I don't blame you for being resentful. I know what you're going through is hard, but you should understand that what I'm doing isn't personal: it's the program. When I caution Jo to stay away from you, I'm only concerned about her welfare. Surely you're aware it isn't proper for a young woman her age to—"

"Associate with the likes of me?" He took another bite of pie. "So you keep reminding me."

"I have never said that," she contended softly.

His features tightened. "Yes, you have." She said it every day: in her tone, in the way she looked at him, in the suspicion in her eyes when he caught her staring. She didn't have to say it; her opinion of him came through loud and clear.

She shook her head. "When did I ever say such a hateful thing?"

He cut off another bite of pie. "You say it without words."

"Then I apologize. I don't disapprove of you, Mr. McAllister. I disapprove of your ways, but I'm trying very hard to give you the benefit of the doubt."

"That's real big of you." Damned if he knew why her respect mattered to him, but it did. These were good people, and he didn't like them thinking he was a criminal. "If this is a dressing down, Miss Ramsey, I'm not getting the point. Be specific. What do you want me to do?"

"Try harder. You do what you're told without complaint, but your heart isn't in it."

"You want me to like my circumstances? That will be a cold day in hell."

"No, I don't expect you to like your punishment. I just want you to be more accepting about it. A year is a long time to carry a grudge against the judge and me. We're trying to make your sentence go as smoothly as possible. It will make it easier for everyone if you'll cooperate."

Polishing off the last of the pie, he rested the empty plate on his chest. She was right. So why was he resisting? These people didn't ask for him to be here, and they'd been decent to him from the start. Other than being kept busy and staying here for the confines of his sentence, he had a reasonable amount of freedom—a lot more than sitting in a cell behind bars. He could have things a whole lot worse.

"All right." From now on he would attempt to make the best of the situation. And he would discourage Jo's interest in him, even though her presence brought Lara back—if only for a few minutes.

She shot him a skeptical glance. "All right, what?"

"You're right about me not liking you. You're headstrong, bossy, and opinionated, and you get on my nerves like a new blister." He paused, waiting for a reaction from her.

If possible, she got even prettier when she was angry. When her chin jutted upward, he added, "But you're only doing your job. I suppose I could try harder to get along."

To her credit, she took the character assassination in stride, only giving him a distant smile. "Well, I'm sorry you feel that way. At first I didn't like you, either. Your annoying refusal to get involved here makes me want to slap you silly. But, though you may not think I believe in your innocence . . ." Color rose to her cheeks, and she took a deep breath. "Actually, I think I do. You don't seem to be the violent sort, and you can be almost nice when you set your mind to it." Their eyes met, and he couldn't quite swallow his grin.

She hurriedly said, "And the judge likes you—you must know that."

"And that burns you."

"No, but I think it could pose a problem. Procky misses his son terribly. Blake lives in Denver, and I'm afraid he doesn't get home often."

"And you're afraid the judge will start to think of me as Blake."

She opened her mouth to reply, then closed it. Well, at least she knew when to stop. She looked so thankful that he let it pass. He wasn't blind, he knew the judge was lonely. Who wasn't?

"Set your pretty head to rest, Miss Ramsey." Lying back, he closed his eyes. "I'll make sure Judge McMann doesn't confuse me for his son."

"Thank you." The relief in her voice was so blatant that it rubbed him the wrong way.

"And don't you confuse me for the man of your dreams."

She gasped, but immediately said snippily, "Don't worry, even my imagination isn't that far-reaching."

He grinned wickedly as she watched the activity going on around her. The silence stretched.

"You ever get a good look at the gangs who ride through here?"

"Not often. Why?"

"Ever hear of Dirk Bledso?" The outlaw was notorious; if he and his murdering brothers had ever ridden through Barren Flats, someone would have noticed.

"It sounds familiar, but there are so many who ride through here." Ragan settled back against the trunk, her brow creased in concentration. "Dirk Bledso. Isn't he also known as the Viper?"

"That's the one."

"I do recall a wanted poster bearing that

name. He rides with his brothers, doesn't he?"

"Yes. How long ago did you see the poster?"

"Three, maybe four years. I remember because Papa and I talked about how vile the brothers looked."

"Vile" didn't even begin to cover it.

Raylene Plummer fastened the ties of her apron and called to Ragan. "We could use your help, dearie!"

Excusing herself, Ragan stood up.

"Thanks for the pie," he murmured.

Lifting his hat, she said softly, "You're welcome." She let the hat drop back into place.

Grinning, he listened for her to walk away. He heard the rustle of her skirt, then unexpectedly felt her fingers brush against his chest as she picked up the empty plate and fork. Her fingers were cool, but they seared his skin right through his shirt, setting his insides on fire.

Tilting his hat back slightly, Johnny studied her swaying skirts as she walked away. Desire rose in him, and he quickly curbed it. They'd declared a truce, not a tryst.

But he had to admit that the latter was beginning to have a dangerous appeal.

Chapter 6

The following Saturday, the air was charged with excitement as townsfolk milled around the stage station, ears tuned to the north. Children balanced on the board-walk railing and scampered back and forth across the road under the watchful eyes of their parents.

Voices hummed as the clock hands inched past two o'clock. Of all days, the stage was late.

The town band warmed up on a carefully erected platform covered in blue and white bunting. Their instruments clogged the air with disjoined harmony. Decked out in his Sunday best, Mayor Rayles paced in front of the dais, lips silently moving as he rehearsed his speech. In his left front pocket a town proclamation awaited the notorious gun-slinger, Dead Eye Mercer.

113

Lowell Homer stepped out of the mercantile, patting his ample stomach. "Fine day, Mayor."

"Couldn't be better!" Carl Rayles indicated the elderly man by his side. "Sheriff Lutz is looking forward to this more than anybody. Right, Alvin?"

The sheriff looked blank. "Eh?"

"You're looking forward to gettin' rid of the gangs!"

Alvin nodded. "Yep. If Mercer cleans up the town, maybe somebody'll take this." He tapped the badge on his shirt.

"Maybe," Lowell agreed. "Nervous?" he asked the mayor.

"Me?" Mayor Rayles laughed. "Looking forward to the excitement. How about you, Shorty?"

"Can't wait." Shorty Lynch stepped out of the store with Mazilea and locked up. "Coming to the picnic afterwards, Carl?"

"Wouldn't miss it! I imagine our guest of honor has many a fascinatin' story to tell."

"Stage is comin'!"

A shout went up, and the band struck up a spirited rendition of "The Star Spangled Banner." Folks craned their necks to see Dead Eye Mercer roll into town. Long minutes passed before they realized the speck of dust they thought was the stage was actually Austin and Raylene Plummer with their sons, coming to greet the stage. The music died away, and the townsfolk resumed chatting.

"How we gonna know it's him?" Florence Banks asked. "Nobody's ever actually seen this Mercer."

"No one has to see him. We'll know," Hubie assured his wife. "Can't miss a legend like Mercer."

"Anyone know what Mercer looks like?" someone else called out.

No, no one did.

"He's mean."

"Mean, and so fast on the draw not a single man's ever lived to tell about meeting him."

"That's why no one knows what he looks like," a voice declared.

The hum rose and fell as anticipation mounted. The suspense was murder, but it wouldn't be long now.

"Has to be a big son-of-a-gun."

"Oh, no doubt."

"Wonder if Mercer wears an eyepatch? Seems I read somewhere he does."

"Probably. He's in a risky business. Could lose an eye real easy."

It was generally agreed the shootist was

big, mean, and fast, and probably missing an eye.

The town had put their money to good use. "I see the stage!"

The band started up, and heads turned. Tubas and horns filled the air with patriotic tunes. Dogs barked, and babies, startled by all the noise, squalled at their mothers' bosoms. It was minutes before someone realized this was another false alarm. This time, a hay-laden wagon driven by a citizen of nearby Brown Branch was passing through.

The tubas died off, followed by the trombones and cymbals. Eyes returned to the north end of town.

"I'm a little nervous." Lillian Hubbard tightened little Trish's hair ribbon.

Haleen Lutz fanned herself with a hanky, her matronly features flushed from the heat. Tiny beads of perspiration lay on her forehead. "Well, I'd like to have Mr. Mercer to supper, but I surely do hope he doesn't plan to stay long. We don't need his likes hanging around. Got enough riffraff the way it is. Don't you agree, Alvin?" She tugged her husband's sleeve, raised her voice, and spoke directly into her husband's ear. "I said, Mercer needs to move on when he's through here. Don't you agree?"

The sheriff checked his watch fob. "Stop

frettin', Haleen. You don't have to yell. It won't take Mercer long to do his job. He's got a reputation to uphold."

Minnie Rayles frowned. "Carl'll make sure he leaves the moment the job is done. I'll have him for pot roast and maybe one of my lemon pies, but I agree with you, Haleen. He cannot be hanging around looking for work."

The mayor's features tightened. "Don't start naggin', Minnie. A man don't just clean up a town, eat post roast and lemon pie, and leave overnight. Ya gotta give Mercer enough time to do what he's gotta do."

"Nonetheless, Carl, Mercer must not be allowed to remain in Barren Flats one moment longer than necessary."

The mayor ground his teeth into the tip of his cigar. "Yes, Buttercup."

The excitement was contagious. The town's troubles were over, no doubt about that! Best money they ever spent.

"He's going to kill the gangs, kill the gangs, kill the gangs," young Mary Hubbard sang, and her sister Trish immediately picked up the chant. The two girls held hands and hopped from one foot to the other. Pigtails flew as they twirled in a circle, forcing others to sidestep them. "Kill the gangs, kill the gangs!"

"Trish! Mary! Who's been filling your

minds with such thoughts? We want the gangs to stop destroying property. We don't necessarily wish the men to be killed." Ragan shaded her eyes, peering down the road.

The judge, Johnny, and the Ramsey family were all gathered to welcome the shootist. She dabbed at the trickle of perspiration on her forehead.

Mary paused, hands on slender hips, eyes narrowed with challenge. "If he's not gonna kill anyone, how come he's called a 'shoots it?' "

Ragan bit back a smile. She glanced at Johnny and blushed when he grinned and murmured, "Why indeed?"

"Shootist, Mary, shootist. It doesn't mean . . . oh, look! Is that the stage I see?"

Eyes shifted northward again and focused on a coach dragging a cloud of dust as it approached.

A cheer went up as word spread that the legend was, for sure this time, about to arrive.

Ragan pulled Holly aside. "Watch Papa closely this afternoon. With all the excitement, he's likely to wander off."

"Ragan! Yoo hoo!"

Ragan clamped her eyes shut, then reopened them to see Everett coming toward her. She spared him a brief glance, then cupped her hand to her eyes and expectantly peered down the road.

Becca poked Johnny, giggling. "Everett loves Ragan."

"Rebecca!" Ragan shot her sister a stern look.

"It's true!"

Ragan glared, but the younger girl only re-iterated, "Well, he does."

"Everett." Ragan smiled as the tall, pain-fully thin telegraph clerk approached. "You've met Mr. McAllister?"

Everett eyed Johnny, then looked back at Ragan. "I've seen him around." He reached out and touched Fulton's shoulder. "After-noon, sir. It's good to see you out and about."

Reverend Ramsey seemed confused, as if he had just awakened and realized there were people around him. He focused on Johnny, a smile breaking across his features. "Why—who's this fine young man?" He frowned. "Ahh, of course . . . the new school-master. Looks as though we have a good one this time. I've brought the children to meet you. Say hello, children."

Fulton Ramsey's daughters exchanged em-barrassed looks, then murmured obedient hellos.

Sliding her arm protectively around her fa-ther's shoulders, Ragan said, "Papa, this isn't the new schoolmaster; it's Johnny McAllister. Remember? He's staying with Procky."

"Oh, yes." Fulton smiled pleasantly, extending his hand. "You'll be good for Paradise," he told Johnny. "An education is extremely important for our young people. They can't read the Good Book if they don't have an education."

Everett edged closer to the small circle. "Ragan, you look mighty fetching today."

"Thank you, Everett." Ragan quickly changed the subject. "We'll be meeting Mercer any moment now. Isn't it exciting?"

"I intend to learn to shoot a gun more accurately." His eyes darted to Johnny, then to the stage finally pulling to a halt in front of the mercantile. "Very soon, actually. Just have to find the spare time."

Judge McMann shouted to be heard over the band. "Better leave the shooting to the experts, son."

Everett ran a finger around the inside of his shirt collar, damp from the building heat. "I can *shoot*, Judge! I just need more practice, that's all."

Four men piled from the top of the stage. A twitter went through the crowd, and all eyes were glued on the descending passengers. But all four turned out to be local boys, and excitement turned into a disappointed buzz.

Then the Thompson sisters alighted from inside the coach, back from their aunt's funeral in San Francisco. For a moment they looked startled at the gathering, then threaded their way through the crowd.

Eyes switched back to the open door. A small, innocuous-looking man stepped off the coach. He couldn't be more than five foot four, and a hundred ten pounds, with thinning brown hair. The new arrival paused, squinting over the rims of thick spectacles.

Then a young boy carrying a portmanteau tied with string hopped down. He scanned the crowd, brightening when he spotted his grandparents.

"There's your grandson, Cap," someone called.

Racing toward them, the child embraced Sylvia Kincaid. The three then set off for a nearby wagon, oblivious to the town folks waiting for Mercer. Clifford's red cap bobbed in the crowd as he lugged the boy's bag.

Eyes shifted back to the front of the coach.

Ragan stood on tiptoes, searching the crowd.

Becca pressed closer. "Do you see him?"

"No. I don't think he came." A sick numbness ran through her.

Disappointment spread through the on-lookers, and the music died away.

"Didn't come? We sent a deposit—he'd better come!"

"Maybe he missed the stage; maybe he's on the next one."

Tempers flared to match the temperature.

"Of all things! The whole town's out to welcome him, and he doesn't show up. What does that say for his credibility?" Minnie Rayles blustered. "Carl? What's going on here?"

"Don't go gettin' yourself worked up, Minnie. Give the poor man time."

Johnny focused on the small-statured, be-spectacled figure threading his way toward Alvin Lutz and Carl Rayles. Mercer? He'd read stories about the gunslinger, but none ever gave a description that he could recall. He watched the man exchange a few words with the sheriff. Shock registered on Alvin's face. He stepped back, cupping his hand to his ear.

A moment later, "*You're* Dead Eye Mercer?"

Johnny winced at the sheriff's incredulous tone. Because of his deafness he always spoke loudly, and his voice carried well through the crowd.

Heads swiveled; jaws went slack.

"*That's* Dead Eye Mercer!"

"That can't be the shootist. That man couldn't fight his way out of a wet paper sack!"

"It's him, all right. Look at Carl—looks fit to be tied."

Johnny saw the man's steely stare. It was Mercer all right; the town just didn't care to believe it.

"Oh, for heaven's sake!" Minnie turned away in disgust.

"Now, Minnie," Muriel Davidson tried to pacify her. "Warren always says it's not a person's size—"

"I don't care what Warren always says. *Look* at him. He can't fight these gangs; he's no bigger than a termite!"

"Send him back, Mayor," Mazilea yelled.

Mayor Rayles held up his hand and demanded silence. When the clamor died enough for people to hear, he lifted his voice above the confusion. "Folks, er . . . now calm down. It seems there's been a mistake—Warren! Stop playing that blasted tuba!"

The tuba strains died away.

"Is *that* Mercer?" someone in the crowd shouted.

"Er . . . yes. Now let's not jump to conclusions . . ."

The crowd pushed forward, and Mayor

Rayles and Sheriff Lutz were forced to step back or be trampled.

"We want our money back!"

"Oh, my," Ragan pressed her hanky to her forehead. "This is just awful."

Judge McMann stood and tried to peer over the frenzied gathering. "They should at least talk to the man—why, this is a disgrace."

Johnny parted his way through the crowd, moving toward the gunman. Granted, Mercer didn't look as if he could whip cream, but looks were deceiving.

"Send him back!"

Johnny couldn't believe it. In their midst was one of the deadliest guns in the west, and they were complaining because he wasn't as big as they had imagined he would be?

He reached Mercer as the crowd formed a ring around the mayor, calling for his removal. By now Mercer stood to the side, stiffly watching the exhibition.

"Adrian Mercer?"

Mercer's eyes narrowed, his hand dropping to his holster concealed beneath a dark blue suitcoat. "Who wants to know?"

Johnny extended his hand. "John McAllister. Pleasure to make your acquaintance, sir."

Mercer ignored the gesture, refusing to

shake. "Seems you're the only one."

Johnny studied the crowd. He wasn't apologizing for others' bad manners. Then he saw Ragan, and his thoughts tempered. This was her town, and it was a troubled town. "They're having a rough time right now; they don't mean any disrespect."

Mercer leaned over and spat. "The hell they don't. Who'd they expect? Wyatt Earp?"

Glancing at the judge who was moving forward, Johnny said quietly, "Do you know Dirk Bledso?"

Mercer kept an eye on the restless crowd. "Sure, I know the Viper. Why?"

"Have you seen him lately?"

The gunman's eyes returned to Johnny. "What's it to you?"

"I have something that belongs to him." A bullet with Bledso's name on it.

Mercer leaned over and spat again. "So?"

Johnny kept his tone casual. "Bledso's a hard one to catch up with. Suppose he and his brothers are still tearing up hell?"

Mercer made a sound like a laugh, but it was easy to see he wasn't amused. "Yeah, those three are real mean."

"I've heard that."

Wiping his mouth with his shirtsleeve, Mercer frowned. "Haven't seen Dirk in a while. Last time I bumped into him was over in Callum County—two, maybe three years ago." The two men turned to look as the noise around the platform swelled again.

"Send him back," the crowd yelled in unison.

Mercer eyed them sourly. "Them people are nuts."

Ragan watched the unfolding spectacle, sick at heart.

"Ragan, roll me to the platform," Judge McMann said. "I'm going to put a stop to this."

Ragan pushed the chair through the noisy crowd, her eyes centered on Johnny and Mercer. What were those two talking about? Her heart sank. Did Johnny and Mercer know each other? Was Johnny thinking about doing something foolish? It would be simple to cause a ruckus and slip off through the crowd. *Don't jump to conclusions*, she reminded herself. She was being as unfairly judgmental as the others.

"Mayor Rayles!" Judge McMann shouted above the noise. The crowd parted and allowed the judge access to the platform.

When the mayor spotted McMann, he stepped down, mopping his brow. "Judge."

He nodded to Ragan. "We got ourselves in a real fine predicament here."

Judge McMann moved closer. "What's the problem, Carl?"

"Well . . . just look at Mercer. He's not exactly what we had in mind." Carl wiped his nose, then shoved the handkerchief back into his hip pocket. Sweat stood out on his forehead.

Heads swiveled to stare at the shootist.

Mercer stiffened, nailing the entire assemblage with a hard look, his hand perched defiantly on his Colt revolver.

Eyes switched back.

"Exactly what about him don't you like, Carl?" the judge asked.

Carl leaned closer. "Look at him, Procky. He's little—skinny as a rail. And reedy—real reedy. We need a man for this job."

Judge McMann's eyes traveled to Mercer. "Seems to me you're being a little unfair, aren't you, Carl? Can't tell a book by its cover."

"I can *that* book, Judge." They turned to look back at the spindly shootist.

"We're sending him packing, and we're demanding our money back," Minnie declared.

"We can't ask for our money back." Carl mopped his forehead with his coat sleeve.

"The man's come all the way out here. We can't ask for our money back just because he's small."

"We'll pay for his fare, but you'll have to get our deposit back, Carl." Minnie snapped open her parasol. "And be quick about it. No use wasting the man's time."

Carl, perspiration running down his face, went to break the unpleasant news to Mercer.

Johnny moved back to stand by the judge as the mayor told Mercer that due to an unforeseen circumstance, his services would not be needed. Ragan joined them a moment later, concern lining her face.

Judge McMann said softly, "Something tells me we're making a mistake."

Ragan turned. "What do you think, Johnny? Could Mercer do the job?"

Removing his hat, Johnny ran a hand through his hair. What he thought didn't matter: by now, there wasn't enough money in the state to make Mercer stay. "Looks and size don't make a man."

"That's true," the judge murmured.

Everett added his two cents. "That's entirely right, Judge. A man's size don't matter—it's his abilities that count."

The crowd dispersed as Mercer got back

on the stage. A moment later, it pulled slowly from the platform

"Well, so much for a shootist!" Roberta straightened her hat.

"It's only a minor setback. We've made a sound decision," Minnie said. "To think of a pint-sized man like that believing he could clean up a town."

Snapping open their parasols, the two women went to begin the picnic.

The following Monday afternoon, Ragan poured lemonade for the Ladies' Quilting Group in Judge McMann's living room. The subjects of Dead Eye Mercer and the raids had been thoroughly discussed, and conversation had turned to the upcoming Founders' Day celebration, held the first weekend in September.

"Why, Frankie can't wait for the pie tasting," Kensil Southern exclaimed. "He's talked of nothing else since he was a judge last year. His favorite is blueberry, but Minnie's pecan holds a close second with him."

The mayor's wife blushed. "Oh Kensil, it's a very average pecan. I use just a dribble of sorghum, you know. That's what gives it that bit of an edge."

"I don't see how your Frankie stays so skinny, eating all that pie!"

"He never has been one to put on weight. Just lucky, I guess."

"Mazilea, you entering your green tomato chow-chow this year? That's always a winner."

"Yes. Shorty's eaten most of it already, but I have some put back, so I'll have an entry. Bringing some pickled watermelon rind and okra, too."

"Oh, you make the best pickled okra around. My mouth waters just thinking about it."

"Alvin's gathering hay and targets for the shooting match. Justine, are your boys shooting this year?"

The blacksmith's wife nodded. "Couldn't keep them away."

"Poor Everett. He'll be in there trying again, though he can't hit the broad side of a barn."

"Yes, dear boy. He really is a dismal shot." Roberta Seeden glanced at Ragan, then back to her sewing.

"Well," Minnie bit off a thread. "One thing's going to be different this year."

The ladies turned their attention to the mayor's wife. "There'll be no liquor at the celebration. I've made that very clear to Carl."

"I wouldn't count on that. How're you going to prevent it, Minnie? You know the men and their spirits. It'll take more than you to stop their fun." Though Haleen's hands were now too arthritic to sew, she always came to the meeting.

"I put my foot down, that's how. I've been checking the cellar every evening after Carl's in bed. Nary a bottle down there. And Florence is watching Hubie to be sure none are sneaked from the saloon."

Florence's needle paused. "The past few years, Hubie's stashed away rum for Carl to pick up on his way home. Now when Carl comes by, I keep a close eye on those two. The only liquor Carl leaves with is what's in his belly."

The ladies laughed heartily, except for Minnie.

Lillian Hubbard frowned. "I'm not sure you can keep alcohol out of the celebration. The men are going to be very upset."

"Let them be," Minnie sniffed. "I don't intend for Carl to get liquored up this year."

"Minnie, you always say that, and every celebration Carl over-imbibes. The men always find a way," Kensil Southern said.

Haleen nodded in agreement. "Men will be men."

"They won't this year, I tell you. I've made my intentions clear to Carl. There's not a single bottle in the cellar—nor will there be between now and Founders' Day."

Sighing at the familiar argument, Ragan set her sewing aside and got up to bring more lemonade for her guests. She glanced out the kitchen window and saw Johnny scrubbing screens. Powerful arm muscles flexed as he worked.

What would it be like to be in those powerful arms, Johnny holding her tight? The thought left her breathless and longing for something . . . yet she didn't know what.

How she wished to fully experience that hunger she saw in his eyes, the need he worked so hard to conceal. Yet he kept his distance.

With each passing day, she knew, knew in her heart, he had been falsely accused. Johnny McAllister was no bank robber. He might be guilty of poor judgment, but she knew a criminal when she saw one. And he wasn't one.

And she was rarely wrong about these things.

Rarely.

Chapter 7

Early the following morning Ragan announced she was out of coffee, so after breakfast, Johnny walked her to the mercantile. When they parted at the door, he smiled. "Don't spend all day in there talking."

"Since when did you get to be so bossy?"

Winking, he tugged the ribbon on her bonnet and walked away grinning. He could feel her eyes following him as he stepped off the porch.

Minnie Rayles emerged from the general store and looked both ways for Carl. The mayor was across the street at the surveyor's office, but it was obvious Minnie didn't know where her husband had gone.

Johnny sauntered toward her and took the two large bags from her arms. "I'll get those for you, Mrs. Rayles."

Minnie had to take two steps with her

plump little legs to his one, and she bustled to keep up. "Thank you, Johnny. You're a sweet man." She reached up and pinched his cheek, and he winced.

Johnny set the sack of groceries on the buckboard seat, his cheek stinging. Tipping his hat, he smiled. "Have a nice day, ma'am."

Minnie tittered. "Oh, I shall. Ta ta!"

Ta ta. How that woman could be so much like Grandma's sister, Aunt Tess, he'd never know. He felt like a nine-year-old around the mayor's wife. Aunt Tess had always pinched his cheek like that when he'd done something to please her.

Leaning against the bank railing, he took inventory of the town. People went about their business as if they hadn't made complete fools of themselves with Mercer. Music already spilled from the open doorway of the Oasis Saloon.

He wondered if there was any real chance Bledso's gang would ever come through Barren Flats. Every other lowlife seemed to.

Removing his hat, Johnny wiped sweat off the headband. It wasn't nine o'clock yet, and it was hot enough to cook an egg on the boardwalk. His eyes swept Main Street as time dragged. Well, if there was anything he had, it was time.

His hand crept down his thigh to feel the space left by his missing pistol. What if he got his chance at Bledso before his gun was returned? The thought plagued him. Judge McMann might let him use an ax to chop wood, but the trust didn't carry over to a gun.

"There is one more requirement you must fulfill before this court is satisfied that the correct sentence has been handed down." Judge Leonard *leaned forward in his chair. "John McAllister, I want your word, as a man, that you will serve the sentence and will return before this bench at its completion."*

"You have my word, sir."

The judge nodded gravely. "I'm an old man. Some folks don't like my sentences—sometimes I wonder myself if they're sound. Tomorrow morning at daybreak, you'll be transported to Paradise, California where you will begin your sentence. I'll expect to see you back in this courtroom at the successful completion of your term."

Johnny nodded. He would be back—unless he ran into Dirk Bledso. In that case the judge's efforts on his behalf would be in vain. If, and when, he met up with Bledso, he would kill him. He'd never get Grandpa's gun back, and that bothered him. But the way Bledso had butchered his family in cold blood disturbed him more.

*   *   *

The consequences of violating the terms of his sentence would be dire. Not only would he break his word to Judge Leonard and forever lose Grandpa's gun, but he'd end up spending the next twenty years in prison, or worse.

Was killing Bledso worth it?

Bitterness gnawed at him, an acridity he couldn't shake.

He had no life anyway. Bledso had ended life as he knew it, in one senseless act. He'd destroyed almost everyone who ever cared about him. Grandpa had loved him, but now he was gone too. He focused on Ragan, who was talking to Roberta Seeden in the mercantile. If things were different, he would have her. Or at least he'd try. But he couldn't have her and kill Bledso. So he'd go on searching, looking. Sleeping in a lonely bed at night.

His gaze meandered the streets, pausing at the telegraph office. The clerk, Everett, what was his last name? Pidgin? Everett Pidgin leaned on the counter, chin propped in his hand, watching Ragan through the mercantile window.

Poor besotted fool. Grandpa said love could sicken the heart as surely as disease sickened the body. He remembered his first infatuation, a dark-eyed Spanish *señorita* in

Mexico. The fascination lasted only a couple of weeks, but intensity made up for the lack of longevity. A man didn't forget a woman like Roxanne Gonzales. He glanced toward the mercantile. Or Ragan Ramsey, for that matter.

Ragan's laughter floated through the open doorway. A man would be hard-pressed not to want a woman like her. Soft, sweet, smelling of rosewater; reeking of domesticity. A dangerous combination for a man like him. *Don't even think about it, McAllister.*

An elusive thought teased him ... Pidgin had mentioned wanting to learn to shoot a gun. *He* needed access to a gun, but he was forbidden to handle a firearm.

Pushing away from the post, Johnny sauntered across the street to the telegraph window. Everett was so engrossed in watching Ragan, he didn't hear the footsteps.

"Hot day."

The clerk's head snapped around, and dark eyes centered on him.

Everett's face was too long, his eyes narrow set. He had a lantern jaw, a five o'clock shadow, thick lips, long sideburns and he was thirty pounds too light for his six-foot-two frame.

The clerk watched as Johnny approached. "Can I help you?"

"No." Johnny casually adjusted the brim of his hat. "Just waiting for Ragan to finish up at the mercantile. Thought it might be cooler over here."

Everett busied himself straightening papers. His open resentment was amusing—no, actually, it was pathetic. Pidgin carried a torch the size of Texas for a woman he could never have. Obviously Everett considered his presence at the McMann house threatening, though he couldn't imagine why.

Ragan was out of his league. Women like her had always been out of his league. She wanted home and family; he wanted Dirk Bledso to pay for his sins. The two didn't mesh and it would be foolish to ever think otherwise. That would be a fatal error on his part, and his goal was to make as few errors as possible. The last one had cost him at least one year, maybe two, of his life.

Lifting the dipper out of the water pail, Johnny took a long drink. He glanced at Pidgin, now busy scribbling on a yellow pad. It was possible they could accommodate one another. He couldn't be caught with a gun in his possession, but he did need to know where he could get his hands on one if Bledso showed up. Taking a final swig, he tossed the remainder of the water onto the ground.

"Founders' Day a big celebration around here?"

Everett didn't look up. "Somewhat."

Johnny leaned against the counter, scanning the building clouds. A shower would settle the dust. "A lot of good food and whiskey, I guess."

Getting up from his stool, Everett sorted a stack of papers. "You're serving a sentence, aren't you?" He avoided Johnny's eyes. "You're a criminal."

Johnny took a deep breath. Pidgin knew his status, but he'd play along. "Yeah. I'm a criminal."

Everett had decided to press the issue. "What'd you do? Kill someone?"

"No, I'm accused of robbing a bank." Everett would have that information, too, if he'd read the wire that Johnny knew Judge McMann received.

Everett reshuffled the same stack of papers. He'd be lucky if there was anything left to deliver if he didn't stop moving them around. "Did you do it?"

"No."

"That's what they all say."

The men fell silent. Everett finally stashed the papers neatly on a shelf, and returned to the window. Johnny glanced toward the mercantile, aware of Everett's curious sideways looks.

"We don't need no more trouble in town. We got enough." Everett pointedly avoided looking at him.

"I don't plan on causing trouble."

"And the celebration and picnic this year? It won't be worth attending."

Johnny didn't doubt that a bit. He'd never been one for socializing. He watched Pidgin tidy up, the young man's face dark with resentment.

"No whiskey this year."

Johnny's brows lifted curiously.

"Whiskey," Everett repeated, frowning. "Minnie Rayles won't let us men have it."

"That's too bad." And interesting.

Warming a little, Everett leaned closer. "It's a crime—but there's not a thing we can do about it. Minnie is just plain mean-spirited. She knows how to take all the fun out of Founders' Day."

"Sounds like it."

"I don't know how Carl stands it. I wouldn't want to marry a bossy woman like Minnie."

"Not many would."

Silence stretched between them. Everett cleared his throat and made another attempt at conversation. "Actually, I don't care all that much for whiskey, but the other men think it's important. Personally, what I look forward to is the shooting contest."

"They have a shooting contest at the celebration?"

Everett nodded. "Big one, every year. The winner this year takes home a brand-new Greener double-barrel shotgun."

"A Greener, huh? Nice gun. Guess you plan on winning?"

"Me? No. I can't hit the broad side of a barn. Hubie Banks will win it. Wins every year."

Play it easy, Johnny reminded himself. *Nice and easy.*

Removing his hat again, he studied it. "What makes you say that? You could practice and get better, couldn't you?"

Shaking his head, Everett appeared to consider, then discard the thought. He glanced at Johnny. "You probably know how to shoot a gun—shoot one real well."

"I do okay. What kind of a gun do you have?"

"A pistol." Everett's eyes drifted back to Ragan. "Women like men who can shoot well."

The subject seemed to be a sore spot with the clerk. Shifting, Johnny said quietly, "I wouldn't necessarily say that. I know women who despise violence."

"Women like their men to be men. And a real man knows how to shoot a gun accurately."

"Most anyone can learn to be a good shot. If a man wanted to learn, I could teach him to shoot a rattlesnake's eyes out at fifty feet."

Everett's jaw dropped, then his eyes narrowed. "You're not allowed to have a gun."

"I could teach a man to shoot without touching the gun."

"You could?" He could almost see the cogs turn in Everett's head. He wanted it, but would he go for it?

"No." Everett shook his head. "I may look like a fool, but I've got more brains than that. You're a criminal; you're not even supposed to be around a gun. I could get in trouble."

Johnny smiled. "I merely mention my services, should you need them."

"I don't need them, thank you. Judge McMann would be real upset if I was to do anything to interfere with his program." He glanced toward the mercantile. "So would Ragan."

"I understand," Johnny said.

Everett picked up another stack of papers. Sweat stood out on his upper lip and his hands shook, causing several of the documents to fall to the floor. He leaned down to pick them up. "I'd . . . I'd like to take you up on your offer . . . but it just wouldn't be right."

Johnny calmly set the hook. "Don't know of a man who wouldn't give his eyeteeth to own a Greener." He chuckled. "Imagine the look on Hubie Banks's face if you were to outshoot him this year."

"Yeah . . ." Everett paused to imagine it. "I'd love to see that, all right. And the look on Ragan's face when I won."

"Well, looks like Ragan and Mrs. Seeden have finally finished their shopping." Johnny casually pushed away from the counter. "Are you sure they said a Greener?"

Everett looked downright sick. "I'm positive. I had the deciding vote."

"How much do you suppose a gun like that's worth?"

"Forty—fifty dollars, at least."

With an appreciative whistle, Johnny adjusted the brim of his hat. "Nice shotgun. If you change your mind about my help, you know where to find me. I'm sure we could work something out." He stepped down off the porch.

"Er . . . Mr. McAllister?"

Johnny turned. "Yes?"

"Can you really shoot a rattlesnake through the eye at fifty feet?"

"Most every time."

He could feel Everett's stare as he crossed the street and took the packages out of Ragan's hands.

She smiled up at him, her pleasant talk with Roberta still evident on her face. "Did I see you visiting with Everett?"

"Just killing time while you shopped."

They fell into step, walking down Main Street. They were almost at the crossroads before Johnny offered his thoughts.

"Why does a woman like you stay in a town like Barren Flats?"

Ragan laughed. "What a question."

"I mean it. I know you take care of the judge and your father, but don't you want more?"

"More?" She appeared to at least consider the idea. "No, not more: maybe different. Why would I want more?"

He shrugged. He'd want more—or would he? He'd spent years looking for his family's killers. He'd told himself revenge was the driving factor, but maybe what he wanted was a family again. Ties. Roots. Belonging to someone.

"You're smart, have a lot to offer."

Her smile was almost impish. "To whom?

A husband? Everyone thinks I'll always be an old maid, but someday I want to marry. Right now, I stay in Barren Flats because my family is here. And Procky is here. He and his wife were second grandparents to me when I was growing up."

They turned toward Judge McMann's street.

"And I have responsibilities here," Ragan said. "Someday I might leave, but I seldom think about it."

"You can't sacrifice yourself forever."

"Family isn't a sacrifice—but then, you wouldn't know about that." She glanced at him, a lighthearted challenge in her eyes. "Since you came from a pea pod."

Wouldn't know about family? She had no idea. He knew what it was like to wake to the smell of ham sizzling in a skillet. Ice on his bedroom windowpane Christmas morning; the sound of Ma humming as she slid a lemon cake into the oven. He knew all right. And it hurt like hell.

"So you'll just stay here and be nursemaid all your life?"

She let the subject of his origins pass. "Not all my life, no. I'll stay as long as Papa and Procky are alive; most certainly until Becca's grown. Procky wants me to go to school later."

"You haven't gone to school?"

"Not to college. He'd like me to study law someday. Says I'm a natural, but I don't know if it's what I really want to do. Besides, I have plenty of time to think about it."

"Can a woman get into law school?"

"It would be a struggle," she admitted. "Just last year, the Wisconsin Supreme Court denied Lavinia Goodell's application to the bar. Apparently they believed women are too delicate and emotional for the profession."

Her chin lifted. "I may have to go to the midwest if I pursue a law degree. The University of Iowa and Washington University in St. Louis opened doors to women almost twenty years ago. But whatever I decide to do, I want to make a difference in people's lives." She slowed, turning to face him. A hot breeze ruffled her hair, tossing it around her animated features. "Are you surprised that I want to further my education?"

"No, nothing about you surprises me." He'd been here long enough to realize she was strong, independent, bossy as hell, and prettier than any woman should be.

She brushed a lock of hair off her cheek. "I want to make a difference, like Procky does. I've watched wayward boys change into responsible, outstanding citizens because he gave them the opportunity to develop to their potential. When I lie back on my pillow at night, I want to know I've helped someone headed in the wrong direction to change—to turn his life around."

She touched his arm. "What about you? What do you want to do once you leave here?"

His plans? He had only one: stay alive long enough to kill Dirk Bledso.

"Johnny?"

"I haven't thought about it."

"You're twenty-seven years old. You can't drift all your life."

"I don't plan to." They reached the judge's front porch, and Ragan reached for her parcels. Their hands brushed in the brief exchange. At the contact, her eyes held his.

"Let's talk about it soon," she said softly. "And someday I'd like you to tell me about your family, too."

For a split second, he thought about telling her everything. He'd empty his soul, tell her what his life had been like the past fifteen years, tell her he knew all about family and responsibility and loving someone. He could tell her he'd stood before the gates of hell, and she would understand his pain.

"Don't hold your breath," he said. What was there to tell? They were all dead.

Her look was indecipherable. Curiosity?
Concern?

"Ragan?" The judge's voice came from the
back of the house as they opened the back
screen.

"We're home, Procky. I have the coffee."

That night Johnny stood at the east window overlooking the judge's moonlit rose
garden. Crickets chirped and an occasional
poor-will called to a mate. A barely perceptible breeze stirred the lace curtains. Johnny
turned when he heard a soft scratching at the
door. The moon shed enough light to see a
furry black paw work its way under the edge
of the door, then stretch more fully under the
crack in search of anything to ensnare on the
other side.

Moving to the door, he lightly touched the
tip of his bare toe to the back of the curled
paw. It began a frantic clawing sweep, trying
to trap the object. He grinned and watched
as the leg stretched as far as possible, grabbing, then retreating to the opposite side. Another tentative try, scooping air, then a
plaintive plea for admittance.

"All right, all right, hold on."

He opened the door a crack and Kitty burst
into the room, scolding him for the neglect
she had endured.

"You're late, cat."

She arched against his leg, then jumped to the sill when he stepped back to the window. He let his hand fall on her head and she pressed into his chest.

"Look out there, Kitty. It's too pretty a night to be cooped up inside. You should be out there socializing, making small talk with the other cats in the neighborhood."

She meowed.

A sound caught his ear and he moved to the north window. The cat changed sills, and rearranged herself in front of him. The muted sound progressed slowly until, illuminated by the moonlight, a small, donkey-drawn cart came into view. Two men walked beside the conveyance, occasionally taking hold of the harness to keep it moving. It passed in front of the house, and the creaking wheels could still be heard as it disappeared into the shadows.

Johnny crossed back to the bed, wondering where he'd seen a cart like that, and thinking of the people he'd seen with donkeys. Plummer had a team of mules. There could be a donkey or two on the Banks's land. The Hubbard girls had a pet jenny, but it was smaller than the one pulling the barrow. He mentally went through the town's animal population.

He could account for six donkeys, but who were these men?

Lying on the bed stroking Kitty's head, he wondered who was taking a cartload of what, where, after midnight?

The cat stretched along his thigh and purred when his hand settled on her back. Strange, how comforting it was to know another living being wanted his companionship. It had been years since he'd had a pet. Fifteen years if the number mattered. He took a deep breath. Fifteen long years.

He had no idea how long he'd slept when the sound of the returning cart awakened him.

Kitty hit the floor and jumped back onto the windowsill as Johnny got up and watched until the mysterious wagon came back into view and bumped back toward Main Street. The donkey moved faster now, and both men rode in the obviously lighter cart.

As the puzzling sight disappeared into the shadows, Kitty jumped from the ledge and ran to the door, trying to paw it open. Johnny stepped over and opened it for her. "Don't go waking up the judge. It's the middle of night, you know." He watched her silently flick down the stairs.

Closing the door, he lay back down and

settled his head on the pillow. Who *were* the men with the donkey? And what had they taken out of town in the cart at this time of night?

Chapter 8

"**I** hear Dirk Bledso's here in Salt Lake City."

Glasses clinked down on the bar, and silence settled over the room. Eyes centered on Johnny in the barroom doorway. He smiled at the bartender. "Tell Mr. Bledso he has a visitor."

A cowboy waved a whiskey bottle in the air, then hurled it against the wall. "Tell him yourself!"

Johnny's hand moved to Everett's pistol. He'd waited fifteen long years for this moment. The taste of victory was sweet.

Chairs overturned and customers faded into the shadows. There he was, just as Johnny remembered. Dirk Bledso, bigger than life and uglier than sin. Johnny looked his enemy in the eye. Mama's face floated in front of him. "Don't kill my babies . . ."

Papa stepped forward, yelling for Bledso to leave them be. Johnny watched the impact as bullets riddled his parents' bodies and they crumpled to the ground. Slowly, methodically, he raised Everett's pistol and sighted his prey. The shot hit the Viper straight between the eyes. His evil grin hung mid-air long after his body lay on the floor. A cheer went up from the townspeople.

The crowd pushed close to the platform, but a hood over Johnny's head prevented him from recognizing faces. Voices rose and fell. He felt the noose drop around his neck. Someone needed to return Everett's Greener.

He'd broken his word, his solemn pledge. Grandpa wouldn't be happy about that.

He sucked hot air between his teeth, and the rope pressed, squeezing, squeezing.

"Say your prayers, boy."

The floor dropped from beneath his feet, and he fought the weight on his throat, struggling for breath. . . .

Johnny's eyes jerked open. Moonlight flooded the room. Sweat rolled off him, and his heart hammered. He lay for a moment, staring into bright green eyes.

Swearing, he struggled to untangle himself from the sheet and Kitty. The cat hissed, startled by the sudden movement. A flurry of sheets and cat ensued. Kitty emerged from the tangle and stretched, lazily arching her body, then sprawled back across Johnny's chest.

He stared at the feline, then pushed her aside. With a protesting mew, she jumped down and stalked to the window. Perching on the sill, she stared back at him with her sleepy jade eyes.

"Dammit," he grumbled. His breathing was ragged, and the image of Dirk Bledso seared his brain. Sisal still bit into his neck.

Hanging wasn't something he allowed into his thoughts very often.

Kitty jumped from her perch and rejoined him on the bed. Purring, she nuzzled his neck, forcing him to pay attention to her.

Settling back on the pillow, he let her stay. For once, her company was more welcome than the darkness. He absently scratched behind her ears. "You know, Cat, when I do kill Bledso, there won't be a man alive who'll blame me. He's a blight on the face of the earth, a scourge to humanity."

Kitty rubbed her whiskers against Johnny's chin and purred.

Stupid cat. Stupid him, for lying in bed talking to a cat. But it was true: Bledso deserved to be shot. The last time he'd disappeared like this, word was that he was dead, his body lying somewhere in the Sierra Nevadas—bones bleached white by the sun.

Then the murdering began again.

Dirk and his brothers stole for the thrill of it. They murdered for the pure joy of killing. How else could a man take the life of a child—two blue-eyed little girls with golden curls . . .

Kitty mewed, nestling against his cheek.

He brushed her affection aside. "*You* kill, Cat. Crickets, moths, mice. Don't look at me like you're passing judgment. 'An eye for an eye'—that's what the Good Book says."

The cat inched closer, head up and eyes focused on him. A purr answered his accusation.

Johnny lay back, staring at the ceiling. There was no telling where the lowlifes were. But wherever they were, he would find them. Someday he would find them.

He smiled, picturing the moment he'd meet Bledso face to face. He wasn't proud of taking advantage of Everett, but there were times when honor was just cause. Everett would get his gun back. He'd see to that.

Kitty mewed softly.

Glancing down at her, he ruffled her fur. "You're worthless, Cat, you know that?"

* * *

When Ragan came through the back door that morning to begin breakfast, there were three cups of coffee waiting on the table. Johnny and the judge already had their hands wrapped around two of them.

She smiled, feeling a rush of gratitude. Any sign of progress with Johnny brought hope.

"You're getting pretty good at making a decent cup of coffee. They'll be hiring you at the Oasis one of these days," she teased him.

The faint hint of a smile showed at the corners of McAllister's mouth, and her pulse raced.

"Don't bet money on it," he told her.

"I wouldn't. Can't quite imagine you in a skirt, anyway."

Judge McMann chuckled, reaching for the cream pitcher. "You two are in a feisty mood this morning."

Bending over Johnny's shoulder, Ragan replenished the cream pitcher. The faint hint of shaving soap left her heady. She turned slightly, her face only inches from his, her breath warm against his clean-shaven cheek. "Good morning."

"You are feeling feisty," he murmured.

"Maybe." She touched his shoulder briefly as she straightened, recalling every single time he'd accidentally brushed against her and sent her imagination soaring. Occasionally, he touched her arm to guide her steps. His hands never lingered, but she felt the effect long after, the way she hoped her presence was disturbing him now.

Sliding into her chair, she allowed her skirt to brush the hem of his trousers. He looked up from his plate, and their glances touched. Seemingly innocently unaware and uncaring, she met his dark gaze over the rim of her cup, luxuriating in the delicious, exquisite warmth he induced in her. Her cheeks flushed as their gazes turned more intimate, her eyes openly inviting his masculine scrutiny, his seizing it with typical male dominance. He focused on her mouth, and shivers of awareness intensified the simmering heat that seemed an eternal damnation.

"More coffee anyone?" the judge asked.

Ragan jumped.

During the meal, while the judge chatted amiably, Ragan's mind was on the dark, handsome man opposite her. She couldn't wait for the meal to be over and for Johnny to accompany her to the mercantile. The moments they spent alone were the highlight of her days.

Shortly after breakfast she approached the work shed, anticipating the outing.

"I'm out of white thread. I'll need to purchase some this morning."

He quietly laid aside the window frame he was rebuilding. "I'll wash up."

The summer heat closed in, and she suddenly felt faint. Was it the heat—or Johnny McAllister?

"We won't be gone long."

He nodded, moving to the water tank to wash.

She wished he would say something, instead of just looking at her with those dark, brooding eyes that made her cold one moment, feverish the next. He fell into step with her on the way to town and she wracked her brain thinking of topics to discuss. Finally, she couldn't stand the strain a moment longer.

"About this morning," she blurted. "I didn't mean to behave so boldly." Actually, she did, but her conscience nagged her. She was in the position of authority; she should never have trifled with his basic instincts—though it had been fun.

"You don't need to explain, Miss Ramsey. You don't think I'd believe you would encourage attention from a prisoner on purpose, do you?"

She was so taken aback by his swift response, she was speechless. Apparently he'd been thinking about this morning's incident, too. "I just don't want you to think . . ."

He turned, and she sucked in her breath as he slowly, deliberately backed her up to a tree. He pressed her against the trunk, his mouth only inches away. The heat of his body against hers took her breath. For the first time, she was aware of the tiny scar at the corner of his bottom lip, evidence of an old injury.

He smiled as her breathing quickened. "Tell you what." His eyes skimmed her lightly. "Why don't we call a truce?" He touched her nose with his forefinger, then gently traced the outline of her face. The sensual caress was devastating. "I'll be good, and talkative, until my sentence is served." The dark gaze that met her eyes simmered with . . . what? Impatience? Anger?

Desire.

"If you'll let up on me. Bargain?"

His words were soft, persuasive. She realized his experience far exceeded hers; he was worldly, she was her Papa's daughter. She licked her dry lips.

His mouth dipped, coming closer. "What do you say, sweetheart? I'll be good—maybe so good that you'll speak to the judge about an early parole?" His lips touched hers briefly, with agonizing precision. "Six months is long enough for a man to pay for his mistakes. Don't you think?" His mouth closed over hers, and she grasped the front of his shirt and held on as he deepened the kiss. When their lips parted, he smiled. "Deal?"

Reaching out, she quickly drew him back. As his mouth took hers hotly, she sighed.

With a appreciative groan, he pulled her closer, his tongue searching for hers. She complied, faintly aware they were making a public spectacle if anyone should come upon them, but at the moment it seemed unimportant. His kiss was so devastating, she could only respond.

When he stepped back his breathing was uneven, making it even harder for what she must do.

"That was nice," she whispered.

"I can be nice—very nice." He zeroed in for another provocative kiss.

She pulled back and said breathlessly, "No—I will not speak to the judge about an early parole." Her eyes took on a teasing gleam. "So if you wish to kiss me, keep business out of it."

While Ragan shopped, Johnny leaned against the livery building and watched the town activity. A few women stood about, discussing such inflammatory topics as which fabrics to use for new dresses and whether milk or cream made fluffier mashed potatoes.

He couldn't be certain, but he was beginning to wonder if the newest raids were the work of the red-bearded bank robber and his gang. He hated to think he'd brought more grief to the town, or Ragan.

He nodded to the Thompson sisters as they crossed the street.

The old timers stopped by, asking him questions. Did he think it would rain? Had Ragan make him one of her strawberry pies yet? How did he like Barren Flats?

Nowadays, he was beginning to notice when old man Parson's lumbago was acting up, or if Widow Keeling was having a particularly hard day adjusting to her husband's passing. He didn't like noticing. It made the people more like family . . . and they weren't his family. They were strangers, and he meant to keep them that way.

He straightened when he spotted Everett strutting up the walk. Good. It would save him the trouble of going to the telegraph office. Had Everett taken the bait?

When the young clerk was upon him, he paused, shifting a sheaf of papers to his opposite arm. "Mr. McAllister."

"Everett."

"Hot today."

"Sure is."

Everett cast a wary glance over his shoulder. Clearing his throat, he lowered his voice. "I've been wanting to talk to you."

"Oh?" Johnny forced a casual smile.

The clerk edged closer, keeping an eye on the mercantile doorway. "I've been thinking about your offer." Everett's voice was low and he spoke without moving his lips, which made it difficult to understand him. "You said you could teach me how to shoot. I figured maybe if you didn't touch the gun, you could tutor me. I'm willing to pay for your services."

Johnny felt a surge of triumph. "I suppose I could help. What do you have in mind?"

Everett glanced toward the sheriff's office. "I know you'd be doing something you shouldn't, but if you give me your word that you won't try and take the gun—"

Give my word that I won't? Johnny shook his head at the man's innocence. "All right. I'll give you my word, and I'll teach you to shoot, but we'll have to be careful. It's not going to be easy to keep this quiet."

Everett grinned. "Leave that to me. Not a soul will know what's going on. I'll arrange everything."

"Fine. When do you want to start?"

"The sooner the better. Founders' Day is six weeks away. I want to be ready."

Six weeks to teach Everett Pidgin to shoot out rattlesnakes' eyes.

"I intend to win that Greener." Everett's eyes shifted to the mercantile. "A woman would be mighty proud of a man who proved to be the best shot in town. Why, if I could shoot out a rattlesnake's eye—"

"You won't. Not every time."

"But *if* I could do it once, that would be enough for me." Everett's look was so earnest, Johnny had to look away. Grandpa wouldn't be proud of this.

Ragan's laughter floated to them as she emerged from the mercantile with Kensil Southern. The two women paused on the top step, chatting.

Everett's mouth went slack. "She's so beautiful, she makes the flowers blush."

Johnny's gaze followed Everett's. He didn't have Everett's poetry, but, yes, Ragan Ramsey was a real beauty. He tried not to let himself think about that. Or the blasted ache in his groin. "I hadn't noticed."

Everett's head snapped back. "You haven't noticed?"

Johnny adjusted his hat on his head. "Women will get you in trouble, Everett. Bet-

ter buy yourself a good horse and forget Ragan." He stepped off the planked porch and
started across the street.

"Mr. McAllister?"

Johnny turned. "Yes?"

"I overheard you the other day at the stage
station. You said a man's size didn't matter.
Did you mean that?"

At times, Johnny felt sorry for the young
man's uncertainties. He didn't like to prey on
them, but Everett was his lifeline.

"A man makes his own way in the world.
Size doesn't have a thing to do with it."

The clerk's eyes returned to Ragan. "That's
how I have it figured."

The sounds of quickly approaching hoofbeats caught the men's attention.

"I'll talk to you later," Everett called, already running down the boardwalk.

Two banditos rode into town, firing into
the air as the town citizens scattered for
cover.

Monday morning, Reverend Pillton posted
a notice that, come hell or high water, services would be held this Sunday, provided the
repair work on the church could be finished.

Immediately after breakfast, Johnny was
sent to the work shed to gather brushes and
rags while Ragan got her sewing materials

together. When she came out the door, he hefted a ladder to his shoulder, and they set out for the church.

"After all the repairs, the church needs a good cleaning and a fresh coat of paint."

"Seems like a lot of trouble to me."

"I'll be at Minnie's if you need me for anything."

"I won't need you."

Shooting him a sour look, Ragan turned north to join her sewing group, and he continued down the lane, grinning. She sure was pretty when she was riled.

Arriving at the church, Johnny found it empty. So much for town participation. He set up the ladder, opened a bucket of paint, and climbed to the highest eve. He painted for over twenty minutes before he heard a hiss from a nearby bush. He glanced down, trying to locate the source.

"Pssssssss. Hey!"

Stepping down a couple of rungs, Johnny leaned to peer over the top of the bush.

"Over here," the voice said.

"Everett? What are you doing behind that bush?"

"I'm hiding."

"Why?"

"I've got the gun."

Johnny glanced at Minnie Rayles's house.

"Stay down. The women can see you."

"Where are they?"

"At the mayor's house."

The clerk duck-walked from behind the bush, a package tucked neatly under his arm. Pausing at the bottom of the ladder, his eye scoured the area for intruders.

Johnny quickly descended the ladder. Picking it and the bucket up, he moved to the opposite side of the building, out of the women's view.

Everett duck-walked behind him, toting the wrapped pistol. When they reached safety, Johnny said, "Okay, let's see what you have."

The clerk hurriedly unwrapped the gun and laid it on the ground.

"Hell, Everett." Johnny looked around to be sure they weren't observed. "That's a big-bore forty-five hogleg. What are you doing with a pistol like that?"

"It was my Uncle Mort's. Aunt Pliss gave it to me when he passed on last year. What do you think of it?"

Johnny studied the weapon: a blue, eight-inch-long six-shooter. The pistol could bore a hole the size of a little finger going in, a silver dollar coming out. "It's not exactly a gentleman's weapon."

"I know." Everett beamed. "It's a man's gun."

Johnny itched to pick up the firearm, but he kept his distance. "Do you have ammunition?"

"All we'll ever need—behind the counter at the telegraph, bottom shelf, way back in the left-hand corner. I keep it there in case I ever have trouble at work."

"It's not loaded now, is it?"

Everett thrust a small paper-enshrouded package at him. "The bullets are in here."

Johnny stepped back, refusing the package. "You carry them."

"We can shoot it right now." Everett duck-walked to the corner of the building and peered around the corner. After a moment he waddled back. "No one will pay any attention to a little gunfire over in the woods. Hubie Banks practices every morning."

Johnny glanced at the stand of scrub oak over the ridge from the church. The area was small, but bushy and dense.

"I don't know, Everett—the women will hear us."

"So? They'll just think it's Hubie shootin', or another raid about to take place." Everett shifted from one foot to the other. "Come on, just five minutes. I'm itchin' to try this thing out." He patted the hogleg confidently. "This is my ticket to the Greener."

Well, one shot wasn't that hard to account for. One shot would hold Everett for a few days, and he would find out where the clerk kept the gun. It would be a cold day in hell before the hogleg would make Everett the object of Ragan's affection, but he didn't have the heart to explain that. Everett would know it soon enough.

"All right, one shot."

"One shot," Everett promised. He waddled alongside Johnny as they moved away from the church building.

"Stand up and walk straight, Everett."

"Oh—sorry." He struggled up.

Moments later, the two men disappeared into the brushy woods.

Ragan's head jerked up from her sewing as the floor shook in Minnie's parlor. "What was *that*?"

"Oh, goodness—another raid." Kensil calmly laid her sewing aside.

A few women dropped to the floor. Several crawled on their hands and knees to the closet, pulling the door closed behind them. One by one, hands emerged to retrieve scraps of material and discarded needles.

The ladies resumed stitching while they waited for the onslaught. When a second shot failed to materialize, their needles paused, ears cocked to the deafening silence.

"I don't hear anything."

Minnie frowned. "Could be Hubie practicing again. That man is obsessed with winning that silly shotgun."

"Don't say anything about my Hubie, Minnie. You're just jealous that he wins the shooting contest every year, and Carl doesn't."

"That's a terrible thing to say, Florence, and I resent it."

"Well, if you—"

"Ladies, please," Ragan interrupted. "Can we please have a little harmony?" The women quibbled over the silliest things.

"Should never have let them get a Greener in the first place. They'll all make fools of themselves." Minnie stabbed her needle through a patch and yanked the thread tight.

"Shush—listen . . . I don't hear any more shots."

"That's strange. They should be here by now."

"Stay down. You never know."

"I'm not staying down any longer. My arthritis is killing me."

"Arthritis isn't as painful as a bullet, Roberta."

"You aren't old enough to know about arthritis yet, Justine. You and Rudolph are just kids. I don't think there's going to be any more shooting. I'm getting up."

One by one, the ladies climbed from under the table and out of the closet. They helped Haleen Lutz out of the back of the closet and sat back down in their chairs and continued to sew.

"These constant interruptions are a nuisance, and I, for one, think it's a crying shame we can't even attend Sunday meeting services without the fear of getting our heads blown off," Minnie said. "The Brown Branch Boys would take care of that."

No one had ever actually gotten his or her head blown off, but Ragan agreed that the problem was still there. However, she didn't know why anyone from the neighboring town of Brown Branch would be of help.

Her thoughts centered on her handsome prisoner. He was far more experienced about these matters than any man in town. Even though it wasn't his responsibility, the raids directly affected him; he could be hurt in one of the rampages. She wondered if he'd ever considered that when he was telling himself it "wasn't his problem." Getting up from her chair, she lifted the curtain to look out of the parlor window.

"Is your prisoner behaving himself?"

Frowning, Ragan searched the grounds surrounding the church. Johnny was nowhere to be seen. She released a pent-up breath when she saw him round the corner with Everett moments later. The men carried paint and ladders.

"Actually, he's been ideal, Haleen. With the exception of refusing to lower his barriers, we couldn't ask for a more model subject."

"I imagine he's rather put out, having to serve this unusual sentence," Minnie said.

"He should consider himself lucky. He could be sitting in jail, or worse."

The mayor cautiously emerged from his study. "Are you ladies all right?"

"Fine, dear." Minnie smiled and joined her husband as he moved to the front door and looked out. "Strange—one jarring blast, but nobody's coming. Must have gotten scared off."

"What would they be scared of?" Minnie asked with a toss of her head. "There's nothing in this town for them to be scared of."

Carl looked both ways once more, and shut the door. "Something must've stopped them."

Estelle Southerland picked through the pile of colorful swatches and selected a purple one. "Maybe they've decided to leave us alone," the seamstress suggested.

Minnie sputtered. "I'm telling you, we need the Brown Branch boys to help us."

Carl paused on his way to the kitchen and turned to stare at his wife. "Who in God's name are the Brown Branch boys?"

"A group of young men who keep the thugs out of Brown Branch, that's who."

"How hard is that? Brown Branch is thirty miles from the border."

"Never you mind, Carl Rayles." Minnie gave her husband a warning look. "It would be money well spent, I say."

Carl glanced at Ragan on his way out. "We better hope those boys, whoever they are, weigh three hundred pounds each and eat glass. Otherwise, she'll order them back on their horses and send them packing."

Ragan bent her head to her work, covering a smile.

Minnie didn't appear to be affected by Carl's lack of vision. She sat back down in her chair. "My, I don't know how you and the judge do it. Writing that book, taking in those desperadoes."

"Johnny isn't a desperado." The denial was out before Ragan knew it. She hadn't decided what he was, but she sensed that below that embittered exterior was a decent man.

One who was badly in need of love, whether he knew it or not.

"Why, Ragan Ramsey." Mazilea's needle paused. "You sound as if you're actually attracted to this man."

"Me?" Ragan's face flamed and she jumped when she jabbed her finger with the needle. "Don't be silly, Mazilea. I would never be attracted to one of the judge's subjects. What a thing to say." She jumped as she accidentally jabbed her finger again.

A series of quizzical looks passed among the ladies.

Noting the exchange, Ragan laid her needlework aside, suddenly feeling quite flushed. "Plain silly, Mazilea, and you know it. Anyone else care for lemonade?"

The sun hung low in the west as Ragan and Johnny started home. Ragan had never seen the church looking better. A couple of more days, and the painting would be done.

"You did a wonderful job on the building. I'm surprised more didn't show up to work today."

She glanced at Johnny curiously. He kept tilting his head as if trying to clear his ears. Usually when she talked, he at least looked at her. Tonight he periodically thumped his head, staring straight ahead as if he were deaf.

"Carl said to tell you he'd be available in the morning to paint the inside, if you're willing to help again."

Johnny turned to look at her. "Milk?"

"Help."

He shook his head. "I haven't in years, but I suppose I can."

She shook her head to clear her own ears. "I noticed Everett stopped by. Did he paint?"

When he didn't respond, she tried again. "I had a lovely day. Minnie made a delicious lunch. She had fresh poke from the garden and pork roast."

He glanced at her quizzically.

"Poke. And pork roast."

"Toast?"

"Roast."

"Why would Minnie poke toast?"

"Minnie didn't poke toast, she served poke and pork roast! What's wrong with your ears?"

He frowned. "Why would she cry about toast? Did she burn it?"

Ragan stopped and faced him, pointing to her ears. "Is something wrong with your ears?"

His face closed. "No."

They walked on in silence, their boots kicking up bits of dust. Grasshoppers jumped back and forth on the road. The sun sank lower, bathing the sky in shades of pink and red.

"Did you hear that loud gunshot earlier this afternoon? We all dove for cover, but apparently the outlaw rode right through town and never stopped."

He continued walking as if he hadn't heard what she said, let alone a loud gunshot.

"Johnny?"

When he didn't answer, she repeated louder, "Hey!"

His head snapped around. "What?"

This was exasperating! Carrying on a conversation with him was like talking to a fence post. Staring straight ahead, she walked faster. "Minnie thinks we should hire the boys from Brown Branch to get rid of the gangs. She says there're no raids in Brown Branch. The people won't allow it."

"It's going to take more than a branch to scare them off."

She paused, staring at him. Were they having the same conversation? "Minnie says the town doesn't have any raids because they have fearless young men in Brown Branch who deal with the problem."

He stopped, his hands coming to his hips

in exasperation. "Sideshow freaks? How does being earless qualify a man to clean up a town?"

"I didn't say *earless* young men—for heaven's sake, what is wrong with you?"

"Nothing." He passed her and walked on ahead.

Fine, just ignore her! Stooping over, she picked up a dirt clod and hurled it at him. It splattered at his feet.

Stiffening, he slowly turned around to meet her sheepish gaze.

"Acting like a child, Ragan?"

The sound of her given name startled her. He always called her Miss Ramsey. She hung her head, ashamed of herself. Usually not much could rile her, but he sure could.

His features sobered. "You really want my opinion on this whole mess?"

Meeting his gaze evenly, she said, "Yes."

"The town is trying to get someone else to solve its problems."

She started to protest, then pursed her lips as he continued.

"The people here need to take the situation in hand, stop acting like frightened children, and take care of the trouble themselves."

"How are we supposed to do that? The gangs burn us out; they—"

He leveled his finger at her. "If this town

doesn't have the gumption to stand up for itself, no one else will." Turning, he walked on.

She watched his retreating back, seething. He had no right to criticize. The town *had* tried to stop the gangs, and their efforts resulted in nothing but more trouble. While he was offering his sterling opinion, why didn't he explain exactly *how* to stand up? What more could they do than what they'd already done?

She blinked as he suddenly bent over and picked up a dirt clod, turned, took aim, and lobbed it back at her. She hopped backward as dirt splayed the bottom of her skirt.

"It's getting dark, Miss Ramsey! The judge's supper is two, that's *two*, hours overdue."

"Stew?" she mimicked. "I *hate* stew."

He acted as if he didn't hear, and walked on.

Swiping the dirt off her dress, she trailed him toward the judge's house. Tonight she was going to write a whole chapter on arrogant men who refused to cooperate. *Deaf* arrogant men who refused to cooperate.

"And there *is* something wrong with your hearing!" she shouted at his disappearing back. You'd think the gunshot that afternoon had gone off in his ear.

Chapter 9

Ragan was snapping beans when Johnny came in the back door Saturday morning. She smiled wanly, one of those womanly acknowledgments that affected him deep in his gut. No wonder Everett was in love with her. When she turned those guileless, innocent eyes on any man who was a man, it was all he could do to keep his mind on business.

"Finished at the church so soon?"

It seemed to be an effort for her to speak. Was she feeling poorly today? Walking to the wash stand, he poured water into the ceramic bowl, watching her from the corner of his eye.

"The hand rail is fixed. I repaired the bottom step while I was at it."

"Roberta will thank you; she's complained about that loose step for months. Her arthritis makes it a real chore for her to climb up or down." She sighed. "And Sheriff and Haleen have stayed home because they're afraid of falling."

"Well, their worries are over. The step's solid as a new stump." He reached for a bar of soap to lather up. The pleasant scent of lye and sun-dried towels reminded him of his mother.

"Dinner will be a little late." Ragan sighed again. "I thought it best to finish the beans before we ate."

Nodding, he was about to leave her to her work, when he noticed her red eyes and nose. It was obvious that she had been crying. She fumbled for her handkerchief, touching it lightly to her eyes.

Leave now, McAllister, before you wade into something that doesn't concern you. He made it to the doorway before her voice stopped him.

"Mr. McAllister?" Her tone had that helpless inflection that usually—no, always—meant trouble.

"Yes?"

"Would you mind helping me finish snapping beans?"

Hell yes, he'd mind. Snapping beans was right under peeling potatoes, which was right behind mending in the list of his least favorites. And he sure didn't want to get involved in whatever had her sniffing and red-eyed.

She briefly touched the corner of her eyes with the hanky again. "The canning has taken longer than I expected, and the judge will be down any moment now." She lifted her eyes and gave him a weak smile. "You know how Procky is when his meal is late."

She met his uncertain frown. "Do you mind?"

"I guess not." Pulling out a chair, he sat down at the table. A sizable pile of beans appeared in front of him. Hell, he'd be here all day.

"Is there a proper way to do this?" Anything like the complicated instructions he'd received on button sewing?

"Pinch the ends off, remove the strings, and snap the bean in two—unless, of course, it's a long bean; then snap it in three pieces."

He picked up a bean and looked at it. He turned it end over end. Was this a long one, or a short one? "How long is a long one?"

"Oh, about this long." She spread her thumb and forefinger to the proper size.

He hadn't known there was a science to bean snapping.

They worked a few minutes in silence. An occasional furtive glance in her direction assured him she was weeping, all right. He didn't know why, and didn't want to know why, because he couldn't do a thing about whatever had her upset. He was getting too attuned to her moods as it was. Before long, they'd be rocking on the front porch together.

Hell—he was stuck in this godforsaken place because of sticking his nose in somebody else's business in the first place.

When her sniffling grew more pronounced, he crossed his arms and asked gruffly, "What are you crying about?"

She glanced up, seemingly surprised that he noticed. "I'm sorry . . . it's . . . it's been a trying day."

He reached for another bean, snapped it, and pitched it into the pan. Trying, was it? She didn't know the meaning of the word. She ought to try teaching Everett to shoot. "Is the judge ill?"

"No, not Procky. It's my father."

Definitely a subject to avoid. Fathers meant family, and family meant feelings he didn't want to be reminded of.

He sighed. "What about your father?" He scooped up a pile of strings and discarded them, mentally groaning when she buried her face in her hands and burst into tears.

Never ask a weeping lady why she's crying.

She sobbed into her hanky, her slender shoulders shaking with grief. His first instinct was to abandon the beans and allow her privacy. It sure wasn't his place to comfort her, even if for some insane reason he wanted to.

She wept softly into her handkerchief, soft, pitiful mewlings like Kitty did when she wanted something. The sound tore at his gut.

Getting up from his chair, he wet the tip of a towel and carried it back to the table. Awkwardly removing the handkerchief, he pressed the damp cloth into her hands.

"Dry your tears," he admonished. "Whatever it is, it can't be that bad."

She held the cool cloth to her eyes.

Squatting beside her chair, he met her teary gaze. "Look. I'm not very good with these things, but if you want to talk, I'm a decent listener."

Wiping her tears, she said softly, "Mama died five years ago today. Papa and I take flowers to her grave every year." She sniffled. "This morning, when I mentioned going, Papa didn't even know who I was talking about."

She dabbed at the moisture filling her eyes. "I don't know why it still bothers me so. Papa's been getting worse for months now. It isn't as if I just woke up today and realized he would never be back." Her chin quivered.

"He's here, but he's not the old Papa . . . my strong, proud Papa."

His eyes softened, and he took her into his arms. She sobbed softly against his shoulder.

"Would you stop that? It makes me want to kiss you, and I'm in no mood to have my face slapped."

She hiccupped, laughing and crying at the same time. Then she smiled at him, and kissed him softly on the mouth.

"Now, that's better," he conceded gruffly, and kissed her back. A long, inappropriate kiss between a criminal and his warden.

He brushed a lock of her hair into place, holding her close. She looked prettier than any woman ought to look with a red nose and teary eyes. "So," he asked softly, "what makes today so difficult?"

"It just seems another part of Papa is gone. I have to admit to myself that both Mama and Papa are gone now."

Removing the towel from her hand, he wet it again. She accepted the cool cloth with a sigh.

"Is your mother's grave around here?"

"No, Papa wanted her buried next to her parents. The family plot is in Searcy County. Jacob's there, too. It's almost a two-hour ride from here."

Two hours? Well, it could be worse; she

could need to go to San Francisco.

She glanced at him.

He averted his eyes and concentrated on the beans. He separated strings from the pods. Measured the two halves of the bean. Dropped one in the pot. Then the other. He looked back at her.

The silence lengthened.

"Hell." He drew a deep breath, and started over. "Shucks, a two-hour ride isn't that far. It's still early, and the days are long."

She bent her head. "No, not that far. But Procky doesn't like me to go alone—not with so much trouble going on."

"No, you shouldn't go alone."

"I know."

Only the occasional snap of a bean and a discreet sniffle broke the silence.

"I'd take you, but I don't have a gun." It was a sore spot with him; a gun was a man's only protection.

"Having a gun isn't a problem. There's the old mining road that hardly anyone uses any more. Papa and I travel it so we won't meet up with any of the gangs."

The prospect of traveling without a gun worried him. A man could run into all kinds of trouble along the way. Wild animals, robbers, no telling what he might encounter. He didn't like being without protection.

He could ask Everett to come along, but somehow he didn't think Ragan would want that. It didn't appeal to him much, either. Throwing a bean in the pot, he made an offer he was bound to regret. "If you want to go, I'll take you."

Hope sprang to her eyes. "Would you do that? Really?"

It wouldn't be his first choice, but her tears touched something inside him, something he thought he'd buried for good fifteen years ago. The way she looked at him, all soft and needy, aroused his protective instincts, even though he fought it. The grateful look she gave him troubled him even more.

Everett was wrong: if Johnny encouraged her, he *could* have Ragan Ramsey. Her eyes made that clear. The appeal was there; clear as a starry night. The last thing he or Ragan needed was to involve themselves in each other's lives. He would be dead or behind bars once he found Bledso. She had her whole life ahead of her.

"I'll take you," he heard himself saying.

The smile that lit her face more than assuaged his doubts. A four-hour ride wasn't much—not considering the gratitude shining in her eyes.

* * *

Judith Ramsey's grave lay in a small grove of scrub oak behind Frank and Lucy Daniel's homestead. Her son's was on the right. Johnny stopped the wagon and helped Ragan down.

"Thank you. I won't be long."

"Take your time."

He stepped to the shade and waited as she laid flowers on her grandparents' graves, then moved to her mother's mound and cleared the weeds that had overtaken the simple wooden cross. Songbirds flittered in and out of the bushes. In the distance, a creek trickled peacefully along the edge of the property. The setting was so restful it was easy to see why Fulton wanted his wife and son buried here.

He studied Ragan's expression as she tidied the site with loving devotion. He thought of his own mother's grave, abandoned now. No one was left to bring her flowers, or clear away weeds. Grandpa was gone, and he hadn't been home in years. If he ever made it back, he promised himself he would cover her grave with flowers. And the little girls', too. He'd buy all the flowers they deserved.

"Were you and your mother close?" he asked.

Ragan got to her feet, then brushed the

grass off her shirt. "Yes, I suppose we were. I was her firstborn, so I had to help out more than the other girls did." She wiped her forehead with her sleeve. The air was close, as if it might storm, but there wasn't a cloud in the sky. "I didn't mind, but sometimes I feel like I never had a childhood."

And not much of a life now. Johnny had heard the whispers around town, the well meaning but careless remarks the women directed at her. Old maid? He found himself tensing when he heard the insinuations. Ragan outshone every woman in Barren Flats, and she should be applauded because she chose to accept responsibility for her father and younger siblings. Instead, the town hens reveled in discussing poor Ragan and her impossible situation.

"What about you? Are you close to your mother?" She returned to pulling weeds around the other graves.

Squatting on his haunches, he watched her work. "I don't have any family."

She yanked a particularly stubborn yucca root. "Everyone has family at one time or another. You didn't just appear on earth one day a full-grown man, did you?"

"Could be."

She turned to look at him. He tried to stop the slow grin that threatened to reveal itself.

"You most certainly did not appear from nowhere, so you have a mother." Sitting back on her heels, she faced him.

"Had a mother."

She waited.

"She's dead."

Ragan's smile faded. "I'm sorry. She must have been very young."

Nodding, he stood up. "Too young to die."

Resuming her work, she tugged a clump of weeds and tossed them aside. "Where's your father?"

"You ask too many questions."

"You don't talk enough." Getting to her feet, she dusted her hands. "There, now. That looks better, wouldn't you say?"

"A grave's a grave." He'd never seen one to brag about yet. He checked the sun. He didn't want to rush her, but it wouldn't be smart to travel after dark. "Only a couple of hours of daylight left."

"I'm through—just let me say goodbye to Mama and Jacob."

He stepped aside as she returned to the gravesites. He caught snatches of her one-sided conversation.

"Papa's not doing so good . . . put up green beans this morning . . . Jo's growing like ragweed . . . miss you both more than I can . . ."

When she returned to the wagon a few minutes later, he helped her aboard. Their thighs accidentally brushed, and he moved away. A kiss here and there didn't commit him to anything other than a kiss; the thoughts that went through his mind when she touched him did. As the wagon rolled out of the small cemetery, Ragan kept her eyes fixed on the road.

"Thank you for bringing me," she said quietly.

He kept his eyes trained on the road as well. "You're welcome."

It had been a pleasant outing, Johnny decided. No harm in a man enjoying a pretty woman's company, as long as he didn't forget his purpose.

He kept to the back roads, as they had on the way there. Although he was accustomed to keeping his opinions to himself, Ragan's tendency for chatter drew him into a spirited discussion about skunks. The debate was whether the stench was worse on animals, or humans.

"Dogs." Ragan faked a gag. "The absolute worst."

"Humans. Apparently you've never taken a direct hit from one."

"Absolutely not—have you?"

"Once. One caught me while I was taking

a bath. My clothes were high up on the bank, and the varmint decided to sit down and watch me. "The dam—" He caught himself. "That old meany kept me pinned to the water for three hours."

Ragan giggled.

He had become creative in his choice of expletives; he hoped she'd noticed. He felt like a fool talking like a sissy. "By then, the sun had gone down, and I was chilled to the bone. I decided to take my chances and climb out. When I did, he turned away from me, pointed that tail to the sky, and he got me. And my clothes. And my horse."

He looked over when she burst into laughter. "You think that's funny? It took me three weeks to get the smell out of my bedroll. The horse smelled so bad we—"

They both looked up as four masked riders darted out of the bushes, and galloped headlong toward them.

"Hell," he muttered. "I thought no one knew about this road."

"Papa and I never met anyone along here before."

Brandishing a gun, the leader motioned for Johnny to pull over.

Ragan pressed against his side, fear evident in her strained features.

"Let me do the talking," he warned as the bandits approached.

She nodded, huddling closer.

Without a gun, there wasn't going to be a fight. He let the wagon roll to a gradual halt. He had no way to fight or defend her, or himself.

The men closed in, weapons drawn. "Put your hands where we can see them!" the leader ordered.

Ragan's arms obediently shot over her head. Johnny lifted his more slowly. "We're not carrying any money."

Climbing off his horse, one of the men approached. Time suddenly stopped as Johnny came face-to-face with the red, bushy beard partially concealed beneath a dirty bandanna—the outlaw from the bank robbery. Recognition turned to perverse humor in the dark, brooding eyes that stared back at him.

It would have been easy for them to find out where Judge Leonard had sent him. But why would they—? Suddenly it all fell into place. They believed that he had the money bag, or that he knew where it was, and they'd came to Barren Flats to get it.

"Well, well, well." The leader leaned in, resting the barrel of his pistol across Johnny's temple. The gunman's stench was worse than his taste in company. "Who do we have here? McAllister, isn't it?"

"We aren't carrying any money," Johnny repeated.

"No?" The hogshead dug into his temple. "Why, I'd swear you look like a man of means."

Johnny's face remained expressionless. Ragan whimpered, and he quenched the urge to reach for her hand. He doubted the man would pull the trigger, not with the money bag missing, but he wasn't a fool.

"I don't have your damned money," he repeated, ignoring Ragan's nudge. This was not the time to enforce house rules.

"No?" The man's fetid breath was hot and potent. His lizardlike gaze darted to Ragan. She inched closer, molding against Johnny's side.

"Johnny?" she murmured.

"Easy," he said. The gun was still pointed at his head; he couldn't afford any unexpected moves. "They aren't going to hurt you." Her hand slipped into his. He held it, tightening his grip. She trembled beneath his touch.

The man's eyes slid insolently over her. "Afraid for your man, honey?" he mocked.

She glared at him, and he casually switched the barrel of the gun to her temple.

She clamped her eyes shut. "Our Father, who art in heaven . . ."

"Shut up!"

She shut up.

Johnny calmly pivoted the barrel back to his own temple and met the leader's eyes. "The lady's nervous with a gun in her face. If you want to shoot someone, shoot me."

The gunman lowered the pistol, a smile lighting his eyes. "Now, why would I want to shoot you?"

Johnny stared back at him.

The other men were restless. One glanced over his shoulder, and rode back and forth beside the wagon. "Come on, Holloway. Stop foolin' around. He ain't got the money. Let's take the woman and get out of here."

Keep your head, McAllister. Ragan's only chance was for him to convince the men they were welcome to her.

"Good idea." The leader's reptilian eyes shifted to Ragan's breasts. He ran his tongue over his dry lips. "We'll take the woman— have us a little fun." He tapped Johnny's shoulder with the barrel of the gun. "Any problem with that, McAllister?"

"Go ahead and take her."

Ragan's gasp cut through the charged silence. She sat up straight, jerking her hand out of his.

The smile was still evident in the leader's eyes. "Take her?"

"Take her. I'll keep the money." If the bluff failed, they were both dead, because there was no way he would let them take her—not without one hell of a fight. Sweat trickled down Johnny's collar and ran between his shoulder blades.

The man's eyes narrowed, then turned deadly. "Where's the money, McAllister?"

Johnny met his stare. "Take the woman, and you'll never see that money again."

"Johnny." Ragan's eyes went from one man to the other. "Do you know this—this vile animal?" Disappointment choked her voice.

"We've met."

The gun clicked, and Ragan whimpered. "Don't shoot him—take me."

"Take her." Johnny smiled.

"You're bluffin', McAllister."

Johnny shrugged. "Try me."

The one called Holloway reached over and jerked Ragan to him. Grinning, he pulled her close, grinding his foul mouth into hers. She fought, struggling to break his hold.

A vein throbbed in Johnny's neck. He'd kill the bastards when he got the chance.

When the gunman shoved her back, she fell against the wagon seat. She met Johnny's eyes, then looked away. Her look of betrayal cut him.

The men moved closer, bunching their mounts to vie for space. "Let us have some of that!" They slid from their horses and approached the wagon, their eyes focused on Ragan.

Holloway eyed Johnny. "Whatta you say, McAllister? Can my men enjoy your lady? She's a fine lookin' filly. Maybe you'd even like ta watch?"

Johnny held tight. In other circumstances he'd blow a man's head off for treating a woman this way, but right now he had no choice but to play his hand out. "Enjoy yourselves, gentleman. When you're through, I'll take a turn."

Color crept up Holloway's neck. "You're bluffing, McAllister."

"I'm her prisoner. Why would I care what happens to her?"

The men exchanged skeptical looks. The leader rammed the gun against Johnny's throat. "Tell us what you did with the bank money, McAllister."

Lunging, Johnny knocked the bandit off balance. With lightning swiftness, he reached for the whip. Swinging it above his head, he brought it down on the four horses standing to the left. The animals bolted, breaking for the underbrush. The wagon shot ahead, pitching the highwaymen to the ground. They scrambled to gain their footing as the buckboard shot off through the thicket.

"There are some old mining shafts about a mile up the road!" Ragan held on to the sides of the rattling buckboard tightly.

"Which way?"

"To the left!"

The buggy clattered along uneven ground, bouncing them like nuggets in a sluice pan. Their teeth rattled, and Ragan held onto his arm with a deathlike grip.

"How far?"

"Not far!"

It seemed a hundred miles before she pointed ahead and shouted, "There!" The opening was nearly obscured by undergrowth, and he would have driven past it if she hadn't pointed it out.

It looked small—too small for the wagon to clear. Glancing over his shoulder, he estimated how long it would take for the men to recover their horses and come after them. Five—ten minutes?

The opening was coming up. "Is it large enough to clear the wagon?"

"I'm pretty sure it is!"

Large enough or not, they were going through. Ragan screamed and covered her eyes as the horse galloped headlong toward the cavern. Thick vegetation grew along the sides of the overgrown mining road, obscuring the shaft.

"Come on, girl," Johnny urged. He prayed the mare wouldn't bolt and refuse to go in.

Johnny shut his eyes as she sheared the undergrowth and burst through the opening. The scream of metal meeting the stone walls was deafening, and the wagon slowly ground to a halt.

Johnny turned to stare at the wheels. Were they ruined?

Dampness encompassed them; they could hear water dripping somewhere inside the shaft.

"Are you hurt?"

"I need to use the necessary," she whispered, pale as a ghost.

Climbing over the seat, Johnny inched his way to the rear of the wagon. The bed was just inside the shaft, and the wheels were sheared to the spokes.

Hoof beats pounded down the road, and Johnny quickly climbed back to shove Ragan to the floor of the seat and crouch over her.

The riders galloped by, then their pounding vibrations receded into the distance.

Ragan's voice was muffled beneath him. "Are they gone?"

"Yes." Helping her onto the seat, he leaned back, taking a deep breath. "If this isn't a hell of a mess."

"Heck of a mess." She suddenly threw her arms around him. Her mouth consumed his, pressing him back in the seat with such force he struggled to breathe. When she lifted her head a few moments later, he murmured, "You pick the oddest times to turn woman on me."

She grinned, leaning her forehead against his. "I'm just so very grateful to you."

"Grateful?" He hadn't expected her gratitude. He thought she'd fly into him like a banshee. "For what?"

Looping her arms around his neck, she nibbled his ear. "For protecting me, silly. Thank you." Her warm breath against his ear made him want her so bad, he could taste it.

Drawing her back to him, he reciprocated the kiss. And again. And again, until his breathing was ragged and he was forced by fundamental reasoning to stop.

Sitting up, she drew a shaky breath, then hauled off and smacked him in the middle of his chest.

"Dammit, Ragan! What's that for?"

"How dare you give those vile men permission to take me!" She smacked him again.

Pinning her hands above her head, he

struggled to control her. "It was a bluff—one that saved your life, lady!" His gaze focused on her lips, and the building heat in his middle threatened to explode.

She stared defiantly back at him. "What would you have done if they accepted your offer?"

He released her hands. "They didn't." He didn't even want to consider the prospect.

Rubbing her wrists, she refused to look at him, so he turned in the seat to take stock of the damage. The wagon was stuck, the back wheels wedged securely in the opening.

He climbed over the front of the buckboard and released the harness. No sooner did the last tether loosen than the mare bolted out of her halter, leaving Johnny holding the reins.

"Damn, now the horse is gone!" He turned to look at Ragan. "She's disappeared down the tunnel."

"It opens up just around that corner. Not much gold was ever found in this area, and the mine shafts are all very shallow." She climbed over the front of the buggy, and they walked out the back of the shaft. Excusing herself, she disappeared into the bushes, returning a few moments later.

"Has the horse come back?" she asked.

"No. She's ten miles down the road by now."

Darkness was closing in, and they had a good hour's walk ahead of them. When they didn't show up for supper, the judge would have a posse out after them.

They struck off on foot.

"I thought you said the opening was wide enough."

"I said I was *pretty* sure it was." She primly straightened her collar.

"Well." He assessed her inappropriate hour-walk-to-town footwear. "I'm *pretty* sure you're going to have a blister the size of Texas, Miss Ramsey. We have a long walk ahead of us."

She seemed unaffected. "You'll have blisters just as big as I, Mr. McAllister."

She speeded up to walk ahead of him, turning to call over her shoulder, "And don't come whining to me for relief!"

"Miss Ramsey?"

She refused to turn around. "What?" Her skirt tail flounced in the dust.

"Those 'vile men' are still out there."

Her footsteps slowed, then stopped. Without turning around she said tightly, "Hurry up. Procky will be worried sick about us."

Lifting his hat, he brushed his hand through his hair, and started walking. The hell with it. The judge could send someone back for the wagon. He fell into step with her, and they walked on.

"For what it's worth, I take responsibility for what just happened. I shouldn't have brought you, not without a gun."

He was surprised when she said, "It's not your fault. I should have known the wagon wouldn't clear the opening." She paused, and he slowed to face her. "I'm also sorry I lost my temper. I know you saved me from certain . . . shame."

"Hell, Ragan. What do you take me for? I wouldn't have let them hurt you." He didn't know how he would have stopped it, but they would've had to kill him first to get to her.

Her face softened. "Really?"

"You know I'll protect you the best any man can without a gun."

She took a step toward him, her eyes softening. "I knew that, silly."

"Look, Ragan." He pulled her back to him, holding her politely. "You're a good-looking woman, and I'm a red-blooded man. I'm not immune to you."

"Who's talking about involvement?" She reached down and pulled his arms around her more snugly.

He gave her a pained look. He couldn't get

involved with her, tempting as the idea might be. But it wasn't going to be easy resisting her. With each passing hour he felt something more for her, something that he'd not experienced with any other woman.

"Can't we just be friends?"

His tone gentled. If things were different—"I'm not in any position to be a friend or anything else to you. I'm a prisoner, Ragan. I'm here to serve a sentence."

He groaned when she lifted her mouth to his. "This is exactly what I'm talking about," he murmured.

"Stop talking and just kiss me."

He took her mouth voraciously and surrendered to the certainty that she was different, and he didn't know what he was going to do about it. But at the moment, he just didn't care.

Chapter 10

⁓◯⌒◯⌒

Ragan jumped as Judge McMann slammed his fist on the desk, rattling Maddy's china cup and saucer. In the years she'd known the judge, she'd never seen him this upset. "I'll not have it! I'll *not* have it! Whatever it takes, we're getting rid of these gangs. You and Johnny could have been killed!"

"I know, Judge, but we weren't—" A knock sounded at the door and Ragan hurried to answer it. The whole morning had been constant interruptions. When word spread that a gang had attacked Ragan and Johnny, the whole town went into an uproar.

"Oh, good morning, Everett."

"Morning, Ragan." The telegraph clerk tipped his hat; his face lined with concern. "Are you all right?"

"Fine, thank you, Everett. It was nothing, really."

"Nothing! You could have been killed." He handed her a wire. "Mayor Rayles said to see that you got this quick as possible. It's from the Hostetler boys over in Brown Branch."

The judge rolled to the doorway. "And not a minute too soon."

Ragan took the wire, scanning the message. "Isn't there some kind of law that keeps you from reading other people's wires, Everett?"

Everett colored. "How can I not read it? I have to write it down as it comes in. Job hazard, you know."

"What's it say?" the judge prodded. "Can they come right away?"

"Mmmm," she mused, rereading the telegram. "Yes, they can come, but you may change your mind when you read this."

"Never you mind—Minnie's already called a town meeting for this afternoon. We'll pay those Hostetlers whatever they ask."

"Well—Mercer was cheap. The Hostetler boys want a *hundred* dollars to do the job."

The judge blanched. "A hundred dollars! The Roman army would be cheaper!"

"That's what I say." Everett nodded.

"Must think mighty highly of their services."

The clerk trailed Ragan and the judge into the kitchen.

"Lands sakes! Do they think we're made of money?" Judge McMann fumed. "Might as well use a mask and gun themselves."

Sighing, Ragan put the telegram down. "Should we give in to this kind of blackmail?"

"It's pure foolishness to ask someone like those dumb Hostetler boys to do anything, but we're desperate. We'll have to pay them what they want."

"Minnie says not to be late this afternoon." Everett swallowed, his Adam's apple bobbing. "Five o'clock. Everyone's required to be there."

"Required?" The judge blustered. "Dadburn that Minnie. Who made her queen?"

"Minnie says we have to do this thing democratically. After the Mercer thing, folks are pretty antsy. The town has to vote on calling the Brown Branch boys, and then figure out how we're gonna come up with the money to pay them."

"Dadburn it—supper'll be late again." The judge nailed a fly with a swatter. "You tell Minnie to make it brief. Lord Almighty. Why even vote? What choice do we have? Gangs riding around, attacking young couples. It's a blasted disgrace." Still grumbling, he rolled himself out of the room.

The thermometer hanging on the Oasis porch registered one hundred and one at five o'clock that afternoon. Anyone with a lick of sense knew you didn't call a meeting at this hour of the day, and more than one person informed Minnie of the fact. Townsfolk wiped sweat, and ordered lemonades from Mildred Crocker, who was cross as a bear for having to work late.

"Everyone sit down and hush up!" The stout-framed woman stood in the middle of the room, hands on hips, hair hanging in her flushed face. "I'm serving up drinks as fast as a body can. I didn't invent this heat."

"I don't know what's worse, Millie, your sour attitude or your sour lemonade. Is there a sugar shortage?"

"No, there's a brain shortage, Jesse. I thought you of all folks would know that."

Ragan pushed Judge McMann's chair through the crowd. Johnny was already seated toward the front with her family. Jo had planted herself next to him. What was she going to do with that girl?

She caught Johnny's eye and frowned her disapproval. A moment later, he got up and moved to the back of the room. Jo turned in her seat and shot Ragan a glare.

The room was abuzz with today's topic. Roberta Seeden's high-pitched voice carried above the noise. "Well, yes, I am concerned when I think that the rest of my life is going to be spent crouching under a table or hiding in a closet. That's not easy for some of us, you know. A hundred dollars is awful, but I'm willing to pay just about anything at this point."

"Maybe you are, Roberta, but there's others in the room who can't pay it. You and Tim got a little money put back, but what about the rest of us? We ain't got that kind of cash."

"Land, it's all I can do to keep the wolf off my doorstep," one man complained.

"You ain't gonna *have* a doorstep if the raids keep up," a woman reminded him.

Calling for order, Judge McMann whacked his cane on the bar. Millie flinched and dropped a full tray of lemonade on the floor.

"Effie, help Millie clean that up—everyone else sit down and let's get this meeting underway. It's twenty minutes past my supper time as it is."

The din quieted with the exception of Effie Willoughby, who crawled on her bony hands and knees, picking up broken pieces of glass.

"Get on with it, Judge," a farmer yelled. "You ain't the only one hungry, and besides that, I got cows waitin' to be milked."

Judge McMann gave him a repressive look. "All right, now. As you all know, Everett sent the wire over to Brown Branch inviting the Hostetler brothers and the Jurley boy to come in and do something about the raids." His eyes moved to Minnie. "Unfortunately, they're available, for a price."

"We know the price, Judge." Carl Rayles's mouth was set, and a deep flush rose from his collar. "Might as well stick a gun to our heads, but they got us over a barrel. We'll have to come up with the money somehow. It's a sad day when we can't even visit loved ones' graves without being harassed."

Clifford Kincaid got to his feet. The small-statured man adjusted the red cap on his head. "I say we offer 'em ten dollars apiece. That's a fair price for anyone."

"That's more than fair, Cap," the judge said. "But they want a hundred dollars."

The room hummed with indignation.

"A hundred dollars? How many are there?" a woman asked.

"Four in all. Three Hostetlers, and the Jurley boy."

"A hundred dollars is outrageous. Can't we offer them twenty-five?"

"We can, but they won't accept it." Florence Banks stood up from where she was helping Effie wipe up the sticky floor. "I've heard about these boys. They're not real bright—but they're stubborn as mules when it comes to money."

"If they're not real bright, why would we hire them?" A woman sitting near the back fanned herself with a paper.

"Bright or not, we'll have to pay whatever they ask," Minnie declared. "We can't go on like this."

"I agree with Minnie! A hundred dollars ain't much when you consider it's our lives you're talkin' about."

"Let's get on with it!"

Clifford used his cap as a fan. "Do something, even if it's wrong. Won't be the first time."

A hat was started around. Amid complaints and disgusted grunts, folks dug in their pockets. When it reached the back of the room, a man seized it and carried it to the front and counted the donations. "Three dollars and eighty-seven cents."

An uneasy silence gripped the room.

"Well, dang!" Austin Plummer said. "I put in a dollar! That means the rest of you yahoos contributed two dollars and eighty-seven cents."

Eyes lowered. Feet shuffled in the back of the room, some in the crowd looking contrite.

"Okay," Judge McMann said. "We're going to have to assess each family a flat fee."

When a few protested, the judge rapped on the bar with his cane. "People! Do we want help or not?"

Holly stood, clearing her throat. "Judge, I understand your need to assess a fee, but Tom and I need every cent we have." She blushed, glancing at her fiancé. "We hoped to marry late fall or early next winter, and we're both saving every bit we can get our hands on."

Others' protests echoed her words. The judge's cane rapped for silence.

A lone voice spoke up. "What's wrong with doing the job yourself?"

Heads swiveled to locate the speaker.

Johnny McAllister met the sea of curious eyes. "Why not do the job yourself?" he repeated.

Ragan felt a stab of relief. She held her breath, praying he would suggest a viable way for the citizens to defend the town.

"I say we assess a dollar a household," Minnie butted in.

Ragan fought the crush of disappointment when heads turned toward the mayor's wife, ignoring Johnny's suggestion. Why couldn't

Minnie keep her opinions to herself just once?

"That's only sixty-seven dollars," someone offered.

"What if there're two families in one household? Would that be one dollar or two dollars?"

"Two dollars! That wouldn't be fair."

"Paying one price for a family isn't right, either. There're only two people in our house, but others in this room have six or seven. They should have to pay more than a dollar!"

"Are you out of your mind? More than a dollar?" Jim Allen was red-faced. "Why, Polly Ann and me can barely keep food on the table for the eight of us. Where are we going to get that much money to give to the dumb Hostetler boys?"

"What's wrong with doing the job yourself?"

Heads switched back to Johnny, then to the judge.

"Shopkeepers should put in two dollars each," a man suggested. "They ought to pick up the slack for those of us who can't afford to chip in."

"Now see here!" Frankie Southern objected. "Kensil and I can't afford two dollars just because we own the mercantile!"

A timid hand raised in the back row. "How about fifty cents an adult and twenty-five cents a child?"

"What are you calling an adult? I'm not paying fifty cents for my fifteen-year-old."

"Friends! Please!" Judge McMann rapped for order again. "You want the help, but you're not willing to pay for it. I'm putting five dollars on the table, and then I'm going home. I suggest you do the same and think about this. I'm not sold on the Hostetlers, but since I can't come up with a better idea, I'm willing to give it a shot." He slapped the bills on the table and motioned to Ragan and Johnny. "It's past our suppertime."

The Brown Branch boys were hired for the job. Within the week they rode into town, looking like the cavalry to the beleaguered citizens of Barren Flats. The oldest boy, Billy, was a big, tall blond whose hair stood straight up at the crown. He was almost scary looking, but the town couldn't be picky.

The second brother, Buck, bore a striking resemblance to Billy. He was dirty, hadn't been near a razor in months, and was a tad shorter and bigger around the middle than his older brother, but a Hostetler, no doubt.

A missing front tooth in no way hindered his friendly smile.

Cisco, the third Hostetler, didn't exactly resemble a choirboy, or his brothers. Ragan studied his swarthy looks and decided the town had another chicken killer on their hands. And a high-priced one, at that. He wore his raven-black hair slicked back and tied with a leather thong. His dark, brooding eyes constantly searched the crowd that had turned out to watch the boys' arrival.

Rantz Jurley, a strange character with Spanish heritage, hung back and waved at everyone as the crew rode in.

"Maizie Jurley's boy," Minnie Rayles whispered. "Dropped on his head at birth. Pure old mean. Maizie's moved him from one town to another to keep him out of trouble. He's lived with every cousin and relative she could convince to take him for a spell. No one's been able to straighten him out."

"Do you know any of these men?" Ragan whispered to Johnny.

"Sure—they're all close friends."

She gave him a prickly look.

When the judge saw the motley group, Ragan heard him mutter under his breath before he turned and rolled his chair back into the mercantile.

* * *

The Hostetlers set up camp in back of the post office. They pitched a tent and hobbled a couple of shaggy pack mules, which brayed day and night. The noise was deafening.

Ragan passed a bowl of gravy to Johnny the second morning, bleary-eyed from lack of sleep. "Well. What do you think?"

He broke open a biscuit and ladled gravy over it. "I think it's going to be a hot one today."

Judge McMann's eyes twinkled.

"What do you think about the Brown Branch boys?" she persisted. "And none of this 'it's not my problem' nonsense. It *is* your problem, whether you like it or not."

He chewed a bite of biscuit and gravy, then calmly drained his coffee cup and pushed back from the table.

Ragan waited. He was going to answer, or she was going to throttle an opinion out of him.

"I think they could use a haircut and a bath."

She calmly picked up the bowl of gravy and threw the contents on his shirt.

Johnny shoved back from the table in shock. Kitty seized the moment and began licking gravy off the front of his shirt. He shot Ragan a look that would have scared most women.

Casually reaching for the bowl of scrambled eggs, Ragan studied it. "Surely you have some teensy, tiny comment?" Her expression hardened. "Don't you?"

The judge hurriedly took a sip of coffee, then backed his chair to safety.

"Ragan—"

Her eyes snapped fire. "Don't you?" She hefted the bowl threateningly.

Johnny set the cat on the floor, mopping gravy off the front of his shirt. "The town doesn't want to hear what I think. They made that clear at the meeting."

"The town might not, but I do." The judge returned to the table, interest lighting his eyes. "I would value your opinion."

Kitty jumped into the judge's lap, sniffing his hand for a treat. Dipping his fingers in the remains of the gravy, he allowed the cat to lick them clean.

Carrying a stack of dishes to the sink, Johnny deposited them in the dishpan. "I don't understand why they want to hire someone else to do their job."

The judge leaned back, studying him. "You're saying you think we haven't tried to defend ourselves?"

"I know how you've been burned out and shot at for years." His eyes met Ragan's. "I know about Ragan's brother, and I know about being scared and helpless. But you can't expect others to protect you. You want my opinion? I think you're a community of gutless cowards who won't stand up for what's rightly yours."

He turned on his heel and left the room.

For a moment, neither Ragan nor the judge could find their tongue.

Finally Ragan picked up the empty gravy bowl, and wiped the table clean.

"Well," the judge observed. "As I said, we have to consider all communication as positive."

That afternoon, Johnny stayed behind while Ragan and Judge McMann visited Main Street to see the Hostetlers' progress. A gang hadn't come through since their arrival, and things were uncommonly quiet.

"Are you sure you won't come?" Ragan pushed the judge's chair past Johnny and through the open gate.

"No. I promised Mrs. Curbow I'd paint that shed for her this afternoon." Johnny closed the gate behind them and latched it.

Work around the judge's house had slowed to the point that Ragan had started to loan Johnny out to the town's widows. Between painting and gardening, he was busy most of the time.

"Mind if Kitty goes with me?"

The judge and Ragan turned to look over their shoulders. He met their stunned gazes easily.

"No, go right ahead. She'll enjoy tagging along."

When they reached Main Street, Ragan braked the chair, eyeing the activity. The three Hostetlers and Rantz ran back and forth from one side of the street to the other, stringing rope across the north entrance.

"What the devil are they doing?" Squinting, the judge leaned forward in his chair, shading his eyes against the sun's glare.

"Looks like they're tying rope to posts at the telegraph office, then tying the other end to the mercantile across the street. Maybe they're going to hang a sign." Ragan couldn't imagine why they'd do that.

Billy snapped orders, while Cisco tied the rope on one side and Rantz tied it on the other. Buck measured out another length and started toward the south end of town, dragging the hemp behind him. He grinned, tipping his hat as he passed the judge. The tip of his tongue protruded through the gap from his missing front tooth.

Billy barely glanced up when Ragan rolled the judge's chair within hearing distance.

"What are you doing, son?"

The boy looped the rope around a post and tightened it. "Strangin' rope."

"I can see that. What's the plan?"

"Gonna strang rope 'crost the road for when the gangs ride through again."

The judge glanced at the rope, then at Billy. "And what's supposed to happen?"

"The gangs'll ride in, and the rope'll catch 'em right here." He gave a hard chop to his sternum.

Rantz snickered as he returned to help. "Knock 'em right off their horses."

"Knock them off their horses?" The judge studied the rope. "That's your plan?"

Buck approached, sweat rolling down his baby-faced features. "Knock 'em offen their horses, and then the sheriff's deputies can arrest 'em and throw 'em in jail."

Ragan was glad that Johnny wasn't seeing this. "Is that wise? The impact could hang a person, couldn't it?"

"Naw—jest knock 'em offen their horse, ma'am." Billy pointed to several coils of rope lying on the ground. "We got us four ropes." He grinned. "We'll catch 'em all, don't you worry none."

Her heart sank.

"Billy, let me see if I understand you." The judge appeared to study the plan. "The gangs will ride into town. You're banking on them being blind; that they won't be able to see the rope strung across the road. When they stupidly ride into the rope, they'll be knocked off their horses, and all the deputies have to do is sashay out there and tie them up. The gangs will just keep riding into the rope until there are no more to ride in, or the four ropes give out. Is that your plan?"

Buck nodded. "Yessir." He flashed a toothless grin.

"Ragan?"

"Yes, Judge?"

"Take me home. I suddenly have a splitting headache."

"Yes, Judge." She turned the chair, and started off.

"String a rope! I've heard it all, now."

"Yes, sir." She bit back a grin. "Can we agree not to mention this to Johnny?"

"Lord have mercy. Maybe the boys will change their minds before they can put the plan into action."

They passed Rantz, who was trekking across the street, dragging a trail of rope behind him.

"Then again, I guess that's too much to hope for."

A commotion had erupted at the saloon. Ragan moved the judge's chair to the shade of the building, and they watched as a crowd of men hustled in and out of the bar, carrying chairs.

"Morning, Shorty, Hubie."

"Morning, Judge, Ragan."

"What's going on?"

Hubie hoisted another chair onto a buckboard. "Hostetler's told us to make space for the prisoners."

"You honestly believe there are going to be some?"

Shorty frowned. "Well, shore. Billy says the jail ain't gonna hold all the gangs."

"Ragan?"

"Yes, Judge?"

"My headache's getting worse by the minute."

Saturday morning dawned dry with a hot breeze. Ragan wiped her forehead with her apron hem, then set eggs and ham on the table. "Is it ever going to rain again?"

She poured coffee, watching Johnny salt his gravy. "It's been three days and no raids."

The judge grunted, reaching for the sugar bowl. "Through no virtue of the Brown Branch bunch."

Undoing his napkin, Johnny laid it in his lap. "I understand those ropes are causing quite a problem." He met Ragan's eyes, and she could swear he was laughing at her. Well, who *wouldn't* laugh? The Hostetlers' idea was downright embarrassing. To think the town had spent so much money on this fiasco.

"Most asinine situation I've ever had the misfortune to witness," the judge grumbled. "Everyone's complaining because they have to park their buggies outside of town. Harold Bradshaw was mad enough to eat nails yesterday. He had to carry fifteen sacks of grain to his wagon because of that danged rope. Lowell Homer turned his wagon upside down when he tried to cut between the mercantile and Sheriff Lutz's office. Dumped the whole load of hay on Frankie's steps. Where the cat hair is Alvin Lutz?"

Ragan carried a skillet to the sink. "He's down in his joints, judge."

"Good heavens, we might as well not have a sheriff."

"Was Lowell hurt?" Ragan asked with concern.

"No, you know Lowell. Hard-headed as a gourd. But the team pulled the wagon on its side and strung hay all the way down Main Street. It's a disgrace, I tell you. We'll be the laughingstock of the county."

Johnny reached for the butter, trying to catch Ragan's eye, but she refused to accommodate him. "Ahh, yes. The old rope trick." He casually buttered a biscuit, then bit into it. "Who knows?" Ragan finally looked at him, and he winked at her. "It might work."

"Five days and no raids." Judge McMann said.

The silence the last few days was unsettling, and Ragan's nerves were on edge. No rope was going to keep the gangs away. The outlaws were only biding their time until they could devise their own plan. In the meantime, everyone in town was inconvenienced.

"Well, it's what we wanted," Ragan reminded him as she turned a shovelful of potatoes in the garden. "You're not unhappy about that, are you, Judge?"

"Of course not. Just wondering if anyone's actually dumb enough to ride into those ropes."

"Actually, one person has. Holly mentioned last night that one of Ted Rowser's boys from Tom's Canyon rode into town yesterday and hit the rope. Knocked him right off his horse—almost hung himself, Holly said. He has a fierce rope burn across his neck."

She wasn't at all surprised at Johnny's snicker. Naturally *he* found the situation amusing, but poor Keith Rowser failed to see the humor.

"Keith was real upset. When he finally got up, he threw a punch at Billy and Cisco. Sheriff Lutz had to separate them and threatened to haul them all off to jail." She knocked a clod of dirt off her hoe, pinning Johnny with a critical look. He was still snickering. "It's not funny. Keith could have been seriously hurt."

Johnny's features immediately sobered. "I don't doubt that. If a rope's taut enough, it'll take a man's head off." He pitched a potato into the pan.

Judge McMann shook his head. "How long is this nonsense going to last? Townsfolk inconvenienced, Lowell tearing up his wagon and losing all that hay, the stage can't get through, and now we've nearly decapitated one of our neighbors' sons." He sighed heavily. "I don't think we can afford the Hostetler boys."

At the sound of gunshots, the judge straightened in his chair. "Listen."

Hoofbeats and rounds of fire sounded near the south edge of town.

"They're coming!" Ragan threw the hoe aside, and reached for Kitty. She thrust the cat toward the judge. "Quick—into the house."

"Wait!" the judge held up his hand. "Listen."

The noise of horses and guns gradually receded.

"They're leaving."

They stood silently, straining to make out the retreating hoof beats.

"Doesn't seem as if they captured the riders," Ragan said.

They all exchanged looks.

"There wasn't enough time," the judge replied. "Let's go have a look."

The Hubbards and Kincaids joined them as they hurried toward the post office. An air of expectancy hung over Barren Flats.

"We made the girls stay home," Lillian explained breathlessly. "We don't want them witnessing all this violence."

People streamed into town to see the first evidence of their hard-earned money at work. Florence and Hubie Banks stood in front of the saloon, discussing what had just happened.

"What's going on, Hubie?" the judge called as they got closer. "We heard the riders coming, then it sounded as if they turned around."

"There were eight to ten of 'em, Judge. They rode up and saw the rope—must have caught 'em by surprise, because they turned around and hightailed it out of town. Jim Allen followed them, and rode back a minute ago and said they were still out there, huddled together on that ridge out near Coyote Road."

Johnny turned to look over his shoulder in the direction of Coyote Road. "They're just sitting there on their horses?"

"Yeah, that's what Jim said. Wonder what they're up to now?"

Billy and Cisco strode down Main Street, smiling. "No need to get upset, folks. We skeered 'em off." Billy gave the judge a smug look. "Our plan worked. The minute they spotted that thar rope, they decided not to try their luck."

Buck chortled. "Skeered 'em to death."

Thundering hoofbeats interrupted them.

Riders appeared, guns blazing. Reining in at the rope, they slashed it with their knives. Then their horses trampled the tattered remains as they galloped into town.

The townsfolk scattered, and the marauders charged toward the saloon. Ragan pushed Judge McMann through the open doorway. The front window shattered and shots ricocheted off the Oasis sign. Glassware exploded and bottles flew from the shelves. Florence groaned as a bullet hit the gold-framed mirror hanging behind the bar. The frame split, and crashed to the floor. A single triangle of glass dangled from the right-hand corner.

The hoodlums rode up and down Main Street, yelling and firing. Then they sliced the rope guarding the north end of town and galloped off.

An eerie silence settled over the stunned population.

"Anybody hurt?" Hubie slowly crawled to his feet, setting a chair upright.

Ragan felt Johnny's hand on her arm.

"Thank you," she murmured.

He moved to help the judge back into his chair.

"I'm okay, son. Thank you. I'm so thankful Maddy isn't here to see this. It would break her heart."

As they descended the Oasis steps, Buck ran past carrying what was left of the ropes. Flashing his toothless grin, he called out, "Jest a small setback. We'll git 'em. Don't you worry none."

"Idiots," the judge grumbled as the crowd dispersed. "We've bought ourselves a hundred dollars worth of idiots." He motioned for Johnny to take him home, and the three were silent as they left Main Street.

*   *   *

"You know . . ." Everett closed his left eye and squeezed off another round. The bullet missed the target by a dismal inch. "I never believed that rope trick would work in the first place."

"Really." No one in his right mind would think the rope plan would work. The idea was laughable, though the town's situation wasn't funny.

It was only a matter of time until a tragedy was sure to happen. A toddler was almost trampled yesterday. Johnny hated to think of another family suffering as the Ramseys had.

"You're jerking your arm, Everett. Hold it steady."

"Sorry."

Squinting first one eye, then the other, Everett took aim and fired again. The bullet missed its mark, and wood chips flew from the base of a nearby scrub oak. At this rate, the clerk wouldn't be ready for the Founders' Day shooting contest in six months, much less six weeks.

"Blast it all!"

Johnny bent to pick up the spent shells. "Rome wasn't built in a day."

"It went up faster than I'm learning to shoot."

The two men scanned the practice area. They'd been at it over an hour now, and Everett had leveled everything in sight with the exception of his intended target.

"Well, Founders' Day is still a ways off."

Everett eyed the barrel of his pistol sourly. "I'm never going to make it." He glanced Johnny's way. "How come you're allowed to move about on your own so much lately?"

He felt a prick of conscience. The judge had sent him to repair the church handrail this morning, but he slipped off with Everett for a few minutes of target practice instead. The judge's trust was misplaced, and he didn't feel good about it.

"Ragan's canning beans today. Judge McMann told me to come alone."

Everett whistled. "You must be gaining Proctor's trust."

"Looks that way." Hell, he could simply walk away from Barren Flats and never be seen again. Hadn't Proctor thought about that? The old man had a heart of gold; he left himself wide open for defeat.

It was a shame he was the one who was going to derail the judge's program if he found Bledso. It wasn't right, seeing how McMann had been good to him. He treated him more like a son than a prisoner. But then, who ever said life was fair? It wasn't for Judge McMann, with his crippled limbs, nor for Ragan's brother, and certainly nor for his family, lying cold in their graves.

Everett settled himself on a log. "You know, Judge McMann and Ragan work hard to prove lawbreakers sometimes deserve a second chance." He slid Johnny a hopeful look. "You wouldn't do anything to mess that up, would you?"

"Now, Everett—why would I do anything to mess it up? I'm living in paradise."

He had good food, a roof over his head, a clean bed to sleep in at night. A woman who cared more about him than anyone had in a long time. He was starting to think of Ragan as his woman. Her kisses came too easily lately, the embraces, the looks that fired his blood. She was the last thing he thought about at night, and the first thing he wanted in the morning. His resolve was slipping. He couldn't have both Ragan and Bledso, and it was getting harder to remember that.

Everett polished the pistol handle with the cuff of his shirt. "No . . . don't suppose you would. You haven't tried anything funny with the gun, or anything like that."

Nor would he try anything funny with the gun, or anything like that. Not until he needed it. Still, the admiration in Everett's voice bothered him. He'd be yet another to be disappointed in him, another who would walk away and say, well, what did we expect from a man like Johnny McAllister?

Lightening the mood, Johnny smiled. "I had the distinct impression you didn't like me when you met me, Everett."

"Well I didn't—not at first."

"Because of Ragan?"

Everett's face flamed, and Johnny felt a little sorry for the lovesick kid. He'd been tempted to impress her a time or two, himself.

"She's some woman, isn't she? Pretty as spring grass. Someday I'm going to marry her. She isn't interested in me right now, but she will be, someday."

The artless declaration disturbed Johnny. Not just because of the stab of envy; it also bothered him because Everett was so gullible, and was sure to be disappointed when his dream failed to materialize. Ragan had made her intentions clear; Everett was just too blind in love to accept them.

"Well—I'm sorry I was so rude to you when you came to town. I thought Ragan would fall like a rock for you, but she didn't." Everett brightened. "She doesn't appear to care any more for you than she does for me."

If the cheerful observation was meant to comfort him, it missed its mark. But then, Everett was a piss poor shot. And Everett had never held Ragan when she was all soft and warm and—

Johnny glanced at the sun. It was getting close to noon, and he still had to repair the church handrail.

He nodded for Everett to precede him out of the grove of trees.

A few moments later Johnny followed, and the two men exited the woods at different points, Johnny turning toward the church lane and Everett heading to town.

Chapter 11

Ragan was churning butter the next morning when young Clayton Miller showed up on the porch looking hungry.

"Mornin' Miz Ramsey."

"Come in, Clayton. What brings you out and about so early?" She motioned the boy to the table, and placed a plate in front of him. Filling Clayton was like filling a hollow stump.

But this morning, Clayton had more than biscuits on his mind. He was breathless with excitement. "Got me a job! The Hostetlers hired me and Junior to—"

"Junior and me," Ragan automatically corrected, pouring a large glass of milk.

"Hostetlers hired Junior and me to tell everybody to bring their cattle to Main Street, quick as they can."

"Cattle?" Judge McMann wiped his mouth, then pushed back from the table.

"You know, cows."

"I know what cattle are, son. Why do the Hostettlers want everybody to bring their cattle to the middle of town?"

"Buck said they're gonna pack the town plumb full of cattle so the gangs can't ride through." His message delivered, Clayton helped himself to two slices of bread and spooned a heap of apple butter in the middle. Folding each slice in half, he set upon them with the gusto of a growing fourteen-year-old.

Ragan glanced at Johnny. He gave no indication that his opinion of the Hostetler's newest plan was any higher than the last one. He kept his head down and avoided her eyes.

Clayton finished the last of his treat, and washed it down with a long swallow of milk.

The judge chuckled. "Have some more, son, there's plenty."

The boy pushed back from the table and stood up. "No thank you, sir. Junior and I are going to borrow Mr. Banks's cart and jenny and spread the news." He puffed out his chest, and would have looked very important if it weren't for the apple butter ringing his upper lip. "I'm to tell folks to bring those cows pronto, 'cause we don't want no more—"

"Any more," Ragan said, handing the boy a clean napkin.

"Any more raids," the boy finished, and swiped his mouth clean. His freckled face beamed. "Thanks for the bread and apple butter."

Ragan stuck a thick slice of ham between two pieces of bread, then wrapped it in a clean towel and handed it to Clayton as she walked him to the door. "All that work is bound to make a body hungry."

"Yes, ma'am. It sure does. Thank you kindly." He tucked the sandwich into the bib of his overalls and jumped down the steps, turning to wave as he headed off. Ragan returned to the kitchen to clear the table.

The judge shook his head. "My Lord. How do those numbskulls think our own wagons and horses are going to get through Main Street if they pack it with cattle? Not to mention the stage, and the neighbors' wagons."

Johnny reached for the butter. "Wonder which one of them is considered the brains behind this operation?"

The judge's mind was still on the cows. "Who's going to keep all those animals from wandering off?" He drew on his pipe. "And the mess. Wonder if those knuckleheads have thought about the mess a herd of cattle that size can make?"

Johnny passed the bowl of gravy. "*Do* they think?"

"When they were handing out brains, those boys must have thought they said trains, and told them they didn't have anywhere to keep one." The judge grunted, laying his pipe aside. "This is turning out to be a blasted nuisance."

Judge McMann was up early the next morning. When Ragan came to work, he was already sitting at the kitchen table, eating a bowl of oatmeal.

Stoking the fire, Ragan slid the stove lid back into place. "I thought you didn't like oatmeal."

"I don't, but I'm in a hurry this morning. Didn't sleep a wink last night. I want to get a look at this cockamamie plan those Brown Branch boys have thought up."

Ragan didn't have to get a look; it already sounded like a cattle drive out there. Cattle bawling, flies swarming—already the flies were awful.

"Why don't you come with me?"

Ragan glanced toward the parlor. "I'll need to fix Johnny's breakfast."

Judge McMann pushed his empty bowl

aside. "Who do you think made this oat-meal? You know I can't cook. John ate with me, then went out to the shed for a minute. We're ready to go when you are."

"But the housework—"

"Just leave the housework. It'll be here when you get back."

Johnny returned, and the three had walked less than a block when they met Julia Cur-bow standing at her gate. Her bright red hair was done up in curls this morning. "Morning Judge, Ragan. Isn't it exciting?" She smiled at Johnny, and Ragan could swear the old woman had set her cap for him.

Johnny graciously returned her smile. "You look mighty pretty this morning, Mrs. Curbow. That right foot bothering you to-day?"

"Why, thank you, darlin'. No, my foot's much better." She beamed. "Once these raids are taken care of, I'm going to make myself a new dress." She eyed Johnny coyly. "A lady can never have too many pretty dresses, don't you agree, Mr. McAllister?"

Johnny shrugged pleasantly and called back as they continued toward town, "That's what the pretty ladies say."

Cattle milled back and forth in front of the saloon. Lowell Homer was trying to move them on down the street. Removing his hat, he scratched his head and told them, "Can't quite figure how having all these cattle in the street is gonna help solve our problem."

The judge shook his head and gestured toward the north. "Is that Plummer coming?"

Lowell shaded his eyes with his hat. "Looks like Austin's brought the whole herd."

The cattle bore down on the town. Occasionally several would break into a gallop, stirring up whorls of dust.

Ragan flattened against a hitching post as one ornery longhorn pushed down the walk, and brushed her with its head. The animal bounded up the land office steps. Lowell struck the beast on the rump with a prod, but the old steer kept going.

When the dust cleared, Ragan ducked into the general store as a shouting match erupted behind her.

"It's a real mess out there, Mazilea," she said. "Tempers are flaring."

"Tell me about it."

"Problems?"

"Those dadgummed cattle. They're stirringup terrible dirt." She swiped the counter with a rag, then moved to the front window, where she rubbed a clear spot on the glass. "Just look at this." She shook the blackened rag at Ragan. "And cows don't buy groceries."

Ragan peered out. Cattle clogged the boardwalks, where red-faced shop owners tried to beat them back with brooms. "Wonder how long the Hostetlers plan to keep this up?" Dust boiled as more and more cattle crowded onto Main Street.

"Oh no!" Mazilea took a step toward the door.

Ragan whirled in time to see a water barrel in front of the store tip over. The barrel spun off the porch, careening off the steps and into the crush of cattle. The lid rolled one way and the barrel the other.

"I'm not risking my life for a barrel," Mazilea declared, watching a big Hereford trample it. "I'm closing the store and going home. No one's going to brave a stampede to buy groceries. I'll have to close permanently if this keeps up."

"Now, Mazilea—people still need flour, tea, and sugar, no matter what they have to do to get it." Ragan handed over her list. "I'll need a tin of baking soda, too."

The storeowner bustled around the room getting Ragan's order together, grumbling all the while. Ragan didn't blame her; the cow stench was enough to put anyone in a bad mood.

"I saw Julia on our way over." Ragan

prowled the narrow aisles, looking over the merchandise.

"Oh? How is Julia? She was in last week, complaining about feeling poorly." Mazilea stuck her head around the corner of one aisle. "You know, she's smitten with your prisoner. Thinks he's the best-looking man she's ever seen. Most excitin', too. That's all she talks about: Jonathan this, Jonathan that."

Ragan frowned. "Yes, she's very taken with him. Why does she think his name's Jonathan?" He did talk to the elderly neighbor from time to time. She felt a prick of envy. Did Julia know something Ragan and Procky didn't?

"She thinks it is. Don't ask me why, but you know how Julia is. Once she gets something in her head, wild horses can't change her mind." Mazilea measured out sugar into a bag. "But then, she doesn't have to contend with him like you do. Maybe she wouldn't be so taken with him if she had to put up with him all the time."

"He's pretty easy to live with." Ragan blushed when she realized how easily she came to his defense. But having Johnny around was not a chore.

"Julia says he likes cats."

"Oh, I wouldn't exactly say that. How would Julia know, anyway?"

"Says he stops and scratches hers under the chin when he passes by."

Well, maybe he did. Kitty *was* awfully fond of him lately. The women turned as Shorty Lynch burst through the door and dumped five loaves of bread on the counter. "Get busy and make up a couple of dozen cheese sandwiches. I'm going back for the pies."

Mazilea stared at the bread. "Hold it right there, Shorty. I just baked those pies last night; they're for us to enjoy for the whole week. So is this bread. Take it right back where you got it."

Her husband stopped to catch his breath. "You can bake more bread tonight. The Brown Branch boys can't handle all the cattle. They've had to ask the town to help. Now, think about it, Mazie. These folks are gonna be hungry. I've been telling everyone to come by here for food." He jerked open the door and disappeared before there could be any argument.

The door opened again, and half a dozen hungry men came in. Mazilea flew into action, and Ragan quickly excused herself and left.

Outside, the din of the animals was deafening. Ragan tried to read Judge McMann's lips when he spotted her. She was able to make out, ". . . are going to camp in town . . . haul water and feed . . ." and "lucky to sleep tonight."

Hopefully she'd filled in the blanks correctly, and she was not the one expected to camp in town, haul the water, and feed the cattle. Lifting the hem of her skirt, she waded across the street.

Everett appeared out of nowhere. "Allow me." He laid out an expanse of heavy butchers' paper for her to step on.

"Thank you, Everett. I'm afraid my skirt is already beyond saving. This is some mess, isn't it?" She picked her way to Judge McMann's side, and Johnny took her elbow as she stepped to the wooden walk in front of the title office.

Everett waited until she was safely inside before he made his way back across the street.

That night, Ragan lay in bed and listened to her father's restless movements. She could hear the cattle in town even from this distance, and the incessant bawling frazzled her nerves.

Every time she squeezed her eyes shut and tried to block out the racket, the vile red-bearded man and his gang arose in her mind.

Who were those horrible men, and how did they know Johnny? She didn't want to admit that it mattered. He would serve his sentence, and be gone before she could wave goodbye. But it did matter. Drat it all; it mattered a great deal.

There was a quiet movement somewhere in the house, and her eyes flew open. She sat up, trying to distinguish the sound from the noisy cattle. A door creaked, and she was instantly on her feet. "Papa. Papa!" She flew through the rooms, outside, and down the porch steps to catch up with Fulton Ramsey, who was already at the gate. He fumbled with the catch. "Papa, it's nighttime; where are you going?"

"They're coming."

"Who's coming, Papa?"

"Listen. Can't you hear them? They're going to hurt my family. I have to protect my girls. Hurry, help me find your sisters."

She turned his frail form back toward the house. "They're asleep in the house, Papa. You come back to bed, too."

Dew soaked the hems of his pajamas, and his bare feet were wet and muddy when she got him inside. "Let's get you washed, and put on some dry clothes."

Holly stood in the doorway in a sleepy stupor. "Is something wrong?"

"No. Go back to bed."

Becca and Jo also appeared. Ragan sent them all back to bed, then led Fulton to the kitchen table and sat him down.

"You know this is never going to end, don't you?" There was no hesitation in his voice now. His eyes were clear and keen. "No one is going to take care of this town, and you might as well accept that."

"We're doing all we know to do, Papa." She rinsed the mud off his feet, and toweled them dry.

"Others can't make decisions for you." He stood up, his chin firm. Ragan followed him to his room, and when he sat on his bed, he looked at her with eyes so sad her heart wrenched. Then he was gone again. "You must listen to me. Noah listened when God told him what to do, and he—"

"I know, Papa, I know." She helped him lie back on the pillow and pulled the quilt over his gaunt frame.

"And he took two of each . . ."

Ragan softly closed the door, the sound of bellowing cattle drowning out her father's words. Tears spilled down her cheeks, and she whispered softly, "I know, Papa. I know."

*   *   *

Cattle packed the streets of Barren Flats for five endless days. It seemed the animals were everywhere. There was talk of little else, and the subject was close to being exhausted in the McMann home.

"If I never hear another steer bawl, it will be too soon," the judge declared after supper Saturday night. "Ragan, I don't even want you to cook a roast anytime soon."

She put a thick slice of apple pie on Johnny's plate. Their eyes met and she yearned to bend down and kiss him. They hadn't found a moment alone for days. Goose bumps welled on her arms when she thought of their stolen embraces: a touch here, an not-so-innocent brush there. "We have to be encouraged that the raids have stopped."

"Hummph. Gunshots are almost preferable to this constant racket and the flies."

"I don't want gunshots *or* cattle." Ragan dropped the knife into the sink. "And if I wanted noise, I'd prefer a good, old-fashioned thunderstorm."

A streak of lightning flashed, followed by a deafening clap of thunder that shook the kitchen floor.

Laugh crinkles formed around Johnny's eyes. "Be careful what you wish for."

The judge chuckled. "Sounds like you

have a connection with a powerful force."

If she had such a connection, she'd ask that Johnny McAllister was an upstanding, solid citizen. That he wasn't a prisoner, and that she could act on these perfectly irrational feelings she was having about him . . .

Another louder crack followed, and Ragan ran to close the windows.

A low rumble began and quickly grew into a roar.

Turning from a window, Ragan whispered, "Tornado?"

Johnny took hold of the judge's chair. Lightning illuminated the kitchen as they headed for the doorway. Closer and closer, the roar increased. The house shook with pounding vibration.

"Earthquake!" Ragan grasped the back of the judge's chair as the porch quivered beneath them.

Johnny paused, grasping the porch rail and listening as rain drummed down on the roof. "The wind isn't blowing. It isn't a tornado, or an earthquake." His eyes swept the sky, then he looked in the direction of town. "It's cattle!"

"Cattle?" Ragan frowned, trying to shield the judge from the rain with the hem of her apron.

"Stampede!" He pointed toward a dark mass that moved toward them.

Ragan's eyes widened at the sight. "The cattle. They're coming straight toward the house!"

Riders rode the perimeter of the giant herd, trying to gain on the lead animals. Rain pelted the outbuildings and ran in rivulets on the parched ground. Blurred images thundered past, trampling shrubs and flowerbeds. The din of pounding hoofs competed with the sound of the driving rain; it was impossible to distinguish one from the other. When the chaos moved past them down the road, Ragan turned to stare in shock at Johnny.

He shrugged. "Plan two didn't work out, either."

The skies cleared, and the sun came out. Lifting the kitchen window, Ragan wrinkled her nose at the strong odor.

"The air smells of sulfur," the judge remarked, standing at the open front door.

"Sulfur? Smells like sh—" Johnny glanced at Ragan, "like the Hostetlers have a manure problem."

Hot, damp air enveloped the house. The stench spread throughout the rooms, saturating furniture and drapes.

Ragan pressed a hanky to her nose. She could just *throttle* those Hostetlers! How would she ever get rid of the stink?

"We might just as well go look at the stampede damage." Judge McMann fanned the air in front of him as he headed out the door and down the walk. "Phew-eee."

Phew-ee, indeed. This was ten times worse than the raids! Ragan hurried to catch up with the two men. Why did they always have to be right in the middle of things?

The three marched toward Main Street, holding handkerchiefs to their noses. Ragan felt something bite her left ankle. She lifted her leg and kicked at a fly at the same time Johnny slapped his neck. The judge shook his foot to ward off two large, green, buzzing insects.

The stench was more pronounced as they turned onto Main Street. The downpour had turned the rutted street into liquified manure. It was impossible to walk anywhere except the wooden walkway without shoes slipping and hems and cuffs sucking up the muck. Flies buzzed, landed, then bit. Mosquitoes attacked in angry swarms. Ragan's nose drew into a permanent wrinkle and she pinched her nostrils tight.

"I've seen all I need to see." The judge wheeled his chair around.

Everett hurried toward Ragan with a clean roll of butcher paper.

"Oh Everett, thank you, but it's no use. There's no way to salvage this dress now." If that boy would just find someone to care for besides her!

The judge patted the clerk's arm. "You better get back inside before these bugs eat you alive, son . . . or you're overcome by the fumes."

Everett obeyed, for once seeming anxious to leave.

People stood in doorways. A few balanced on hitching posts, and some high-stepped their way across the street.

On the other side, Rantz and the Hostetlers were surrounded by an angry mob.

"How do you expect us to conduct business in this stinkin' mess?" Shorty Lynch demanded.

Trish Hubbard buried her nose in her mother's skirt. "I'm going to spit up, Mama. Honest."

Lillian guided her youngest to the side of the general store and held the little girl as she doubled over.

"Now, folks." Buck Hostetler waved his arms above his head. "Folks, let me have your attention, now. There's no harm done here. Don't get excited."

"No harm? Our town stinks like a damned privy, the road runs with cow manure, and the flies are eating us alive! What do you mean, no harm?" Rudolph Miller's massive form towered above Buck. He crossed his beefy arms over his chest and stared. "What are you gonna do about this mess?"

"Well." Buck glanced at Billy. "Give us a minute to think about it." He took off running when Rudolph came after him.

Florence Banks slapped a fly off Hubie's back, then pinned Billy with a withering look. "You'd better do something, and do it quick, young man."

Billy swatted a fly. "Now, folks—"

"Clean up this mess!" the crowd roared.

Billy lifted his manure-stained hand for quiet, and started to pace importantly in front of the crowd. "The way I see it, this is your town, and we gotta have more cooperation outta you." He motioned for Bucky to come back and stand by his side.

"That's what we paid *you* fer."

"And what we want you to do," Buck continued, ignoring the jeers, "is for each family to come up with a barrel of lime and a rake." He paused, making a dramatic, wide-armed sweep of the area. "Line those barrels up and down the street—the whole street, both sides—and dump the lime in piles from north to south. Then everybody rake the lime until it covers the whole street. That will take care of the smell and the flies."

The crowd fell silent.

Buck, sensing confusion, went on. "The sooner you get back here with the rakes and lime, the sooner we'll get rid of the stink. Once we get rid of the stink, then me and my crew can get on with another plan."

"We've had enough of your plans, Bucky," someone called.

"Go back to Brown Branch!" Timothy Seeden yelled. "Thanks to you, we live in Manure Hollow."

Billy's hands shot to his hips resentfully. "I *said* we're going to clean this up. You'll get your money's worth."

Jesse Rehop approached Judge McMann and his party. "I think I've had about all I want for my money. How about you, Judge?"

"Disgraceful," the judge snorted. He nailed a fly on his knee and brushed the squashed remains aside.

Carl Rayles moved to the front of the crowd. "People! Listen! Billy's suggestion isn't a bad one. The lime will quell the odor, and when the manure is covered, the flies will quieten down. I say we bring in the lime and take care of this disgusting problem as quickly as possible."

The town finally agreed they had little choice. The flies were eating them alive.

The barnyard stench imprisoned Barren Flats as the citizens set to work. The first barrel of lime arrived, and the men raked it from boardwalk to boardwalk. Flies scaled the walls and clung to screens and windows.

An occasional "Blast those stupid Hostetlers" marked the strained silence.

By late afternoon, some progress was noted. The flies still buzzed, but the lime made it possible to walk without the aid of a handkerchief blocking the nostrils, even though it caked trouser cuffs, skirt hems, and boots.

The judge, Ragan, and Johnny stood at the edge of town, watching the cleanup.

Everywhere they looked, a thick layer of white dust crusted the ground. "Looks like a summer blizzard," Ragan murmured.

"Doesn't smell like snow." Johnny's observation made her smile.

Mazilea was in front of the general store, sweeping the porch in a mad frenzy. Leaving Johnny and the judge to their own devices, Ragan approached the harried shopkeeper.

"Can I help, Mazilea?"

Mazilea shot her a hopeless look. "President Grant couldn't help with this one! Just *look* at this. That . . . that stuff is everywhere. On my floors, in my curtains, clogging the air. I can't sweep it out, dust it off, or mop it up." To prove her point, she picked up a broom and attacked the white substance marring the porch. Her efforts merely rearranged the white powder. "Someone ought to tar and feather those stupid Hostetlers."

"What in the ding-dong devil are you doing now, Billy?" The judge stood up in his wheelchair, a vein throbbing in his neck. Buck and Billy were digging a hole in the middle of the road.

"Easy, Judge," Johnny said.

"Idiots! Simpletons!"

Buck glanced up, and swiped his shirt sleeve across his sweaty forehead. He flashed a toothless grin. "We're diggin' a ditch clean 'crost here, so when the raiders come, they'll fall into it. Then we'll all run out and capture them."

Johnny laid a hand across the judge's shoulder. By now, Proctor's face was red, and the blood vessels pounded in his forehead. "At least a ditch doesn't stink," Johnny reminded him in a low undertone.

The judge looked at him, aghast. "You

can't mean you think any of this nonsense will work!"

"No, it won't work. But you're already out a hundred dollars. What do you have to lose?"

"Billy," the judge began again, "that is about the dumbest idea I've ever witnessed. And I've witnessed some dumb things lately. How will the stage or our own wagons get through?"

The boy paused, scratching his head. Buck looked blank as he considered the question.

"Have you given any thought to the damage this ditch will cause to animals? If a horse hits that hole, it'll break its legs. If you think cow manure stinks, wait until you have a ditch full of rotting horse carcasses."

"Well," Billy viewed Judge McMann as if he were the simple-minded one. "The horses will jump *over* the ditch. Jest the riders will fall into it. I think. Least ways, that's the way I have it ciphered." He looked at Buck, and they both nodded.

"Yep, that's how I got it ciphered, too." Buck agreed. He scratched his crotch.

The judge looked at Johnny, who shrugged.

"Maybe the gangs are idiots, too." He looked around at the townsfolk. They didn't deserve this. These were good people.

Mazilea and Shorty were trying hard to eke out a living in this forgotten little town. Their trade was affected in every way by the marauders. Jim and Polly Ann, down the street from the judge, were trying to raise their boys to be upright citizens, and as far as he could tell they were doing a good job of it.

The Homers, the Plummers, Widow Keeling, Julia Curbow—all were suffering.

"Now see here, Judge." Billy was clearly getting put out. "We got us a job to do, and we intend to give Barren Flats its money's worth. You're jest gonna have to step back and let us do what we was paid to do."

Closing his eyes, the judge took a deep breath. "Billy, with all due respect, I believe it is time for you to go home."

A few bystanders stepped forward, ready to back up the edict.

"Yeah, Billy. It's time for you to go on back to Brown Branch." Mayor Rayles said loudly, and others joined in.

"Go home, Billy."

"We don't need you here!"

"Take your stinkin' idees back to Brown Branch."

All eyes switched to the road as the sound of approaching hoof beats interrupted the conversation. Billy, waist-deep in the ditch, turned to see what was causing the ruckus. Horses bore down on the town in a swirl of dust.

"The stage! It's the stage!" someone yelled.

Wide-eyed, Buck scrambled out of the channel and took off running down the middle of Main Street, his boots kicking up manure and lime behind him. Johnny reached for the judge's chair and moved it to safety as the stage approached. The crowd scattered, ducking for cover.

Billy threw his shovel aside, dirt flying as he tried to climb out of the ditch. He turned toward the stage, wildly gesturing at the vehicle bearing down upon him.

Stumbling, he went down on one knee, still frantically signaling the driver. But the team didn't slow. When the driver finally spotted Billy, he sprang to his feet, throwing on the foot brake as he frantically hauled back on the reins.

The coach whipped past Billy, knocking him face first back into the ditch as the horses bounded over the trench. The animals whinnied and the old stage threatened to break apart as it slammed to the ground, rocking wildly side to side until it ground to a halt in front of the mercantile.

A passenger's head popped up in the window, hat askew, his eyes bulging with fright.

As the dust settled, Johnny calmly rolled the judge's chair to the gaping hole, and the two men peered over the rim.

Billy slowly pulled himself up out of the ditch, his dirty, sweat-streaked features clearly shaken. He looked at the judge, then broke into a lame grin. "See: horses jumped that ditch clean as a whistle."

Chapter 12

Lantern light spilled from the livery doorway. Mellow rays fell across the white-covered ground, softening the thick coating of lime. Johnny rubbed warm oil into a saddle, listening to the activity outside.

The Hostetlers had cleared out, and Barren Flats was settling down for the evening. Haleen's annoyed voice drifted to him, fussing at Alvin for tracking lime on her clean floors. If the smell of potatoes and onions frying in someone's skillet hadn't reminded him it was suppertime, his stomach would have.

The Brown Branch boys' fiasco had left little impact on Barren Flats. Life went on; the familiar was taken for granted—unless you didn't have a home to go to, or a mate to fuss at. Your own table to sit down to at night.

Johnny glanced up when he heard a sound. Jo stood in the doorway, framed by lantern light. The warm rays caught the red in her hair, and he was struck again by her resemblance to Ragan. Like her older sister, Jo was going to be a beautiful woman.

He turned back to his work. "Shouldn't you be home for supper?"

The young girl crossed the hay-strewn floor, pausing in front of a buckskin's stall. "I'm on my way there now. I saw the light, and hoped it might be you." She reached out to pat the mare's nose. The animal whinnied her appreciation, nuzzling the offered hand for a treat. "Aren't you eating supper with the judge and Ragan?"

Johnny massaged oil into the finely tooled leather. "I wanted to finish up here before I went back." The smell of hay and saddle leather mingled with the scent of fresh lime.

"You working for Rudy now?"

"No. Just lending him a hand." There were just so many widows' sheds that needed painting, and he welcomed the chance to keep occupied.

Giving the mare a final pat, she moseyed over to sit close by. "Got a minute?"

He had more minutes than she could count. "Better run along home, Jo. Your sisters will be worried about you."

"I won't stay long." Settling her skirts, she looked around the stable. "I've got a problem, and I don't know who to talk to about it."

Johnny continued to polish the leather. "Can't be much of a problem at your age."

"It's a boy problem." She turned doleful eyes on him, and sighed. "Benny Dewayne Wilson."

He flashed her a grin. "Benny Dewayne, huh? What's Benny done other than set you to thinking about things a girl your age shouldn't be thinking?"

"Benny doesn't even know I exist." She sighed again, crossing her hands in her lap. Her hangdog expression tugged at his heartstrings. Ragan had the same look when she had to do the mending.

Dipping his fingers into the oil, he gazed at her. "How do you know he doesn't?"

"I just know. He never looks at me, and if he does by mistake, he makes a horrible face, or does something mean like yanking my hair."

"Sounds to me like he's noticed you."

She heaved another sigh. "Not the way he notices Emma Tracy. He eats lunch with Emma. I hear them laughing sometimes."

"Laughing doesn't mean anything." He thought about how he laughed with Ragan. She could put him in a good mood real easy. "Just because a man spends time with a woman doesn't necessarily mean he's got his eye on her."

Jo brightened somewhat. "Emma is quite homely. I don't mean to be harmful, honest. Emma's my very best friend, and I truly love her. She's funny, and thoughtful, and doesn't have a mean bone in her body. But I suspect you'd have to tie a pork chop bone around her neck to get the dogs to play with her if you went solely on looks. "

Johnny listened to her worries, smiling on the inside. Lara and Lily would have had these problems by now. And a hundred more.

He was aware of Jo's eyes dissecting him as they talked. How was he going to discourage her interest without hurting her feelings? Jo brought out his brotherly instincts and he felt partial to her, protective.

When she continued to gaze at him, he asked, "Do I have lime on my face?"

"No." She smiled. "You're very handsome, you know." Her eyes went all dreamy. "Almost as handsome as Benny." She sighed heavily.

Aha—so *that's* the way the wind blew. Johnny chuckled and pushed the stopper back in the oil bottle. "Well, I have a confession to make, Miss Jo. I thought you might be getting a crush on me. Guess I was making a mountain out of a molehill, what with Benny Dewayne and all, huh?"

She started giggling, the snickers ballooning until she was in the grip of a full-blown laughing fit. Holding her sides, she laughed until his stern look finally halted her.

"*What*?" Did she find the idea that amusing?

Pointing at him, she laughed until tears ran down her cheeks. "You thought—you thought I was smitten with you?"

"Well . . ." He colored, putting the bottle of oil back on the shelf. Ragan was the one all the time harping on him to discourage Jo's attention. It clearly wasn't needed.

Jo doubled over, and her youthful shoulders shook with mirth. "I think you're a wonderful man, but *I'm* not smitten with you! I want you for Ragan, not for me." Her pretty features sobered. "I want Benny Dewayne."

He felt three times a fool. He'd been sweating bullets over her, taking all kinds of heat from Ragan, and she was working him for her sister!

Women.

They were all alike. A man didn't stand a chance around them.

Ragan rounded the corner, high-stepping through the lime as she made her way to the stable. Supper was on the table, but both Johnny and the judge had wandered off. She'd had to come clear to the other end of town in search of the men. You'd think they'd have enough sense to stay close when told supper was five minutes away.

Her footsteps slowed as she neared the livery. Jo's laughter drifted from the open doorway. What was she doing here at this time of day? She should have been home an hour ago. Stepping closer to the doorway, she listened to her sister's and Johnny's low voices.

"I fail to see what's so funny, Jo." Johnny hefted the saddle onto the side of a stall. "Besides, you should let your sister pick her own men."

"She won't do that. She's so busy taking care of the judge and Papa she forgets all about herself."

"Still, it's not your place to hustle men for her."

She touched his arm. "Don't be upset. I like you a lot. And you're just perfect for Ragan."

Jo trailed Johnny to the back of the livery, where he hung a bridle on the far wall.

"She's never going to find a man she loves in this old town—never, not here in Barren Flats. You hear how the town whispers about her being an old maid, and how she'll always have to put her life on hold so she can take care of Papa and the judge?" Jo continued. "But I see how she looks at you, all starry-eyed and love-struck."

Yeah, he'd seen those looks—even encouraged them. But he couldn't marry Ragan, no mattered how good that sounded—and it sounded better all the time. It sounded too good, and he couldn't do anything about it.

"You're talking nonsense, Jo. You know why I'm here."

Her chin lifted. "Of course. You're accused of robbing a bank."

"And you want Ragan marrying a bank robber?"

"Did you do it?"

Stepping around her, he moved to the back stall.

"Did you rob that bank, Mr. McAllister?"

He stood in the silence, listening to the gelding shuffle in its cubicle. An ache settled around his heart, a pain so hurtful he wanted to tear it out, rid himself of the constant reminder. Jo made him want family, want a life of his own where his every thought wasn't consumed with hatred.

"Did you, Mr. McAllister?"

Johnny closed his eyes. "No."

A soft breath left her. "I knew it! And you're exactly the kind of man I want for my sister." A delicate hand came up to touch his shoulder. "And though you won't admit it, even to yourself, I believe you'd like to be that man. I've also seen the way you look at Ragan. All soft and needy-like."

Shaking his head, he said softly, "Your sister deserves more than I can give her, Jo."

"My sister deserves love, Mr. McAllister, and I'm bettin' you could love her better than any other man could even think about."

How simple her trust was. How much he wanted to deserve it.

"You remind me of my sisters, Jo."

"I take that to be real special. Where do they live?"

Johnny sat down on a haybale, removing his hat. "My sisters are dead. They were murdered, along with my ma and pa."

Jo's face registered shock. "How awful for you." She reached for his hand. "That must be powerful hard to accept. Do you know who killed them?"

"Yes, I know. Dirk Bledso and his brothers."

Jo shook her head, wordlessly sharing his pain. "They must be awful, vile men. Do you have any other family?"

"None." He stared into space; Bledso's

ugly face swam before him. "Bledso took them all but my grandpa. He's gone now, too."

"You must be very angry about that."

Getting up, Johnny adjusted his hat to his head. "Yes, I am. I'm going to kill Bledso and his brothers."

Jo's eyes widened. "Mr. McAllister!"

"That's what I intend to do."

Her pretty features knitted with concern. "But . . . then you would be hanged."

Johnny got up and tossed a forkful of hay into a stall. "That's why you can't be getting your hopes up about me and your sister."

"The Good Book says, 'Thou shalt not kill.' "

He turned to look at her, his features tight. "I don't claim to be perfect, Jo. I'm just telling you not to get any ideas about Ragan and me. Even if I'm cleared of the bank robbery, I still have a score to settle. I'll never be free to marry Ragan."

Sagging against the side of the livery, Ragan pressed her knuckles against her mouth. Tears smarted her eyes.

The poster she'd seen of the murdering cutthroats floated to her mind, and she recalled how innocently she answered Johnny's questions that day about Bledso and his brothers, assuming he was simply making idle conversation.

But he had been dead serious.

She didn't for a minute believe he had robbed that bank—but was he capable of something more horrendous? Was he capable of killing a man in cold blood?

If he were out to kill Dirk Bledso, then the judge's work was in vain. Her work was in vain. Should she tell Procky what she'd just overheard, or should she plead with Johnny to reconsider before he destroyed not only the program, but more importantly, his life?

Turning away, she walked back to the house, struggling to regain her composure. If she told the judge, he would surely be forced to confront Johnny about the matter. But what if Johnny were only trying to scare Jo? Yes, scare her! That was very possible.

If Johnny kills Dirk Bledso, he's as good as dead.

Biting her lower lip, she sidestepped Minnie Rayles.

"Oh, hello dear. I was—"

"Not now, Minnie. I'm sorry, I have something cooking on the stove." Hurrying up the judge's porch steps, she entered the house, slamming the screen door behind her.

* * *

"Dearly beloved, avenge not yourselves, but rather give place unto wrath: for it is written, Vengeance is mine . . ."

The words lodged in Ragan's throat.

"Go on," the judge said, rocking in his chair. The evening air had cooled pleasantly; the scent of wild grapevine was sweet in the air.

She glanced up to see if Johnny was paying attention. If he was, he gave no indication. Her heart ached with the terrible knowledge of his secret.

"*I* will repay, saith the Lord," she read a little louder.

Judge McMann insisted on daily Bible readings. Some days he'd take the Bible from its stand right after breakfast, and other times the devotions were observed in the late afternoon following his nap.

On soft summer evenings such as this one, he often asked if Ragan would mind staying to "sit a spell" before she left for home. Tonight Ragan's chair was turned in order to catch the light from the inside lamp on the entry table.

Johnny rested his back against a porch column and idly moved the stem of a dried weed in front of Kitty, who was sitting at his feet. The cat's head moved from side to side, her paw occasionally stabbing the pretend prey.

Smiling, he surrendered the weed to the cat and picked up a slingshot he was whittling for one of Jim Allen's boys. He held it to catch the light, tracing his fingers over the wood to check for smoothness.

Christian Allen had cajoled Johnny into showing him how to down flies with a rock and a slingshot, then had entreated him, "Make one for me, Mr. McAllister. Pleeeease."

When the other five surrounded Johnny with pleas for him to provide them with a weapon, too, he'd been outnumbered. He was fashioning the second one tonight.

He held up the sturdy forked stick and sighted Ragan in the Y, moving it forward and back. Laugh lines appeared around his eyes, and he winked at her.

"Procky's asleep, and you're not listening," she said crossly. She snapped the Bible closed.

The judge flinched, but didn't awaken.

Johnny laid the slingshot aside. "I am listening—heard every word."

"You are not!" Eyeing him sourly, she opened the Bible and read. "I will repay, saith the Lord—"

He finished by memory: "Therefore if

thine enemy hunger, feed him; if he thirst, give him drink: for in so doing thou shalt heap coals of fire on his head," he supplied before she asked.

"Oh."

If Johnny could quote the Good Book by heart, why didn't he apply its teachings to his life? It had been on the tip of her tongue to tell Procky about Bledso all evening, yet she'd held back. Why? Was she afraid Johnny would leave Barren Flats if the judge confronted him?

Chirping crickets and the sound of tree frogs blended with the judge's even breathing. She forced her mind back to the scriptures. When she thought of Johnny pursuing revenge, the tightness in her chest nearly squeezed the life from her.

The moon settled over the housetop, bathing the old porch in its amber light. The judge snorted, then settled deeper into his chair.

She sat up straighter. "What's that noise?"

"The judge snoring."

"Not that." She turned to locate the barely perceptible squeak. "That sound, like a wagon's coming." She got out of her chair and walked to the end of the porch.

Johnny joined her and peered down the darkened road. "It's a cart."

"Whose cart?"

"I don't know. It comes by once or twice a week."

Ragan strained to make out the cart's moonlit silhouette. "It looks like Carl Rayles's rig. What would the mayor be doing out at this time of night—and who's that with him? Minnie?"

"It's not Minnie. It's another man."

She turned to face him. "How do you know so much about that cart?"

"I told you. It passes by here two, three times a week. It's usually close to midnight, but lately it's been coming by earlier. It turns just past the house and heads out toward Coyote Road."

She turned back to have another look. "I never noticed it before."

The squeak gradually receded into the distance.

"That's strange. Where do you suppose it goes?" She wasn't convinced it was Carl, but it did resemble the cart he used to haul wood for town events.

"Looks like it heads toward the water tower."

"I wouldn't think Minnie would allow Carl out every night."

"Maybe she doesn't know he's out."

She glanced at him, and they both grinned.

"Whatever he's hauling, he's not bringing it back with him. When they return, the wagon bounces. And the men ride back, not walk."

"Odd."

They returned to their seats. Ragan closed the Bible; Johnny tied a rawhide thong onto the slingshot.

Judge McMann's chest rose and fell in steady rhythm, and he exhaled with a light whistle.

"There's lemonade if you want it."

"No thanks." He studied the piece of wood. "Why didn't you tell him?"

Ragan rearranged the buttons in her sewing basket. "Pardon?"

"Why didn't you tell the judge what you overheard in the barn earlier?"

Her gaze flew to his. How did he know? Had Jo seen her?

Clearing her throat, she said quietly, "I trust that you'll do the right thing." She desperately wanted to believe that.

The judge stirred, and Ragan set her sewing basket aside. A moment later he drifted off again.

Getting to her feet, she held out her hand. "Let's walk," she said softly.

They stepped off the porch, and walked the flagstone path to the gate. Johnny unlatched it, and on the road, they walked in silence for awhile.

"How did you know?"

"I saw the hem of your blue dress as you left."

"You know you'll put an end to the judge's program if you follow through with this plan."

"I know that."

"But you're willing to do it? To put the judge's program in jeopardy?"

A muscle in his jaw tightened. "I don't want to hurt the judge, but nothing will change my mind."

"You know what the Bible says about vengeance."

"If you're suggesting I feed the hand that killed my parents and my sisters, forget it, Ragan. I'm not proud of what I'm going to do, but there's no choice for me. I watched Dirk Bledso destroy everything I loved. I heard my parents plead for their children's lives. I smelled the blood when he slit their throats." He paused, turning to look at her, and his eyes narrowed. "Years, Ragan. For years I've hunted him. I won't rest until he's dead."

Emotion choked back her words. Until this moment, she hadn't known she was in love with him. But she was desperately in love.

Somehow he'd found his way into her heart, and the thought of losing him to Dirk Bledso was more frightening than anything she'd ever faced.

"If I asked you to give it up, would you?"

He touched her cheek with his knuckle. "Don't ask me." His gaze softened. "If I could, I would. But there are some things a man has to do. This is one of them."

"But I care for you—care very deeply."

He smiled sadly. "I never intended for anyone to care what happened to me. That way, when the time came, I could do what I had to do, and no one but the guilty parties would be involved. I'm sorry you're part of it now."

His touch, fleeting as it was, profoundly affected her. Warmth spread from her cheek throughout her body and into her heart, where it somehow gave her courage to speak. Her answer came from her soul. "I don't want you to do it."

It was moments before he answered. "It's what I have to do."

She blinked back tears as he turned and walked back to the house. The sight of his lone figure tore at her heart. That was to be Johnny's McAllister's life: alone and lonely. Did she blame him for his bitterness? Not at all. Did she understand his pain? In every

imaginable way. If Bledso had murdered
Papa and her sisters, she would have the
same hatred festering in her heart. But she
wouldn't let it destroy her. That hatred *would*
destroy Johnny McAllister.

Even worse, now that she'd fallen in love
with him, it might well destroy her, too.

Chapter 13

⌒◯◯⌒

Founders' Day approached, and Barren Flats shifted into full swing for the yearly celebration. Held the first weekend in September, the holiday provided a time to let down. The raids were still coming on a weekly basis, but as Carl Rayles declared, "No ill-mannered, foul-smelling roughnecks are gonna spoil this year's festivities."

During the August town meeting, they'd voted to place guards at opposite ends of Main Street for the big day. Men would spell each other, allowing all to enjoy the celebration.

For the past three weeks Johnny and Everett had practiced out by the water tower, near the first of the old mineshafts. Most of the town's men now regularly visited the small stand of timber behind the church to

275

practice for the contest, so it was much too risky to go there to shoot.

The mining road was further away, and the spot of scrub timber was small but secluded. Hopefully no one would be concerned about gunfire coming from out this way, since hunters often foraged the area, scaring up grouse, jackrabbits, and other fresh meat.

And since several of the men had declared their intentions to practice for the upcoming shooting contest, most any gunfire was considered commonplace these days.

Everett fired off another round, ducking when the wild shot snapped a limb and sent a hail of dead branches crashing to the ground.

Johnny threw his arms over his head, protecting himself from the shower of dried acorns. He straightened, pinning Everett with a stern look. "You're still jerking your arm."

Everett fired again and grazed a chicken that had gotten out of its pen and wandered away. Feathers flew and the bird set up an ear-splitting squawk, beating its wings through the undergrowth.

"Shoot." Everett slipped another round into the cylinder.

Gathering the spent shells, Johnny eyed the target. Everett might as well forget the

Greener. There was no way in hell he would ever win it.

The clerk took studious aim and Johnny's hand shot out to relocate the barrel. Everett glanced up, frowning. "Thanks." He fired, shearing the top off of another scrub oak. The shrub caught fire, and fizzled out in a puff of smoke.

Johnny shook his head. "I say we quit for the day." Everett had been shooting for over an hour, and he was wild as a March hare today. "We'll try it again tomorrow. It's getting close to suppertime." He thought about the roast he'd smelled in the oven earlier. Ragan would be mashing potatoes and making gravy. She'd smell like vanilla, and her face would be rosy from the heat. "We'll come back tomorrow."

"Okey dokey—just one more shot." Everett leveled the pistol and closed one eye.

"Don't aim over there!" Johnny reached out to move the gun barrel, but it was too late.

The bullet flashed and drilled toward the mouth of the abandoned mineshaft. A second later, a horrific explosion knocked both men flat on their backs. Timber and rock shot straight up in the air as the mineshaft belched rubble like an angry giant.

Shielding their bodies from the falling debris, they watched in horror as the blast snapped all four legs on the water tower and the tank slowly folded in half, crashing to the ground.

A tidal wave swamped the embankment.

Female shrieks erupted. Horses squealed, and men shouted blasphemies as the ground rumbled beneath them.

"Earthquake!"

"That's no earthquake; that's an explosion. Look at the smoke!"

Men, women, and children ran down Main Street, past the churchyard, over the rise, and out to the old mining road.

"It's the shaft!"

"It's the water tower!"

"It's the shaft *and* the water tower!"

Johnny and Everett, lying amid the ruins of rock and timbers, listened to the pandemonium.

"My God, the water tank's gone!"

"What are we gonna do for water?"

"What the hell happened?"

"Oh hell, Everett." Johnny shut his eyes and laid his head back in the mud. He didn't know what could have been in that mineshaft, but whatever it was made a hell of an explosion. He opened his eyes, then shut them again. Everett had blown up the town reservoir. Groaning, he touched a bleeding cut on his forehead.

Hubie Banks and Carl Rayles dashed into the clearing, panting, each wielding a shotgun. When they spotted Johnny and Everett lying prostrate on the ground, they stopped dead in their tracks. Hubie's eyes focused on the hogleg still clutched in Everett's hand, then shifted accusingly to Johnny. Eyes switched to the demolished mineshaft, the crumpled water tower, then back to Johnny.

Struggling upright, Johnny cradled his aching head. "*What* was in that shaft?"

"Whiskey," the men answered in unison.

"What was whiskey doing in that shaft?"

"We were hiding it from our wives." Carl leaned down and sifted through the rubble, and picked up a jagged piece of glass with the letters "iskey" visible on it. Hubie looked as if he would burst into tears.

"Everett! Are you responsible for this?"

Everett roused enough to weakly lift his head, then fainted dead away.

"Son?" Judge McMann tried to make himself heard above the hullabaloo.

Hubie and Carl were carrying on like crazy folk. Red-faced and shouting, the men accused Johnny of ruining Founders' Day. Minnie and Florence paced back and forth in front of the Oasis, fit to be tied.

"Is it true? Were Carl and Hubie hiding liquor in that old mineshaft? Did you and Everett blow it up?"

Johnny glanced at Jim Allen and Austin Plummer as they passed by with Everett's supine form on a stretcher. He touched a knot the size of a goose egg on his forehead. "Whiskey could never blow up like that. What else was in that shaft?"

"Dynamite."

Johnny stared at Austin. "*Dynamite?*"

"Everybody knows there's dynamite in there. When the miners didn't find any gold, they left it and moved on."

"Everybody knew about this dynamite, but you still stored whiskey in there?"

"Well, sure. Dynamite's not agonna blow by itself. Safe a place as any for the liquor. Why'd you and Everett go and blow it up?"

He'd like to deny that he had anything to do with the accident, but that would leave Everett to face the town's wrath alone. As furious as he was at Everett, he couldn't let him take all the blame.

"We didn't know liquor *or* dynamite was stored in the mine, Mrs. Rayles."

"Hubie Banks!" Florence screeched. "How dare you store that whiskey in that mine shaft! Did you think Minnie and I wouldn't find out?" Hubie ducked when she landed a solid blow to his back with her umbrella.

Minnie was up in Carl's face now. "The very nerve! I distinctly told you there wasn't to be any liquor at this year's Founders' Day celebration. Did you think I wouldn't notice?"

The solemn expression on Judge Mc-Mann's face bothered Johnny more than the town's outrage.

Ragan's expression was grim as she dabbed cotton on Johnny's facial cuts. "Hold still," she admonished softly when he flinched from the sting.

He met her eyes, holding her gaze. He'd disappointed the judge; he'd made her unhappy. He didn't know which one he regretted the most. "We didn't know there was anything in that shaft," he repeated. "Everett wanted to improve his aim, and I told him how to do it. I was trying to help him win the Greener."

"You're aware of the terms of your sentence." He winced as Ragan dribbled whiskey on his open cuts. "You have a couple of places that should be sewn up. Someone will need to go for Marta when she finishes with Everett."

"What are we gonna do for water?" someone shouted.

"Judge, what are you going to do about this?"

"Yeah, Judge—he's your prisoner!"

Florence and Minnie lit into Carl and Hubie again, and the noise level rose until Johnny couldn't hear himself think.

Judge McMann wheeled his chair into the Oasis, motioning Johnny to follow. The crowd spilled into the saloon, still ranting among themselves. Judge picked up a glass and banged it on the bar, trying to restore order.

"Settle down! I can't hear myself think!"

Eventually, the hubbub quieted enough for the hearing to proceed. Accusing eyes centered on Johnny, now standing beside the judge.

"Excuse me—pardon me." Jo threaded her way to the front to stand beside the accused.

"Go sit down," Johnny said under his breath.

"No."

"Jo!" he snapped. She didn't realize what trouble her show of support would cause.

Ragan took a stance on the opposite side. The two women took hold of his hands and held on tight.

"Both of you, sit down. This doesn't concern you."

They ignored him as if they didn't hear.

The judge rapped for order again. "Folks! The least we can do is hear John's side of the story."

He wished he had one. Wished the town's animosity wasn't directed at him. Wished Ragan and Jo weren't risking their reputations for him.

The judge turned to look at him. "Son?"

He wished like hell he could erase that betrayed look off Proctor's face.

"I was teaching Everett to shoot."

A hush fell over the crowd. Hubie Banks stared daggers at him.

"Everett was practicing for the contest, the bullet went wild, and the shaft exploded."

His stomach tightened when he felt Ragan's grip tighten in support.

Shaking his head, the judge looked away. "You could both have been killed."

"We didn't mean to cause any trouble."

Everyone present knew the incident had not only depleted the town's water supply; it had also put the judge's program in serious jeopardy.

Jim Allen slowly got to his feet. "What are you going to do now, Judge? McAllister isn't supposed to handle a gun."

Judge McMann's eyes focused on Ragan's hand resting in Johnny's. She met his visual warning with respectful defiance. He looked back to face Johnny.

"Teaching someone to shoot isn't the same as handling a gun. You don't have to plow and plant a garden to explain how it's done. But the matter is out of my hands. The town's water supply is gone; it's up to the residents how they want to punish the culprits."

"Everett should be here! He's in on this, too," Millie Crocker complained.

"Everett's out cold," someone pointed out. "No tellin' when he'll come around."

Ragan tightened her hold on Johnny's hand and spoke. "It's only water. I know how precious water is to the community, but nobody was hurt or fatally injured in the accident."

The crowd fell strangely quiet. Anger was still evident, but it was obvious that tempers had begun to cool. Would they demand that Judge McMann send him back to Judge Leonard? If so, Judge Leonard would order him to prison.

"I won't let them send you back," Ragan murmured.

"How can you stop them?"

"I'll think of something. I can't imagine why you would betray the judge, but I know you well enough to believe you must have a reason."

The judge rubbed his forehead. He looked very tired. "Austin, will you accompany Mr. McAllister to Rudolph's stable and stay with him until we can determine what to do about this matter?"

The farmer slid out of his seat and made his way to the front. Giving Johnny's hand a final squeeze, Ragan released it, smiling. What he saw in her eyes was almost worth the misery.

Austin took his arm and walked him though the crowd. Julia Curbow reached out to pat his shoulder as he passed, her eyes warm with affection.

"You're a good boy. You were only trying to help. The Almighty will send adequate rain to replace the water in the tower—we'll make do."

Nodding, he allowed Austin to lead him away. It wouldn't take long to find out if the rest of the town shared Julia's opinion.

Common sense told him they wouldn't.

"Austin?" Ragan stood in the livery doorway, holding Kitty in her arms. The town had been meeting for more than an hour now.

Austin glanced up. "Any decision yet?"

She shook her head. "May I have a moment with Johnny?"

The farmer got up from the pile of hay, reaching for his battered hat. He looked worn out, older than Ragan remembered. Austin used to give her brown sugar treats when she was a child. She'd always sought him out in a crowd, holding tight to the old farmer's callused hands. When he reached the doorway, he turned to look back. "Can I trust you to be alone with him? You won't do anything foolish, will you?"

"I give you my word."

"That's good enough for me. Gonna get a dipper of water. A little thirsty tonight." He left the barn, and Ragan listened to his footsteps fade into the shadows.

Johnny refused to look up as she approached.

"I brought Kitty."

He raised his head, frowning, then dropped his gaze back to the floor.

Lowering the cat to his lap, she sighed. "I thought you needed a friend."

"Darn cat. Nothing but a nuisance." He reached for the animal, scratching her behind the ears.

He could deny he loved that cat all he wanted, but Ragan knew differently. He could deny that he cared for her; but she knew differently. She took a seat beside him.

"You shouldn't be here," he told her.

"Why not? I have a stake in your future."

He kept his eyes down, his features sober. "What future?"

"Your future—our future."

He slowly turned to meet her gaze.

"Our future," she repeated softly. "We could have one, you know. If you weren't so hell-bent on destroying it."

"You don't need a man like me. Ragan, be realistic. You need a man you can be proud of."

"How do you know what I need? Maybe you're more man than you imagine yourself to be."

He studied his hat in his hands. "I'm a man who's not worth all this trouble. Get that through your head."

She reached for his hand.

He still refused to look at her. "Didn't anyone ever tell you a man's supposed to make the first move?"

"I don't hold with all those rules." She smiled. "And by the way, you haven't kissed me today."

"Come on, Ragan—you can't be seen kissing a convicted bank robber."

She feigned surprise. "Don't tell me you haven't thought about it."

A grin played at the corners of his mouth. "I thought about it."

"When?"

"This morning, when you were dusting the parlor. Your cheeks were pink, and that piece of hair was in your eyes—"

"What piece of hair?" She unconsciously smoothed back a strand.

"That piece that's always in your eyes."

"So, hush up and kiss me now." She leaned closer, drawing his mouth over to meet hers. He tasted cool and sweet.

"Ragan, dammit, I'm bad for you." He drew her closer, holding her. "Why can't you see that?"

"You'd like nothing better than to convince me that you're bad to the bone, but so far, you haven't even come close. I've seen you with the town widows and Papa."

Settling against his shoulder, she sighed. "You're a gentle man at heart. You've made some foolish mistakes, and this thing with Everett is just plain poor judgment, but we're all guilty of poor judgment at one time or another. I think since I'm in—" She caught herself. "Very fond of you, I'm entitled to steal a kiss once in awhile, and also to be curious about why you decided to violate the terms of your sentence." Her gaze met his in the dim barn interior. "Wouldn't you say?"

His eyes focused on her lips, and she knew he was thinking about kissing her again. Knew it with every fiber in her soul. And there was nothing that she wanted more.

"You're fond of me."

"Yes, I am."

"That's crazy—"

She laid a finger across his lips. "You can't stop me from liking you very much. We may not always see eye-to-eye on everything—"

"Name me one time we've agreed on anything."

She couldn't, and she couldn't think of a single instance when they'd tried. But it didn't matter.

"Believe me, I've tried to deny I feel anything but compassion for you. But today, when I realized you could very likely be sent to prison for more years than I care to think about, I realized that my feelings went much deeper than that. I don't expect you to be in love with me, but I think it's important that you know there is someone in this world who loves you."

"How did your feelings go from fond to love so quickly?"

She blushed, but her eyes locked with his. "And I will be heartbroken if you carry out your threat to kill Dirk Bledso." Her heart was in her eyes, now. "Don't do it, Johnny.

Don't let Bledso take your life, too. Anger is eating you alive. I understand your need to avenge your family's deaths, but by doing so, you will be giving Bledso the victory. Is that what you want?"

"Bledso *slaughtered* my family."

"An eye for an eye?"

"That's right."

"Why not 'vengeance is mine, saith the Lord'?"

He stood up, running his hands through his hair. "Stay out of my problems, Ragan."

"I almost wish the town *would* ask the judge to send you back."

He stared at her in disbelief.

"It's true. If they send you back, Judge Leonard will sentence you to prison."

"That's what you want?"

"It's not what I want, but I don't want you dead, either. If you're in prison, you won't be able to continue this insane search for Bledso."

"Do you know what you're wishing? If I'm sent to jail, I could be there a long time."

"Death is longer. If you kill Bledso, they'll hang you. If you serve your time in prison, you walk away a free man. Free, Johnny." She reached out to take his hands. "Free to fall in love, free to marry, free to live again."

"Meanwhile, Bledso is also free. Free to go

on killing. I can't buy your argument, Ragan." His eyes softened. "I wish I could."

She rose and stepped over to him. Hooking her arms around his neck, she pulled his mouth down to meet hers.

The contact was electric. All reason left her, and all she wanted was his embrace. She was prepared to do whatever she had to, to spend a lifetime in his arms.

They stepped apart when they heard the barn door open, and Austin appeared in the shadows. "Judge wants to see you, McAllister."

"I desperately hope he sends you back." She softly kissed him once more, then whispered, "Don't do it, Johnny. Whatever the judge decides, don't continue this search for Bledso."

The citizens of Barren Flats wore solemn faces when Ragan and Johnny entered the Oasis. Judge McMann looked drained, his complexion pale. This couldn't be good for him. What would she do if something happened to him? The day had been taxing beyond belief.

He motioned toward a couple of stools. "Sit down."

Johnny sat down, and Ragan stood beside him. The room fell silent.

"The town's made its decision."

Johnny nodded. Prison. Ten years wasn't that long, but twenty was unthinkable. Ragan's hand tightened on his shoulder, and he knew he was only kidding himself. Ten years without her would be an eternity.

"Everett regained consciousness a few minutes ago. He sent word that he, and that he alone, was responsible for the accident."

Johnny took a step forward. "That's not true, Judge. I took advantage of Everett."

The judge peered over his spectacles at him. "In what way?"

If he told them he wanted access to a gun, that admission would seal his fate. If he didn't, Everett would shoulder the blame. He couldn't do that to a friend.

Ragan spoke up. "Isn't it obvious, Judge? Mr. McAllister is feeling a sense of guilt for his part in the accident. He was befriending Everett, and feels they both share equal blame."

Proctor eyed her impatiently. "Mr. McAllister is capable of speaking for himself."

"He's capable, but he won't do it."

"I—" Johnny began.

Julia Curbow was on her feet in Johnny's defense. "The gun was never in his hand. Everett swore to that."

The town murmured in agreement.

"Speak up, son. Did you handle the gun?" Procky asked.

"No."

The judge smiled. "I'm glad to hear that." He looked at Ragan, then at Johnny. "The town has decided to let you stay."

"Yesss!" Jo bounded to her feet, and Holly pulled her back down to her seat. She flashed Johnny a smile.

He couldn't let them believe a lie. "Judge, I—"

"Order! We aren't accepting testimony from the accused. We have made a decision."

The judge's voice was firm. "The decision to let you stay in no way excuses what you've done, John. But it seems we need that water tower more than we need a piece of your hide. You and Everett will begin to rebuild the tower, at your own expense, and you'll start come daylight tomorrow morning."

"Yes, sir." Johnny exhaled in deep relief. He hadn't known until now how much he wanted to stay. Building the tower back wasn't a problem—leaving Ragan would have been.

After supper, Johnny excused himself and went to the porch. Seating himself in the rocker, he went over the day's events. The town had gone easy on him. He didn't deserve their clemency, but he was grateful for it. Rebuilding the tower would take every cent he had, but he didn't begrudge the lost funds. It could have been much worse.

The screen opened, and the judge wheeled out. Kitty trailed behind him. When His Honor saw Johnny, he nodded. Proctor had been unusually quiet during supper. Johnny had the feeling that the town might have forgiven him, but it was evident Proctor hadn't.

"Thought I'd get a breath of air. The house is hot tonight."

Johnny got up to give the judge his favorite seat. "It's cool out here." He helped the judge from the wheelchair, into the rocker, then sat down opposite him.

Kitty bounded onto his lap, and he smiled. The cat purred and rubbed against his shoulder, wanting attention.

"Get down, Kitty."

"She's not bothering me, Judge."

Pulling his pipe from his pocket, the judge packed it with tobacco. Johnny stroked Kitty's head. The two men sat in silence on the porch, enjoying the faint breeze.

Proctor struck a match, and the flame illuminated his weary features. Johnny wished he hadn't been the one responsible for the dark circles under the old man's eyes tonight.

"I'm disappointed in you, son."

"I know, Judge. I didn't set out to endanger your program. I was wrong, and I apologize."

Fanning the match out, Proctor drew on the pipe stem. The pleasant cherry scent perfumed the air. Kitty settled herself on Johnny's lap and stretched out. In a few moments, she was purring softly.

"It isn't so much the program. I knew when I started it, I would have setbacks. It's more about you. I want you to get back on your feet—start living life to its fullest."

He drew deeply on the bowl. "I know you must wonder why I allow myself to be wide open for defeat, but there's something you need to understand. Giving a man more freedom is the only way I can be assured he can be trusted, that he does what he does because he wants to, not because he's made to."

The judge settled back in his chair. "I want to feel, beyond a doubt, that the person I'm working with can be rehabilitated. In your case, I had no doubt that you were a man of your word, that I could trust you."

Johnny wished the judge's words were filled with condemnation; it would have been easier. He heard failure instead, and knew he had put it there.

"You can trust me, Judge. I give you my

word: there won't be any more problems."

The judge snorted. "Hubie and Carl should've known better than to store that liquor in there in the first place."

"Well." Johnny leaned back, absently stroking Kitty. "I suppose you can take comfort in the knowledge that Hubie and Carl have a much bigger problem than a dry Founders' Day."

The men chuckled at the thought of Minnie and Florence lighting into the mayor and his bumbling accomplice in front of the whole town.

Then, Johnny said quietly, "I am sorry, Judge. I won't give you any more trouble."

Drawing on his pipe, the judge set the rocking chair into motion. The gentle squeak mingled pleasantly with the sounds of tree frogs. "I'm an old man. I've learned to roll with the punches. It's Ragan I'm concerned about."

Johnny didn't have to ask why. The judge had witnessed her openly holding his hand that afternoon. Proctor didn't want her hurt. Neither did he.

The old chair creaked back and forth. "She's like a daughter to me. I love that girl, and wouldn't take kindly to anyone who would cause her a moment's grief." The old man's eyes drifted shut. "Do we understand each other, John?"

"Yes, sir. We understand each other."

"Good." His head bobbed, his pipe resting loosely in his hand. In a few minutes, soft snores filled the porch. Johnny leaned over and gently removed the smoke from his hand.

Ragan pushed the screen open with her hip, balancing a wicker basket.

Johnny got up to help. "I'll get that for you."

She smiled. "Thought you might walk me home."

"I'd like that."

A full moon lit the path to the Ramsey place. As Ragan walked hand in hand with Johnny, the companionable silence was a far cry from the turmoil of the day's events.

"It's been quite a day, hasn't it?"

"I could have lived without it."

"Johnny." She paused in the middle of the road, moonlight playing across her feminine softness. "I'm glad you're staying."

He couldn't resist teasing her. "Three hours ago you wanted me sent to prison."

"I want you alive."

His hand tightened on hers, and they walked on. "I'll be staying a while."

"For me?"

"Could be." He drew her into his arms and kissed her. A hot, thoroughly possessive kiss that, hopefully, left no doubt why he was staying in Barren Flats.

"What about Bledso?" she murmured against his mouth.

He wished he knew. "Maybe someone will mistake him for a polecat and shoot him."

She drew him back for another long, leisurely kiss. "Just so it's not you."

Well, he had some time before he could go after Bledso, anyway. Maybe someone *would* mistake him for a polecat and kill him. Stranger things had happened. It would be nice to think about settling down in a place like Barren Flats, with a woman like Ragan Ramsey.

When they set off again, Ragan giggled. "Some thought the blast was an earthquake. What did you think?"

"I didn't have time to think. I was flat on my back, looking up at the sky."

They broke into infectious laughter. Each time one gained control, the other burst out laughing again.

"I thought Florence was going to beat Hubie with that umbrella!"

"She did! I saw her whack him a couple of times on the way back to town."

"She was as mad as that old hen that Everett nicked during the practice." He told Ragan about Everett's wild shooting and his attempts to teach him to hit the target. And why he was teaching him in the first place. It was hard to confess his motives, even to her, but he was proud of the friendship he had established with Everett.

"At least the mystery of the donkey cart is solved," Ragan said.

"I wonder how many late-night trips Carl and Hubie made carrying that liquor out there."

"More than they'd admit, I bet. There was a lot of fuel for that fire." They broke into laughter again.

When they arrived at the Ramseys', the house interior was dark. Ragan stepped up on the porch, and peered in the front window. Everyone had retired for the night. "I didn't realize it was so late. I hope the girls weren't worried about me."

Johnny set the basket on the step. "Do you have to go in this soon?"

"Well," she sighed, coming back down the steps. "It's been a long day, and you have to be up earlier than usual in the morning." She met his gaze, and burst out laughing again.

It took a second for him to join her. "Not funny," he said reaching for her.

"Shhh." She giggled, laying a finger across his mouth. "We'll wake the family."

He slowly pulled her to him, lowering his mouth to taste each sweet-smelling fingertip that still held the flavor of supper. When she murmured her pleasure, he drew her into his arms. "You're beginning to grow on me, you know that?"

She leaned closer, offering her neck. Pushing her hair aside, he kissed the fragrant skin, resting his mouth against her ear. "You smell good, too."

Closing his eyes, he drank in her essence. Moonlight, and the faint scent of the judge's tobacco on her dress. She fit him as if she were made for him. Maybe God was trying to make up for a wrong.

"It's Maddy's lemon water. I sneak a dab here and there." Her breathing switched tempos. "Procky said he didn't mind—it makes him think of his wife."

Turning her into him, he kissed her, lightly at first, then drawing her deeper into his embrace. She was all woman. Beautiful, desirable. His, if he wanted her.

And every inch of him did want her. Yet even if she were willing to marry a convicted man, he still couldn't have her and Bledso. Which was more important to him? Revenge or loving her?

Whispering his name, she returned his kiss with a hunger that inflamed him. When their lips parted, she rested her head on his shoulder. "What am I going to do about you?"

"I don't know, but for what it's worth, I'm real 'fond' of you, too," he murmured.

"You are?"

"I am."

"That's not good enough," she whispered. "Say you're fond enough of me that you'll stay alive for me."

He pulled her to him again, his mouth closing over hers. He wanted to live for her, more than he'd wanted anything for a long time. But something inside refused to let him give up his quest for revenge. A lifetime of hatred was difficult to put aside.

That night when he lay back against his pillow, the faint scent of lemon still lingered on his skin.

Kitty turned around on his chest a couple of times, then plopped down on the pillow. Switching her tail, she eyed him sleepily.

Could he give up his quest to kill Bledso?

Once the issue had been so clear-cut, but it was murky now.

Maybe his family's vindication wasn't in seeing a worthless, no-good piece of humanity eradicated, but rather from seeing him productive and happy, going on with his life.

It was a new thought; one he'd never imagined before. He closed his eyes, the taste of Ragan still on his lips.

But was it enough for him?

Chapter 14

The Founders' Day celebration was threatened by a rainstorm during the night. Thunder and lightning shook the ground, but by morning the skies cleared and a bright sun shone on the town. The grass dried, and outdoor activities began in earnest. Teams strung red, white, and blue bunting across both ends of Main Street, and store owners tacked patriotic streamers to storefronts.

Men swung heavy scythes, and weeds disappeared like magic. Women set up long tables in the churchyard and arranged chairs. The south end of Barren Flats began to look like a county fair.

Ragan waved to Jesse Rehop as his wagon rumbled past, loaded with benches for the spectators at the shooting contest. As the team of mules topped the rise, Jesse turned and yelled over his shoulder.

"Hey, Cliff. Come up here!"

Carl Rayles and Shorty Lynch dropped what they were doing and followed Clifford Kincaid up the hill.

Ragan frowned. What were they gawking at? Johnny and Everett were building the new water tower just beyond the rise. She could hear the ring of hammers from where she stood.

"Excuse me, Minnie. I'm going to see what's so interesting over there." She laid a tablecloth aside and walked up the rise to join the men. She could hear their conversation as she approached.

"Now, that's a fine piece of work. Makes the old tower look downright embarrassing."

"Shore does. Didn't know Everett had it in him."

"Don't think it's so much Everett as it is McAllister. I was watching them work the other day. McAllister seems to know what he's doing with a hammer," Carl offered.

The four men eased closer to the edge and peered at the construction.

"Built real sturdy-like. Take a heck of a wind to topple this one."

"Or a big blast." Shorty winked at Carl.

"Admiring the new tower, gentleman?"

Ragan tried not to let her pride show, but it was near impossible. The new tower was more than lumber and nails; Johnny was building a work of art. The Barren Flats water reservoir would soon be the talk of the county!

"Yes sir," Cliff said, "that boy's a real carpenter."

Ragan swelled with bliss, and she had to be careful not to strut as she walked back down the hill to rejoin the women. She glanced back over her shoulder, grinning when she heard Carl yell at Johnny and Everett to stop work and come join the Founders' Day Festivities.

"C'mon up here, Everett!" Cliff echoed. "You need to get in a little practice before that shootin' contest this afternoon."

The thought of Everett throwing his hammer aside and vaulting over the sawhorse tickled Ragan.

The change in Everett was one more good thing the town could attribute to Johnny McAllister.

These days, Everett walked with a new confidence. The strenuous physical labor had produced muscles that were invisible a month ago. Long hours in the hot sun had tanned the clerk's skin to a nut brown, and the hard work had perked up his appetite.

He'd packed a good ten pounds on his lanky frame, and the extra weight suited him well.

By nine o'clock, Main Street was full. Neighbors welcomed relatives from surrounding counties, and friends gathered in small groups.

After lunch, Ragan saw that Julia Curbow had Johnny cornered near the watermelon table, introducing him to all her friends.

"Jonathan, this is my best friend, Lydia, from Cedar Gulch."

Then a moment later, "Jonathan, this is my best friend, Lucia, from Brown Branch." The spunky widow dragged Johnny through the crowd, showing him off. "And this is my best friend, Mona Joann, from Tom's Canyon."

When Johnny passed Ragan for the third time, she teased in a loud whisper, "Why Jonathan, you are just the sweetest man; let me introduce you to my best friend."

Johnny finally escaped Julia's clutches and found a shady spot for himself and the judge. The two men seemed to be deep in conversation when Ragan noticed them. She considered taking her two favorite men a glass of lemonade, but decided they had more important things on their minds.

"I'm proud of you, son. You made a mistake, but you're paying your debt. One slip isn't going to impede your progress. And you've been good for Everett."

Everett was busy entertaining several of the town's eligible young women. The new water tower had made the telegraph clerk somewhat of a celebrity.

"He's a hard worker."

"That boy was raised in a strange family. His daddy took off soon after Everett was born. An uncle moved in and helped Everett's mother and grandmother put food on the table, but he was an overbearing man and never had much good to say about the boy. Everett's mother never quite took to her son, although she raised him with strong moral convictions and he always did well in school."

The judge sighed, giving Kitty a final pat. "Suppose that's why Ragan's always been so good to him. Everett latched onto her like a lifeline."

Johnny smiled. Who could blame him?

"From working with you these past few weeks, he's a different boy. Actually, he's no longer a boy; he's a man now."

When Everett spotted the two, he excused himself and walked over to join them. "Afternoon, Judge."

"Afternoon, Everett. Turned out to be a nice day."

"Yes sir, real nice. Can I get you a cool drink, sir?"

"No, think I'll just go over and help myself to another piece of Mazilea's chocolate cake. Lordy, that woman can cook." He wheeled off, heading for the desserts.

Everett fell into step with Johnny, and they walked to the area where the shooting contest was scheduled to start in little under an hour.

"How's your aim today?" Johnny asked.

Everett shrugged. "Not worth a hoot."

Johnny grinned. "Just remember to keep that arm steady."

"I'll try, but however the contest turns out, I'm not doing it for Ragan anymore."

"No?"

"She's in love with you."

Johnny shook his head. "Once my sentence is served, I'll be moving on."

"You'll break her heart."

The last thing he wanted to do was break her heart, but he cared for her enough to walk away.

"When I leave, Ragan can go on with her plans. She'll go off to school, and someday she'll find a man deserving of her love. I'm not the settling-down kind."

Clearing his throat, Everett dropped his voice and glanced around. "Shoot fire, I'd hate to see you leave myself. I've never had a real friend before...hope you don't mind."

"I don't mind, Everett. I was thinking the same about you."

What are you going to do, McAllister? Put your life on hold forever; let a woman like Ragan slip through your fingers so you can pursue scum like Bledso?

Bledso wasn't worth a hair on Ragan's head. Why the *hell* couldn't he let it go and get on with his life?

Finally it was time for the shooting contest. All the other men, their faces drawn with concentration, had taken their three shots at their targets. There'd been some mighty fine shooting.

Now, all eyes were centered on the last contestant.

Silence gripped the area.

Everett clutched the pistol and steadied his arm. Sweat beaded his lower lip. Staring down the sight, he slowly squeezed the trigger. His arm jerked upward, and the bullet landed somewhere on his target.

Carl Rayles checked the board for accuracy, then shook his head. "Well, that was close."

Everett craned his neck to see. "It was?"

"Weren't bad. Take your second shot." Mayor Rayles stepped back, his eyes on the large X.

Hubie Banks paced behind the benches, his eyes glued to the target. The brand-new Greener double-barrel shotgun, displayed in a leather-tooled case, rested on a nearby table.

Everett closed one eye, squeezed the butt of the pistol between both fists, and sighted. His eyes closed as the shot rang out.

"Hit it square in the middle this time!"

"Let me see that!" Hubie Banks pushed through the onlookers and snatched the board from the mayor's hands. He studied the bullet holes, then silently handed back the target.

Everett's eyes narrowed. "You're not the judge, Hubie. Go sit down."

The saloon owner stalked off.

Everett returned to his mark and, taking careful aim, fired his last shot.

"Half inch to the left of the X," the mayor called out.

"Dang!"

"Still pretty good shootin'. Definitely in the running."

The mayor added Everett's target to all the rest, and the men began to put away their guns. "That's it for the contest, gentlemen. I'll announce the winner of the Greener before the fireworks tonight.''

Everett flashed Johnny a relieved grin, and Johnny released the pent-up breath he didn't realize he was holding.

Toward dark, the festivities started to wind down. Women gathered the leftover food and packed it away, and lanterns were lit. Older children played stickball, or captured fireflies and put them in glass canning jars.

Mothers with small babies spread blankets on the ground, and settled down to nurse their infants before the annual fireworks display started.

The brand-new shotgun went to Hubie Banks again this year, but Everett came in third. The telegraph clerk shook Banks's hand and warned him that next year would be different. He turned and met Johnny's eyes in the crowd, and with a huge grin, saluted him.

While the prizes were distributed, Johnny wandered through the crowd until he located Jo, sitting with Fulton Ramsey. During the day, he'd noticed Ragan's father seemed more lucid than usual. Tonight his eyes were bright as he watched the activity going on around him, even though it was getting close to his bedtime.

Seating himself on the ground beside Jo, Johnny grinned at her. She smiled back.

"Guess who I just saw at the lemonade stand?"

She lifted her brows. "Who?"

"Benny Dewayne I-can't-live-without-you Wilson."

Her eyes lit with excitement. "Is Emma with him?"

"No, I saw her talking to Austin Plummer's boy." He leaned closer. "Benny looked like he could use a pretty girl's company."

Jumping to her feet, Jo tidied her hair. "Really?"

Chuckling, Johnny said, "Go on. I'll stay with your father."

Jo hurried toward the lemonade stand, fussing with her hair as she walked.

"Enjoying the day, Mr. Ramsey?"

Fulton turned his head. He smiled vaguely, digging in his vest pocket. A moment later he produced a wooden giraffe and pressed it in Johnny's hand. "God watches over them."

Johnny nodded. "Yes sir, he sure does."

The old man's face sobered. "But he also expects his people to look after themselves."

Johnny studied the older man. Ragan favored him in some ways. Same blue eyes, same shaped nose. Those eyes focused clearly on Johnny now, not clouded as they usually were. "Because I didn't stand up to the gangs, my son was taken from me. You can't let that happen. Give me your promise that you won't let that happen again."

"Mr. Ramsey—"

Fulton took Johnny by the arm, his eyes burning with conviction. "If I had stood up, the town would have followed me. If we had stopped the raids, Jacob would be alive."

Johnny was relieved when he caught sight of Ragan crossing the lawn, balancing three pieces of watermelon in her hands. Concentrating on the melon, she called out, "Anyone still hungry?"

Her smile faded when she looked up and saw Johnny's somber expression. She glanced at her father, then back at him. "Is anything wrong?"

"No . . . your father and I were talking."

She frowned. "Talking?"

"Yes, your father was talking about your brother."

"Oh, Papa." Ragan set the watermelon slices aside, and leaned down to adjust the light throw draped across Fulton's legs. "Do you want to go home now? Are you tired?"

Fulton rummaged in his pocket and came up with a wooden fish. He handed the treasure to her. "Two fishes and five loaves of bread were all that were needed to feed the multitude."

"Come, I'll—"

He suddenly flashed her a smile, his eyes clear again. "No, daughter, I don't want to go home. I'll stay for the fireworks, thank you."

Chapter 15

⁓ ⟲⟳ ⁓

"I thought I might find you here." The following Monday morning, Ragan set her bundles on the general store floor, and knelt beside Johnny, who was loading nails into a sack. Their eyes met, and she drank in the sight of him. He looked so handsome this morning, his dark hair damp with rain. "Good morning."

He leaned around the counter and checked that Mazilea was at the front of the store before leaning to steal a brief kiss. "I thought you had baking you wanted to do this morning."

She pressed her forehead against his. "Bread's cooling on the counter. It's raining."

He checked Mazilea's whereabouts again, then stole another kiss. "Did you come all the way over here to remind me that it's raining?"

"Of course not. But that means you can't work on the tower."

He dropped the last nail into the sack, and stood up. "Not until it lets up. Everett's catching up on some work at the telegraph office, so I decided to come for the supplies. Do you need something?"

She rose to face him. "You." Slipping her arm into his, she led him toward the front door. "Come with me."

"Where are we going?"

"You'll see." Breezing by the register, she called, "Mazilea, put two dozen nails on Johnny's account."

The store's owner was busy sacking cornmeal. She tied off a bag and stacked it on the shelf, waving an acknowledgment as they went out the door.

The couple stepped onto the porch, and Ragan popped open her umbrella. The sky was dark; the steady rain that had fallen since daybreak drummed on the tin roof.

"What's this about?" Johnny asked, ducking under the canvas awning.

Flashing an impish smile, she inclined her head toward the end of the street. "Follow me!"

They darted down the steps and across the street, sidestepping mud puddles. They were halfway down Main when the sky opened, and rain fell in torrents. By the time they reached the judge's house, there wasn't a dry thread on either of them. Racing up the porch steps, Ragan flung open the door, propped the dripping umbrella on its handle, and dashed into the foyer.

Johnny, close on her heels, closed the door behind him. They stood in the hallway, dripping on the polished oak floor.

"I'll clean that up later." Ragan impatiently grabbed his hand and proceeded up the stairway, dragging him behind her.

The noise prompted the judge to wheel his chair to the parlor doorway. "That you, Ragan?"

She stopped midway and turned to lean over the railing. "It's me, Judge. Johnny's going to carry some boxes down from the attic."

The judge frowned, patting Kitty who was stretched lengthwise on his lap. "Can't imagine where she gets all her energy," he said to the cat. Shaking his head, he returned to his journals.

Johnny and Ragan exchanged conspiratorial glances, and she continued up the stairs.

Rain pattered off the eaves of the musty-smelling attic. Ragan lit a candle and set it on a nearby trunk. Rubbing her arms, she smiled. "Procky hasn't quite gotten used to the idea that he can't run up and down the stairs anytime he wants to anymore."

Johnny returned her smile. "Should he check on us?"

"Maybe." She shivered again, glancing around. "We should probably get out of these wet clothes," she murmured, trying to still her chattering teeth.

"Fine with me. Right now?" He reached for the top button on his shirt and pretended to fumble with opening it.

She blushed, ignoring the innuendo. "We'll warm up in a few minutes."

He grinned at her.

She tried to ignore that, too. "You know what I mean."

His gaze scanned the cramped quarters. "So, what boxes do you want carried down?"

"I don't; I just thought the judge might think it improper if I entertained my beau in the attic."

"Your beau?"

She picked up an old blouse, and started drying off. "We are courting, aren't we?"

His gaze sobered. "I'm not in any position to be courting."

"That's for me to decide."

He stepped deeper into the attic, his eyes scanning the discarded furniture and crates.

"Do you spend much time up here?"

"Some. It was Maddy's sewing room. She said it was the only peace and quiet she could find, so she came up here most every day and sat in that corner by the window to read, or sew, or to just think about things. I've sorta picked up her habit. I do quite a lot of thinking up here, myself."

Johnny bent to look out the window. "Not much of a view. All you can see is the porch roof."

"I didn't bring you up here for the view." He turned around, and her eyes met his. "I have something for you." Taking him by the hand, she moved toward a table on the other side of the window. The surface was cluttered with sewing notions and stacks of cotton material. Scissors, thread, pins, a tape measure, and patterns attested to its recent use.

Ragan picked up a wrapped bundle and handed it to him. "Go ahead, open it," she said with anticipation.

Johnny unwrapped the package, and removed two new shirts. Holding them up, he stared at them.

"Do you like them? I finished them after breakfast this morning."

"They're nice."

"Just nice?"

He looked at her, confusion evident in his eyes. "What are they for?"

"For you, silly." She moved around the table, tidying up. "I had all this material just lying around. I made the judge shirts for Christmas, and I thought you'd enjoy having something new, too." The two shirts he owned were threadbare, and they'd been washed so many times that the colors were faded to nothing.

He seemed to be struggling with accepting the gift. Had she embarrassed him? That wasn't her intention—far from it. She longed to take care of him, the way a wife cares for a husband. She wanted to give him the family he longed for.

Thunder shook the old house, rattling the windows. Rain sluiced down the glass panes.

Johnny held one of the shirts up to his chest for fit. "I can't pay you for your work."

"Pay me?" She paused, hands on her hips, and stared at him. "I wouldn't accept money. They're a *gift*."

"I don't remember the last time I had a gift—or a new shirt, for that matter."

"Well, you have two new ones, now. I have a good eye; I think they'll fit," she said as he stepped in front of a mirror and held a shirt up to himself. With a devilish grin at her in the mirror, he unbuttoned his shirt and removed it. Her breath caught at the wide expanse of chest and dark hair.

His eyes caught her studying his reflection, and his smile widened. Slipping the new shirt on, he assessed his image.

"What do you think?" she asked eagerly. He looked powerfully handsome in the blue and black plaid.

"You did a good job."

"Thank you, sir."

"Want to come over here and button it for me?"

Blushing, she stepped over and began fastening the garment. His gaze captured hers, and her breathing quickened. "You're making this very difficult," she murmured.

He lifted a brow. "Sorry. Maybe you would rather unbutton?"

Her cheeks flamed. "Oh, you." She swatted him.

Drawing her closer, he bent to kiss her. She looked up at him, her heart hammering. "I love to make things for you."

"You want to know something?"

She nodded, loving him so overwhelmingly she felt that she might explode.

"I like you to make things for me."

They were the most heartfelt words she'd ever heard from him. And the most welcome.

His lips closed over hers while rain hammered the roof. She murmured as their tongues touched, pressing closer. Her wet bodice molded tightly against his chest. She could feel his heart beating rapidly and hers matched the erratic tempo. The rain's steady song wrapped them in a sensual cocoon.

Resting her cheek on his shoulder, she savored the moment. There had been too few good ones lately. "You've been so quiet the past few days. Withdrawn, the way you were your first few weeks in Barren Flats. I thought we had moved past that."

"I'm sorry. I've had things on my mind."

"Still Dirk Bledso?" she guessed softly.

Gently releasing her, he moved to stare out the window at the falling rain.

How could she reach through this shell he'd built around himself? How could she make him see that all he wanted was right here, standing beside him, with her heart in her eyes?

"It's funny," he mused.

Coming up behind him, she wrapped her arms tightly around his waist. "What's funny?"

"I'm twenty-seven years old. I have no home, no family, my horse was sold for restitution, and someone other than family has Grandpa's pistol."

She heard what he couldn't say, that he

had no purpose other than to kill a man. "Papa would say a man makes his own purpose."

"Your papa's wiser than I am."

Johnny was silent as he stared out at the rain.

Was she getting through to him? It was hard to tell. His hurts were buried so deep. But she wouldn't stop trying until she did.

Johnny turned from the window and drew her back into his arms. Closing her eyes, she held him tightly, surrounding him with her love.

The rain slacked off shortly before noon. The sun popped out, and the air grew steamy. Ragan mopped her forehead with her sleeve, but smiled when she saw the rainbow over the shed. Johnny was inside, working on window frames for Widow Keeling's house. He was inundated with projects now.

New church pews were in progress. A special Transformation Fund had purchased the lumber, and the church members donated the other supplies.

Town projects were mounting up, too. Minnie had put in her bid for a speaker's platform in the open space east of the churchyard. After donating one hundred dollars, she challenged others to do the same to build back the town. Donated materials were accumulating at an amazing rate. Barren Flats had enough work to keep Johnny busy for years.

"Johnny! Ragan! Judge McMann! Johnny! Ragan! Judge McMann!"

Ragan's heart lurched to her throat, and she reached the front door just as Everett burst through the gate.

"Johnny! Ra—"

"Everett, what's wrong?"

Johnny rounded the corner of the porch, hammer in hand.

The judge's cane pounded the oak floor. "What in the world—? What's happened?"

Kitty darted out the door in front of him, and disappeared under the rail.

Everett stood at the foot of the porch steps, his sides heaving, gasping for breath. He waved a paper in his outstretched hand. "Just came in . . . for . . . the judge."

Johnny took the paper out of his hand and handed it to Judge McMann.

"It's a telegram," Everett managed between gasps.

"We can see that, son. Who died?"

"No one *died*. They found the money."

"The money? What money? Just take a minute to get your breath." Judge McMann scanned the wire, then reread it.

"Well, well, well." He turned to Johnny, his weathered face breaking into a smile. "It's from Robert. They've found the bank money pouch. Located it in a pile of brush two miles out of town."

"That's . . . that's what I was trying . . . to tell . . . you." Everett pressed his side, nodding vigorously. "Word just came in."

Julia Curbow came through the gate like a shot, then Millie Crocker, followed by Maggie Anglo. Shorty Lynch and Hubie Banks followed Roberta Seeden.

"Is it true?"

"What does it mean?"

"Did they find the money?" Shorty demanded. "Is Johnny cleared of the charges?"

"Whoa now." Judge McMann raised his voice and rattled the paper for attention. "Let me read this again, so there'll be no mistakes." He bent over the paper and took his time reading the message for the third time.

"Says right here the money's been found and it'll be returned to the rightful owners, the patrons of The First Territorial Bank of California in Canyon City." He looked up. "Sadly enough, that doesn't mean John's sentence will be excused."

A chorus of disappointed murmurs rippled through the audience.

"Seems to me that if they found the

money, that'd be good enough," Julia said.

Hubie turned to look at Johnny. "Guess that proves you've been telling the truth all along."

Johnny took off his hat. "I had nothing to do with the bank robbery, or the money. But like the judge says, finding the money doesn't prove that."

Disappointment colored Everett's features. "I was hoping Judge Leonard would at least reduce your sentence."

"I was hoping that, too." Ragan came down the steps to join Johnny. They locked hands, and Ragan didn't care that Roberta's brows lifted.

"Well, the boy's a damned fine carpenter, and I believe he's innocent of the charges." With that declaration, Hubie turned and headed out the gate. Shorty followed.

"A hard worker," Julia added as she turned to leave.

"Deserves a break."

"Got a bad deal."

"Building a helluva tower."

Julia waved her fingers at Johnny as she left. "Keep your chin up, Jonathan. You're a good boy."

"Thank you, Julia."

Ragan squeezed Johnny's hand, and he squeezed hers back.

"I still think we could do something about this," Everett mumbled.

By mid-October, the new water tower was finished and pronounced far sturdier than its predecessor. Barren Flats declared Johnny, in Mayor Rayles's words, "The finest carpenter this side of the Mississippi River."

As far as Ragan was concerned, Johnny was the finest everything, and she didn't let a day go by without reminding him of it. Each week drew them closer, and she dreaded the day he'd ride away. If only she could make him understand that Bledso had already stolen fifteen years of his life; he shouldn't allow him to have more. She fell more in love with this complicated man every day, but did he return her love enough to abandon his quest for vengeance?

He caught her in the barn late one rainy afternoon, in a playful mood.

"Johnny—"

Backing her against a stall, he kissed her, long and so completely her knees threatened to buckle.

"I am going to miss you so much when you leave," she whispered when they came up for breath. *Please God, let him realize that what we have together is more important than seeking retribution.*

"I'm not going anywhere for a while." Moving her deeper into the shadows, his mouth took her roughly, possessively. She clung to him tightly, wondering how she could ever let him go.

"You were saying?" he asked a moment later.

"Mmmm." Coherent thoughts were impossible. "I was saying—" He kissed her again, and she gave up on conversation.

"In conclusion, I feel the program, while experiencing occasional setbacks, has proven effective. In the future, I recommend that the penal system offer rehabilitation to those first-time adult violators exhibiting the willingness and common sense to change."

Judge McMann closed the folder, and sighed. Outside a cold fall rain beat against the window panes. "And that's that."

Ragan drew a stitch through the pillowcase she was embroidering. "Feels good, doesn't it."

"Indeed, it is gratifying to know the book is completed. And with only a twenty-percent failure rate, the program was definitely a success."

Ragan glanced at Johnny, who was adding more wood to the fire. "So what do you think?"

"Me?"

"Yes, you, silly. Did we leave out anything?"

"No, except you don't know the outcome of my case."

Ragan glanced at the judge. "We feel certain we do."

"My life," the judge declared, lifting the manuscript to study it. "This is the most important thing I've accomplished for society, with the exception of marriage and fatherhood, in my lifetime. I wish Maddy were here to share this."

Ragan smiled, taking another stitch. "She doesn't have to be here. She knows, Judge."

Proctor's gaze moved to Johnny, even though he still addressed her. "Don't ever forget what's important in life. Love, family, loyal friends. It's very easy to lose sight of the things that count."

Ragan bit off a thread and tied it. "Can't agree more."

"Well." The judge yawned. "It's past my bedtime. I assume you'll be mailing the manuscript first thing in the morning?"

"First thing in the morning, Judge. Then I have an errand afterwards. Did you know that Mary Linder is getting married in two weeks?"

"Yes, her mother cornered me after church.

I hadn't realized Mary was old enough to get married."

"She's seventeen, Procky."

"Couldn't be—she was just born a few weeks ago."

Ragan grinned. "Mary's not feeling well, and in order for Estelle to have her gown finished on time, she's asked me to stand in for Mary's final fitting tomorrow. I'll mail the book, then stop by the seamstress's on the way home."

"Take your time; no hurry." The wheels on the chair squeaked as the judge rolled into the kitchen calling for Kitty. "Come on, old girl. It's bedtime."

Early the following morning, Ragan watched Everett unlock the telegraph office.

"You're sure up and around early this morning."

"I want to get this mailed early."

"Stage won't be here until late afternoon."

"I know, but once I mail it, I'll relax."

"Proud of it, huh?"

Ragan grinned. "Very proud."

She had enjoyed writing more than she'd ever imagined she would. The hours of research, then putting words to paper, was all very gratifying.

She hovered over Everett's shoulder while he weighed the heavy manuscript and figured proper postage. With a dramatic swoop, he held it over the mailbag. In a loud, authoritative voice he announced, "I now declare this project officially completed."

By now, a group had assembled to watch the historic moment. When the parcel hit the bottom of the mailbag, they broke into a round of applause.

Ragan took a mock bow. "I hereby faithfully promise to remain humble, although the book is destined to elevate Judge McMann and me to the ranks of the famous." She bowed again to another round of applause.

Still laughing and accepting congratulations, she left the post office. Bumping into Jo, who was on her way to the mercantile. She said, "Hi, there. What brings you to town so early?"

"Papa wants an apple pie, and we're out of cinnamon," the young girl explained as Ragan fell into step with her.

"Then by all means, we are off to buy cinnamon." The two sisters locked arms and giggled as they skipped down the center of Main Street.

Ragan felt lighthearted today, carefree. The money had been found, and Judge Leonard was bound to reduce Johnny's sentence if Johnny kept up his present cooperation.

"What are *you* doing in town so early?" Jo asked.

"Oh, I mailed the book this morning."

"Really!" Jo stopped to hug her. "Congratulations!"

"Thank you!"

They fell back in step, and Jo looked at her, grinning. "Have you seen Johnny today?"

"I see him every day, nosy."

The sound of hammers and saws coming from the church attested to his whereabouts. Johnny had mentioned over breakfast that the new pews would be done in time for the next Sunday's services.

Jo sighed. "He sure is good, isn't he?"

"Yes, he's an excellent carpenter. And a good listener, and a wonderful friend." Ragan's cheeks flamed. *The man I adore.*

"You're blushing."

"I am not. It's just warm this morning."

"Huh uh. You're beet red. All I said was that he's good. That made you blush?"

"No, Jo. Drop it."

"You don't think I'm old enough to understand, do you? Well, I am. I love Benny Dewayne, and I know what love is."

Benny Dewayne! Ragan resisted the urge to tell her sister this was puppy love, not the love of a man for a woman. That would come someday, and Jo would realize the difference. The way she'd discovered the difference when Johnny came into her life.

"It's true: Benny Dewayne is my absolute one true love. There's never been a truer love, except for maybe Holly and Tom, or you and Johnny. But Benny Dewayne and I—"

"Are much too young to be talking such nonsense." Ragan walked ahead, leaving Jo to try to catch up.

"I *wish* you'd talk to me about you and Johnny. I am old enough."

"Jo, there's nothing to tell. I admit, I care about Johnny—"

Way too much.

"And sometimes I think he cares for me—"

Not nearly as much as I'd like.

"But there're many reasons we can't be together at this time."

None strong enough that we couldn't overcome.

"I *know* he loves you," Jo stated.

"You don't know that."

"Yes, I do. I just feel it in my bones, Ragan."

Ragan sighed. Arguing with Jo was like arguing with a stump. "Feel it in your bones—you sound like Grandma Ramsey. I have to stop by Estelle's. Mary Linder is ill, so I'm going to do her final gown fitting. Want to come?"

"I guess so. I hear the gown is lovely."

"It is if Estelle's making it." The two sisters climbed the outer stairs to the seamstress's two-room apartment over the title office, and knocked on the door.

"You'd think Mary would want to come for the final fitting, ill or not."

"You know Mary. If she can get someone else to do it for her, she will."

A short while later, Ragan stood in front of the mirror, staring at her image. Mary's bridal gown was exquisite. Yards of tulle and lace, puffed sleeves, and a delicately embellished neckline. Estelle was simply gifted with a needle and thread. Ragan turned, studying the way the dress lay in perfect symmetrical folds. If she married Johnny . . .

Her thoughts wavered.

When she married Johnny, she wanted a gown exactly like this one.

"It's beautiful," Jo murmured, fingering the delicate Queen Ann lace. "Estelle, you're marvelous."

"Speaking of wedding lace." The seamstress eyed Ragan. "When are *you* getting married, young lady?"

"Someday."

"Well, it better be soon or I'll be too old to

make the dress." She swatted Ragan's backside affectionately. "Turn. Step back." She bent, adjusting the hem.

"Is Mary feeling better?" Ragan asked.

"I believe so. She wants me to thank you for the favor. I think she just has wedding jitters, but you know she's a little spoiled. Too pampered, I say. Good thing you gals have the same tiny waist. Don't know of anyone else who could oblige her."

A sudden ruckus outside drew their attention.

Ragan caught Estelle's eye in the mirror and frowned. "A raid?"

Estelle shrugged and knelt, slipping a pin into the hem. "I hope not. Don't have time to put up with one today."

Jo opened the door and peered down the stairway.

"What's going on?" Ragan turned in front of the mirror, admiring the gown.

"Nothing that I can see."

The seamstress and Ragan joined Jo on the porch and they cautiously descended the stairs.

Jo peered around the corner. "I still don't see a thing."

Estelle shrugged again. "Must have been a false alarm. Be careful with that hem coming up; Mary will have a fit if it gets soiled."

Ragan lifted the skirt and turned to follow. "Jo, could you help with the train back there, please?" As Jo gathered the trailing hem, the sound of thundering hooves approached and they all turned in alarm. Four riders were coming in hard, their dusty coats whipping the wind.

"Outlaws!" Ragan grabbed for Jo's hand to pull her back up the stairway and the riders galloped straight at them, firing pistols into the air.

Ragan frantically tried to push Jo ahead of her to safety, but the lead rider swooped down and scooped the young girl into his arms, laughing.

"Jo!" Ragan screamed, grasping her sister's arm.

"Ragan!"

Horrified, Ragan felt her sister's hand slip through her desperate clutch. For an instant she met the evil eyes of the red-bearded horseman, and her stomach heaved as she recognized him.

"Put her down!" She leaped forward and grabbed her sister's skirt. The outlaw threw back his head and laughed harder as Jo thrashed about, fighting him. The horse reared, and he jerked back on the reins, then swung Jo up in front of him, wrenching her from Ragan's grip. Kneeing the stallion, he galloped off with Jo's frantic screams filling Main Street.

Estelle fell back against the stair railing, holding her hand to her heart. "Oh my . . . oh my!"

Ragan ran after the horseman. "Stop. Oh, stop! Come back!" she screamed, watching in terror as the gap between herself and her sister widened. "No, no, not Jo! Please, not Jo." She stumbled and fell to the ground. The train of the wedding dress caught between her feet as she tried to regain her footing. "Not Jo, please dear God, not Jo," she sobbed.

The three accompanying riders shot the bank's front window, shattering the glass, then wheeled their horses and hightailed it out of town.

Ragan got to her feet and ran, oblivious of Mary's beautiful gown. Though she thought her lungs would burst, she ran faster and faster. Johnny—she had to get to the church. She had to find Johnny!

Chapter 16

Ragan stumbled up the church steps, screaming Johnny's name. She could hear her voice, but it was as if it came from somewhere far off.

Johnny dropped his saw and charged toward her, meeting her halfway up the aisle.

"What's happened?"

Nothing registered in her brain. His mouth moved, but she couldn't make out his words.

He shook her, but she didn't feel his hands on her arms. He shook her again. She knew he was trying to reach her, but she couldn't break free. Powerless to speak, she opened her mouth, aware she was crying hysterically. His look of stark fear finally brought her to reality.

"Ragan!" His eyes searched hers. "Calm down and tell me—what's wrong?"

"They have Jo!"

"Who has Jo?"

"That red-bearded outlaw and his men!"

He grabbed her arm, and they were running. Out the door, down the steps, across the churchyard.

He ran faster, pulling her along, shouting to the town's men as they passed each business. "Hubie! Shorty! Carl!"

People spilled from doorways and followed Johnny and Ragan down the street.

Rudolph Miller ran out of the livery to meet them. "What's going on?"

"One of the gangs has Jo!"

"Dear God!"

Timothy Seeden fell into step. "Why would they take Jo?"

Johnny's features hardened. "They don't want Jo; they want me, Tim. I'm going after her."

Carl Rayles took two steps for every one of Johnny's. "Now hold on, son. We need to talk about this. You can't go after her alone."

"Then form a posse."

"A posse!" The men exchanged dubious looks. "Where's Alvin? Someone get Alvin— he needs to handle this."

Ragan wanted to scream. Didn't anyone care about Jo? What if the men hurt her? What if they did the unspeakable? She couldn't bear to think about the horrifying possibilities.

"Now, see here. It's foolish to just ride out of here not knowing where we're going. No telling where they've gone with her." Hubie avoided Ragan's eyes. "Thank goodness, here's Alvin. Sheriff, what do you think we should do?"

"Eh?" Sheriff Lutz approached, cupping his ear. "Somethin' goin' on?"

Hubie leaned closer and held his hand to his mouth. "What do you think we should do about this?"

"About what? What's happened?"

Johnny struck off for the stable. "I'm going after Jo. Anyone who wants to come with me better find a horse."

"Now son, don't do anything rash," Mayor Rayles cautioned. "We're all worried about Jo, but we've got to think this thing through, not go off half cocked and get ourselves killed. Why—you don't even have a gun."

Jesse Rehop unbuckled his holster. "He does now."

Carl frowned. "What are you doing with a gun?"

"I wear it while I'm working, in case I meet up with a rattler." Jesse met Johnny's eyes. "You take it, son, and good luck to you."

Julia wrung her hands. "Jonathan isn't

supposed to have a gun. Don't you men get him in more trouble!"

Rudolph Miller settled the matter. "For heavens sakes, Julia, if this situation doesn't warrant a gun, I don't know what does. " He looked to Sheriff Lutz. "Don't you agree, Alvin?"

"Eh?"

"IT'S ALL RIGHT FOR MCALLISTER TO HAVE A GUN. HE'S GONNA NEED ONE IF HE GOES AFTER JO."

"Snow? You outta your mind?"

"JO, ALVIN!"

"Oh."

"Deputize him, Sheriff."

The elderly lawman stepped forward. "Johnny McAllister, I hereby deputize you— now it's a temporary thing, you understand. It don't set aside your sentence in any way. And it don't give you the right to risk your life, but it'll allow you to carry Jesse's gun." He paused, glanced at Ragan, then frowned. "Which one of the Ramsey girls did you say was missin'?"

"*Jo*," a chorus of voices yelled.

Alvin gave them a sour look. "Don't have to yell. Raise your right hand, sonny."

Johnny was quickly sworn in. Julia clapped her hands at the completion of the brief ceremony. "I'm so proud. Jonathan will make a wonderful sheriff."

"Deputy, Julia," Carl Rayles said impatiently.

Johnny turned to Rudy Miller. "I'll need a horse."

"You got it."

"Now, son." Lowell Homer put his hand on Johnny's shoulder. "I can't let you ride out of here by yourself. Jest wouldn't feel right."

"I'm going after her, Lowell, with or without the town's help."

Ragan's heart pounded so hard in her ears she could only catch snatches of the men's conversation. Why didn't someone offer to go with him? Why couldn't this town, just once, stand up and fight! She reached out and caught Johnny's shirtsleeve. "I'm going with you."

"You're staying here." Strapping the gun around his waist, he searched the crowd. "Anyone coming with me?"

The men hung their heads, shuffling their feet.

Johnny turned and strode toward the barn.

Jerald Hubbard tried to intercept him. "Be reasonable about this, McAllister. We're all married men. We have families to consider."

"And children to raise." Jim Allen fell into

step. "You know we'd help if we could, but who'd see after our womenfolk if something was to happen to us?"

Mayor Rayles hurried to keep pace with the others. "I feel certain they won't harm the girl. The gangs have never actually harmed anyone, just made a nuisance of themselves."

Johnny shook off his hand. "This is more than a nuisance, Carl."

Ragan's stomach balled into a tight knot. Jo would be frantic, scared out of her wits.

"Rudy, where's that horse?" Johnny shouted as they walked into the livery.

Ragan suddenly realized his danger. What would she do if he didn't come back? What if she lost both Jo *and* him to the red-bearded stranger? She put her fist to her mouth to keep from screaming. *Why didn't somebody do something?*

Everett stepped from the barn's shadows, holding the reins of two saddled horses, his gun at his hip. "I'm going with you."

Nodding, Johnny reached for one pair of reins and swung aboard.

"Johnny!" Ragan grabbed his hand, and her eyes beseeched him, so frightened she couldn't think.

His hand tightened on hers. "Go home and be with your family. I'll find your sister."

"Tom will want to help search for Jo."

"Tom isn't here, Ragan, and time isn't on our side."

"Please, Johnny be careful." If she were to lose either one of them, she couldn't bear it. "Come back to me," she whispered, tears streaming down her cheeks.

Gripping her hand, he said quietly, "I'll be back."

The two horses galloped from the livery a moment later and headed out of town.

"Any idea where they might have gone?" Everett called.

"No. What about you?"

"My hunch is Sutter's Ridge. It's an easy ride over the border."

"How far to Sutter's Ridge?"

"Two or three miles."

They whipped the horses faster. It was the first time Johnny had been on a horse since the day of the bank robbery. The chestnut gelding was smaller than his sorrel but well muscled, and he caught the horse's rhythm easily. His eyes scoured the road, looking for fresh tracks.

"Looks like they've been here." Everett pointed to a set of fresh prints leading into the canyon.

Johnny circled the area, studying the ground. It almost looked as if Holloway was marking the way, as if he wanted to be tracked.

Everett followed close behind.

Reining up, Johnny got off his horse. The tracks were too obvious. Something was wrong.

"How far do you think they'll go with her? Across the border?"

"Hard to say." Johnny removed his hat. "They've left a trail obvious enough for a simpleton to follow."

"That's what I was thinking. Why do you think they've done that?"

"I have a hunch they're laying a trap for me."

"You?"

Johnny nodded. "The red-bearded man committed the robbery I'm accused of."

Everett turned to look at him. "Are you sure?"

"Positive."

"What do they want with you?"

"They think I have the money. The day of the robbery, I was standing on the bank porch when Puet and his gang came out of the bank with Judge Leonard's daughter as hostage. I made an attempt to save her, and somewhere in the process I ended up with the bank bag. The pouch was lost a couple of miles down the road. I never saw it again, but Puet believes I still have it."

"And that's why they took Jo? They want to trap you?"

"That's how I have it figured."

Everett studied the ground, worry etched in his face. "What do you think they'll do to her?"

Johnny didn't want to think about that. "We have to find her."

He didn't want to think about the anguish on Ragan's face when he left her standing in the livery, either. He knew now that he was in love with Ragan, and everything else had ceased to matter. Not Bledso, nor vengeance—nothing but Ragan and her happiness concerned him.

He couldn't go on like he was anymore, always searching, bitterness eating him alive. He wanted to let go of the past and choose to stay with the woman he loved: make a home, start a family, be a part of Ragan's family. And Jo was part of that family.

Everett studied the horizon ahead. "Look over there."

"Smoke?"

A faint breeze caught the scent and carried it in their direction.

"Do you think it's them?"

Johnny mounted and kneed the gelding forward. "Stay close."

"Don't worry. You couldn't lose me if you tried."

Within a hundred yards of the outlaw's camp, they slid out of the saddle and crouched low. Male voices and laughter carried clearly. The smell of fresh coffee scented the air.

"Don't seem too worried, do they?"

That's what bothered Johnny. They didn't seem worried at all.

Everett dropped to the ground, then pulled himself on his belly to peer around a bush. The ring of mesquite surrounding the small clearing provided almost no covering. "That's them, all right. I see Jo."

Johnny eased closer. Puet and two other men stood around the campfire, eating and drinking coffee from tin cups. Jo, her hands and feet bound by thick rope, sat at the edge of the clearing.

"What do we do now?" Everett whispered.

"Why, come in and join us, gentlemen. We've been expectin' you."

Johnny looked behind to see a fourth outlaw with a gun trained on him. His hand automatically dropped to his holster.

"Don't try it, mister. One shot, and the girl's a goner."

Johnny and Everett stepped into the clearing a moment later, hands above their heads.

Jo's eyes widened when she saw them, and she struggled against the heavy ropes.

"Well, well, well." Puet stepped away from the fire. "You took the bait. Had you figured to be smarter than that, McAllister."

Jo whimpered, trying to work free of the ropes. One of the gang members leaned over and smacked her hand. She gave him a withering look, and he backhanded her. Tears welled in her eyes.

"Stay where you are, McAllister." A hammer clicked, and Johnny froze. He couldn't help Jo with a bullet in his chest.

"Let the girl go."

Puet laughed, and his eyes fixed coldly on Johnny. "I want my money."

If they knew it'd been returned to the bank, he'd have nothing to bargain with. "Let Everett take the girl and you can take me. I'll lead you to the money."

The outlaw's eyes blackened with fury. "I'm tired of your games. You're a burr under my saddle, McAllister. If Billy hadn't been so stupid that day, he wouldn't have mistaken you for me; that money would be in my saddlebags, and I'd be long gone from here."

Billy took the slur personally. His lower lip

jutted out. "I *told* you Holloway, I was jest tryin' to get out of there—"

"Shutup!"

"You fellas will never get away with—" Everett grunted, toppling to the ground when Billy struck him from behind with a rifle butt.

Johnny's eyes locked with Holloway's. "Let the girl go." They'd kill him when they discovered he'd lied, but at least no one innocent would die.

"You're giving me orders? You're not in any position to give orders."

A fist slammed into his gut, and Johnny doubled over.

"Let the girl go," he repeated tightly. "She doesn't have anything to do with this."

He saw the next blow coming and felt a bone in his nose give. *Ironic. He was going to die by an outlaw's hand, after all.* A hard upper cut to his right jaw sent him sprawling. His face hit the ground, and he tasted blood and dirt. The pointed toe of a boot rammed his side, and he groaned.

"Where's your people, McAllister? That gutless town refuse to help their own?" Pain coursed in black waves, and Johnny realized he was losing consciousness. He couldn't . . . had to rescue Jo . . .

"Aw, come on, Holloway. He ain't got the

money. Let's kill him and git it over with."

"Not yet! Make him watch us pleasure the girl," the fourth man said, wetting his full lips. "Then shoot all three of 'em."

Holloway laughed, grinding Johnny's face into the dirt with the heel of his boot. "First he'll tell me where that money is."

Johnny moaned in pain. "Touch her, and you're a dead man, Puet . . ."

The outlaw jerked him by the hair of the head and yanked him upright. "Fun's over. Where's the money?" A vein bulged in the side of the Puet's neck.

"If you kill me you'll never find it." And he wouldn't be able to save the others . . .

Puet shoved him down, and the kick connected solidly. Pain shot through Johnny's chest, and he rolled to his side. "You like this, boy? I can keep it up all day without killin' you." He delivered another blow to Johnny's ribs.

"Hey, you! Red Beard!"

Puet glanced up at the sound of a male voice. A fraction of a second later, an egg splatted in the middle of his forehead. He blinked, raising his hand to the sticky yolk. "What the—"

A row of wagons rolled from the line of mesquite. Grim-faced men, women, and children, toting large pans, buckets, and sling-shots advanced on the campsite.

"Uh-oh." Billy's hand dropped to his holster.

The other outlaws moved in closer. Squinting, the youngest one stretched to study Holloway. "That *egg* on yore face?"

"Shutup, you idiot!"

Suddenly all hell broke loose.

Potatoes zapped through the air. The vegetables slammed into their marks, and the outlaws dropped to their knees, clutching their groins. Their rifles fell to the ground, unheeded.

The citizens of Barren Flats stood up in their buckboards, hurling potatoes. When the potatoes ran out, they threw rutabagas. Then onions: big, fat onions that felt hard as bricks on a man's skill. Arms flailed the air as the outlaws tried to shield themselves from the vicious onslaught that pelted the men to the ground.

Then eggs. Eggs with yolks as thick and sticky as gelatinous glue. Rolling on the ground, the gang shouted obscenities as the unrelenting attack kept up.

"Make em' stop, Holloway!"

"Shutup! Ouch!"

"Shoot 'em!"

"You shoot 'em!" Puet shielded his head

with both arms. "I cain't get to my . . . *ouch!* . . . gun!"

Mazilia and Minnie crawled into the campsite on their hands and knees, scooping up the men's weapons, swiping pistols from holsters, utilizing their bargain day shopping skills to disarm the hoodlums.

Ragan dashed toward Johnny, dropping to her knees to check his injuries. When he opened his eyes, she smiled. "Hello, darling."

He struggled to focus. "Why are you wearing a bridal gown?"

"I didn't have time to change."

Struggling to sit up, he fell back. "What in the *hell* is going on?"

"No swearing, darling. Remember?" She leaned down, about to kiss his bloody forehead, but gave him a loving pat instead. "Lie still, I need to see about Jo." She rose, gathered the folds of Mary's lovely satin and lace skirt in a wad, and bolted off to untie her sister.

"Mess with my Jonathan, and you mess with *me*, misters!" Julia Curbow stood up in her surrey, loaded another batch of eggs in the slingshot, then hauled back and let fly.

Martha, perched daintily on the seat beside her, clapped with delight. "Atta girl, honey. Let 'em have it!"

The outlaws shrieked and wallowed in the mess, trying to protect themselves.

Shorty Lynch and Carl Rayles galloped by on horseback, balancing a hornet's nest on a long pole between them. As they reached the floundering outlaws, Carl dropped one end of the pole, Shorty leaned over, pulled the rag out of the hole, and tossed the nest. Angry hornets boiled from the paper womb and Carl and Shorty grinned as they galloped off, looking back over his shoulder.

The outlaws hammered their heads, batting at the stinging insects.

The youngest one's high-pitched wails troubled Blanche Payton.

"Poor child," she tssked. "Poor, poor child!"

"Don't feel sorry for that boy," Stanley admonished. He loaded a slingshot with another rutabaga. "His mama's prayers are the only thing that keeps these from being bullets."

In the midst of the chaos, Jo and Ragan raised Johnny to his feet. Clifford Kincaid and Austin dragged Everett to a nearby wagon. The telegraph clerk opened his eyes long enough to grin, then passed out cold again.

A wagon wheeled by carrying Jim Allen and his sons. Ragan heard the unmistakable sounds of "oinks" and whirled to see the wagon rattle to a halt beside the writhing outlaws. Jim's two oldest boys sprang from the bed, dragging a barrel between them.

The outlaws' eyes widened when they spotted Jim's two youngest curly-headed boys racing toward them. Flinging their arms over their heads, they shouted curses as slop rained down on them.

"You little snots!" Puet bellowed. "We'll get you for this!"

Jim's two older boys dropped the gate on the wagon, adjusted a wide plank, and hogs poured out.

The pigs squealed, making a beeline for the dinner table. The men's screams equaled the rooting sows'.

As Ragan and Jo supported Johnny past Judge McMann's wagon, they paused briefly.

"Jo, you all right, girl?"

"I'm fine, Judge. Just a little shaken."

"Johnny?"

"Fine, Judge." He grinned, trying to focus with eyes that were swelling shut. "Glad to see the town's decided to stand up for themselves."

"Me, too." The old judge beamed. "You look a sight, boy. You sure you're all right?"

Ragan smiled. "He needs a little tender loving care."

"Which you'll be only too delighted to provide."

Ragan smiled from ear to ear. "Only too happy."

"Well, don't just stand there, woman. Get your man home, and see to his wounds. Then take Mary's dress off." He looked at the soiled gown, shaking his head. "Pitiful."

Ragan blew him a kiss, and the three went on.

The judge sat back, drawing on his pipe. "Well, Alvin, I have to say it does my heart good to see the town finally stand up for themselves."

Alvin cupped his ear. "Eh?"

"Stand up for—never mind, Alvin. Let's go home. I'm getting too old for this kind of excitement."

"I'd say." Alvin flipped the reins on the horse's rump. "It's gettin' on my dinnertime."

Chapter 17

"My, my." Estelle stepped back, taking stock of the damage the next morning. The town's women stared at Mary's soiled wedding gown, shaking their heads.

Ragan frowned. "It's bad, isn't it?"

Minnie nodded. "Curdles the blood."

"Mary will be devastated."

"Oh my, yes . . . and with her weddin' only a few days off."

Minnie dipped a cloth in a pan of wood ash, lye, and water and dabbed at a splotch of yellow egg yolk. "Estelle, I hope you can sew fast."

"I don't like the thought of it, but I can make a dress in three days if I set my mind to it."

"Better start settin' your mind. This one's a goner."

The seamstress fussed about at her sewing table. "Never saw such foolish goings on. Why didn't someone think to defend the town with guns? Eggs? Rutabagas? Pigs? And a *hornets' nest*! Never saw the likes. It's a wonder they didn't get their own fool heads stung off. What's this world coming to?" She measured off a length of fabric and carefully stretched it out on the table.

Ragan didn't know what the world was coming to either, but she sure was proud of the citizens of Barren Flats. They'd stood up to Holloway Puet and his no-good gang in a remarkable show of solidarity. But best of all, they'd stood up for Jo and Johnny. Their loyalty made her heart sing!

Fireworks went off outside, and a cheer went up. Barren Flats was in a festive mood this morning. Holloway and his gang were prominently displayed in a large jail cage in the middle of Main Street. The four men sat in the bottom of their wagon, reeking of pig slop and muck, and nursing some pretty ugly welts.

"How's your young man, Ragan?" Estelle cut into the length of silk, critically eyeing the measure. "I don't know how I'll ever get Mary's new bridal gown done in time," she grumbled.

"Johnny's fine. He has some cuts and bruises, but he'll heal."

The way he'd responded when she'd gently kissed each abrasion before applying salve assured her he was none the worse for wear. He'd insisted his injuries were well worth the trouble, considering all the attention she gave them.

"Good heavens, will you look at that? Those outlaws are carrying on something awful," Minnie exclaimed.

"What's going on now?" Ragan moved to join her at the window.

Below in the street, Holloway let out a string of curses that fouled the air. Julia Curbow calmly walked over to the water barrel, dipped up a bucket, and doused the salty-talking outlaw. The women at the window cheered.

Stumbling backwards, the dripping victim sat down hard on the floor of the wagon. His cohorts doubled over laughing, then shrieked when Julia dipped a second bucket and doused them.

Ragan shook her head at the commotion. "I guess Alvin's not going to do anything to stop this public debacle."

Minnie giggled.

"Minnie!" Ragan scolded.

"They're only gettin' what they got comin'."

"Julia's not about to give up her post anytime soon, either." Ragan frowned as the judge's elderly neighbor dipped yet another bucket of water and stood waiting to administer punishment to the next prisoner who acted up.

The band below struck up a merry tune. Warren lugged his tuba across Main Street to join in and Hubie Banks and Austin Plummer locked arms, breaking into a merry jig.

Toward the end of Main Street, Shorty Lynch held a ladder while Rudy Miller nailed up a crudely lettered sign. It read: AIN'T GONNA TAKE IT ANY MORE! ENTER AT YOUR OWN RISK.

Ragan anxiously scanned the area. Where was Johnny? He was already gone when she arrived at the judge's this morning. She wanted to celebrate Barren Flats's unqualified acceptance of him.

Minnie let the lace curtain drop back in place. "I think we finally have our town back—thanks to Johnny."

Estelle turned to look over her shoulder. "Hand me that thimble, will you dear?"

"Ragan Ramsey!" Johnny's voice roared from the street below.

Ragan whirled and hurried back to the

window to see him striding toward the building. Behind him, Everett and a contingent of male supporters urged him on.

Estelle left the sewing table, frowning. "Now, who's doing all that caterwauling?"

Ragan grinned, so proud she thought she just might burst. "That's my man."

She watched behind the curtain as Johnny paused before Estelle's stairway, looking up at the second floor. "Ragan? Are you up there?"

Ducking back, with a teasing gleam in her eyes, Ragan motioned for Estelle and Minnie to keep quiet. "Shhhhhhh."

"Why? What's goin' on? Is he angry with you?" Minnie whispered.

If he was, he hadn't mentioned it while she tended his injuries last night.

"Ragan Ramsey!"

Everett, Shorty, Austin, and Rudy cheered Johnny on from the street.

"Go after her, McAllister!"

"Show her who's boss!"

Estelle frowned. "Oh my. There's gonna be trouble, I can feel it." She gathered the cut material and scooped scissors and spools from the table in the center of the room.

"Law, now he's taking the stairs two at a time." Minnie backed to the wall.

The door burst open, and Minnie's hands

flew up to cover her mouth. Johnny towered in the doorway, his bruised and battered face a mask of determination.

Ragan slowly backed up.

Covering the distance between them, Johnny scooped her off her feet and kissed her. A long, red-blooded, totally improper kiss that made Estelle drop into a nearby chair, looking faint.

When their lips finally parted, Ragan sucked in her breath, staring back at him wide-eyed. "Are you upset with me?"

He kissed her again, hard, pulling back only briefly to set her down and give her a stern look. "You could have been killed out there."

"So could you—and I wouldn't have wanted to go on living without you."

His eyes softened. "And I wouldn't want to go on without you."

"Honest?"

"Honest." His mouth took hers in a kiss that threatened her sanity.

Tittering, Minnie returned to lean out the window. The men below were hooting and catcalling, making a royal nuisance of themselves. "Stop all that racket, Carl Rayles! Have you lost your mind?"

Carl waved a stein in the air, grinning

up at his spouse. "Come on down here and join us, Minnie Winnie."

"Minnie Winnie!" She slammed the window shut. "That old fool's been in the liquor again."

Estelle fanned her face with a hanky.

Ragan was oblivious to the commotion.

Johnny's gaze held hers. "There was so much going on yesterday, I think I forgot to mention how pretty you looked in that wedding gown."

She blushed. "Oh, that. Mary wasn't feeling well, and Estelle knows we're about the same size, so she asked me to put on the dress while she pinned the final fitting. I didn't have time to change back into my clothing when the trouble started."

"Humph." Estelle had recovered enough to return to the sewing table. "Seems to me there's a lot of yakking going on. Seems a certain young man around here might ought to ask for a certain young woman's hand in marriage. Then, that certain young woman could have her own bridal gown—providin' I ever find the time to make it."

A slow grin started at Johnny's eyes and moved to the corners of his mouth. "Well, Miss Ramsey? What do you think about me staying on in Barren Flats? Making the town my home."

Ragan caught her breath. "Oh, Johnny—are you serious?"

"They tell me I'll be a free man in a few days. Sheriff Lutz says Everett is eager to testify that Puet confessed to robbing the bank, and that I had nothing to do with it. There's a sizeable reward on the outlaws' heads. Seems the bank at Canyon City was only one of many they hit. Everett and I are going to split the money." His voice softened. "My share will be enough to buy a small spread, and get a new start."

Ragan sighed. A new start—that sounded so nice. She affectionately traced his nose with a fingertip. "What about Bledso?"

"There's only one thing I want in my life. And I'm holding her in my arms." He caught her closer to him and held her tightly. "You're the only thing that matters to me."

"Oh, darling, how I've longed to hear you say those words."

Their mouths clung, and Ragan thought she might burst with happiness. Johnny was staying, and Bledso was finally in the past.

"Well?" He kissed her softly. "What about it? Ready to make this permanent?"

"You and me?"

"You and me."

"Is this a marriage proposal?"

He kissed her again. "If you want, I'll get

down on my knees and beg you to marry me."

"Oh dear. And I've promised myself I'd never entertain the idea of marriage to a man who has two black eyes and a split lip," she teased.

He shrugged. "Family problems."

She nodded solemnly. "Oh. In that case, I accept."

He lifted a skeptical brow. "Just like that? What about your schooling? Your plans?"

"I've decided that I don't want to go to school. I want to write."

"Write? Books?"

"Novels. I enjoyed doing research for Procky, but I've discovered what I really love is the writing part. Putting words on paper, writing what's in my heart." She hugged him tightly. "And there's no reason I can't do that right here in Barren Flats." She suddenly pulled back. "You really *do* want to stay in Barren Flats?"

He smiled, touching his nose to hers. "It's my home, isn't it? And the judge needs looking after. Then there's that damn cat to consider." His mouth made delicious forays up and down her neck.

Minnie and Estelle pretended unusual interest in a spool of thread, allowing the young folks their privacy.

"Until you came along, I hadn't let myself think about marriage, family, and home," he whispered when the kiss came to an end. "All I could think about was killing Bledso. But you've changed that; all I can think about now is you."

She tucked her head beneath his chin. "Oh, Johnny, I love you."

"I love you too, Ragan. I'm sorry it took me so long to admit it." Lifting her off her feet, he swung her around, laughing. "I *love* you, woman!"

"My, my," Estelle mumbled, stuffing another pin in the corner of her mouth. "This is goin' to be a headache. I suppose now you'll be wanting *your* wedding gown yesterday."

Proctor McMann's parlor was overflowing late Saturday afternoon, the twenty-fifth day of October.

Ragan had insisted the wedding ceremony be limited to immediate family, but that didn't keep Minnie and Mazilea from filling the sitting room with baskets of mums, and baking for two days straight prior to the service.

All of Barren Flats was invited to share the joyous occasion of Johnny McAllister and Ragan Ramsey's nuptials with a celebration immediately following the ceremony. A large picnic and street dance was planned and predicted to go on until the wee hours of the morning.

Fulton Ramsey sat on the bride's right, and Holly stood on her sister's left, looking pretty as a peach in a gown of baby blue silk organza. Jo and Rebecca were bridesmaids, each holding a colorful bouquet.

The best man, Kitty, sat on her haunches to the right of Johnny, a black bow tie around her neck. Everett, Carl Rayles, and Rudy Miller served as groomsmen.

Judge McMann beamed on the gathering with a grandfatherly smile.

"Do you, John Franklin McAllister, take Ragan Ramsey to be your lawfully wedded wife? Will you love her, honor her, keeping her only to yourself, as long as you both shall live?"

When Johnny turned to Ragan, she saw his promise clearly written in his eyes. "I do."

"Do you, Ragan Ramsey, take John Franklin McAllister to be your lawfully wedded husband? Will you love him, honor him, keeping him only to yourself, as long as you both shall live?"

"I will."

The wedding party laughed when Kitty

batted her paw at the judge's shin, adding her resounding, "Meeeow."

Judge McMann closed the Bible. "Then it is my great and personal honor to pronounce you man and wife. May God's love shine on you and your marriage. May your days be long upon this earth, and your blessings too many to count. And, I will personally add, may you be as happy fifty years from today as you are at this very moment. Now come here and give this old man a kiss from the prettiest bride Barren Flats ever produced."

Smiling, Ragan handed her bouquet to Holly, pecked the judge on the cheek, then turned into the waiting arms of her husband.

Red and white banners proclaiming the McAllister/Ramsey marriage lined Main Street. The smell of beef roasting over an open pit filled the air. The women were turned out in their Sunday best, and fiddles tuned up near the bandstand.

Beneath the beautiful star-studded night, Johnny McAllister stepped onto the gaily decorated gazebo and claimed a dance with his bride.

Shorty Lynch good-naturedly handed Ragan over with a knowing wink. "Take care of her, son."

Johnny's eyes locked with his bride's. "I will, Shorty."

Ragan settled into her new husband's arms, marveling at life. Not long ago she had believed she would never find true love, and that Johnny would drift through life, never knowing love or family ties. Tonight, he was here in her arms, and her joy was immeasurable.

Johnny gazed down at her, his desire barely concealed now. "Hello, Mrs. McAllister."

"Hello, Mr. McAllister." She shivered in anticipation of what was to come. What was it like to make love with a man? To be made love to by this man? She'd asked Holly what to expect, but Holly didn't know. Then she'd broached the subject with Kensil, but the older woman only blushed and said she'd get used to it. She didn't want to "get used to it." She wanted it to be wonderful.

She felt giddy with anticipation.

"What makes my beautiful wife smile?" Johnny murmured.

"Her handsome husband."

He chuckled, pulling her closer. "Happy?"

"Very happy."

His breath was warm against her ear. Closing her eyes, she relaxed as he waltzed her around the floor. Happy? The word was much too mild for the wild excitement churning inside her. She was ecstatic, delirious. Her emotions escalated from one delicious high to another.

He touched her ear with his tongue.

"You dance marvelously," she said.

"I get by."

He did more than get by. He masterfully guided her about the dance floor, holding her effortlessly in his arms. Her feet felt light as a feather as she matched his steps.

She suddenly frowned. "Who taught you?"

Pulling her closer, he whispered. "Someone who was not nearly as beautiful as you." His hands increased the pressure on her waist, and she thought she would die of anticipation.

"You dance well yourself." He leaned in closer, his tone playful now. "And who taught you?"

"The judge." When she was fifteen and clumsy, having no idea that dancing with a man could hold such wonder, such pleasure. She laid her head on his shoulder.

"Johnny?"

"Yes." She could feel his smile, as if he read her thoughts.

Her voice sounded very needy, even to her own ears. "I'm very tired."

"You are?" He held her closer, as one would a child. He kissed softly up her neck, his lips moving along her hairline. "Do you want to go to bed now?"

She nodded, feathering kisses along his warm neck. Oh, she did. Very much so. He smelled so good, uniquely him. What soap did he use? She couldn't think of anything that smelled this masculine, this sensual in the McMann household.

"Well," he touched his mouth to hers briefly. "Why don't I make our excuses, and we'll retire early. How does that sound, Mrs. McAllister?"

Just the two of them. Man and wife, alone at last. Oh yes, that's what she wanted.

"If you like, Mr. McAllister," she said with a broad smile. She was his wife now. There was no shame in a wife desiring her husband.

Sweeping her up into his arms, he carried her out of the gazebo. They swept past Shorty Lynch and Rudolph Miller, past Roberta, who turned to stare, past Minnie and Kensil, striding right past Mazilea and Muriel, whose forks paused in mid-air at the sight, and headed straight down the middle of Main Street.

The men hooted and hollered, stomping their boots on the dance floor, nosily expressing their approval.

Julia watched the romantic exit, clasping her hands ecstatically. "Now isn't that just adorable. That's *my* Jonathan."

Martha took another bite of wedding cake. "Honey, he's *just* too precious for words."

Ragan turned Johnny's face and rubbed noses with him giggling. "We're acting so rudely. I thought you were going to make our excuses."

He turned to shout over his shoulder. "Excuse us! We're leaving now."

When they reached the hotel, he took the stairs two at a time, then strode down the hallway and kicked the door on the left open with his boot. As he carried her across the room their mouths fused, then he settled beside her on the bed. They were unable to break apart for a good long time. Conversation wasn't uppermost on either of their minds.

Resting on his elbow, he traced the neckline of her dress. She studied his eyes as his hand stopped at the hollow of her neck. Tiny laugh lines appeared. "Not fair. Too many damn . . . darned buttons."

"You *do* remember the judge's rules."

"Hell, yes." He grinned. His eyes returned

to the row of buttons. "Did you and Estelle conspire on this?"

She leaned closer for another kiss. "Buttons are pretty."

"Not this many. There should be a limit on how many can be sewn on a wedding dress." He slowly released the top one, his tan fingers contrasting with the white material of the bodice. Strong, masculine knuckles lightly brushed her heated skin. He paused, waiting for permission to continue.

She caught his hand, and their eyes met. "I love you so very, very much. Do you know how long I have waited to find you?"

"Not nearly as long as I've waited to find you." He kissed her ever so softly. She trembled beneath his touch, and he immediately stopped. "Are you frightened?"

"No." Never frightened of him, frightened of the strange new feelings he aroused. Desire suddenly made her weak.

He rolled them to their sides, and his mouth was everywhere now. She drowned in the delicious sensations coursing through her body. She adored him, wanted him to assuage this incredible, exquisite ache he was creating. She slipped her fingers through his hair, grasping the thick waves, as the agitation heightened.

"Johnny?" she whispered. What was this

feeling? It was wonderful! She strained against him, needing to be closer.

"Not yet, sweetheart ... slowly." His mouth closed over hers, crushing her lips. Her fingers tightened in his hair, and the ache grew. Deep, deep inside where no man had ever touched.

Moonlight streamed through lace curtains. Sounds of celebration floated up from below. Desire spread like rich, warm honey through her. She strained closer, wanting, needing something ...

One by one, he worked the tiny buttons free until only her chemise impeded his touch. Lifting her slightly, he slipped the silken straps down her arms, his lips following the trail of bare skin.

She murmured his name, drowning in the emotions his mouth awakened.

The chemise was off. He looked upon his wife for the first time, and his eyes softened with reverence. "You look exactly as I knew you would look."

Her eyes met his in the room's dim interior, her breath coming in short gasps. "You thought about me this way?"

with the heat of his words. Every touch of his mouth ignited her.

"Every single moment," he murmured, his voice ragged with need.

Cupping his face, she returned his kiss, pleading against his mouth, "Don't stop."

His masculine chuckle brought chills of delight. "I couldn't stop if I wanted." His fingers traced her breasts, stroking, exploring.

Her body was on fire. How could a mere touch bring such perfect pleasure? Did he know how he pleasured her? Could he possibly ever know what his love meant to her?

His fingers found the hem of her gown, and his hand slid up her leg to unfasten her garter belt. He slowly eased one stocking off. His hands were gentle, confident.

Hungry.

His uneven breathing matched hers, now, and his need fed hers. Her body tensed. She tried to stem the urgency that threatened to consume her.

His shirt was rough against her nakedness. Emboldened, heady with passion, she reached to unbutton his shirt.

"Do you mind?"

moment later the fabric whispered to the floor. A mat of dark hair covered his muscled chest. Her fingers slid into the soft cloud, and she kissed his skin. His stomach tightened beneath her questing palm.

He unfastened her other stocking and slid it free. She wiggled from the gown, his mouth holding hers captive. When she was free of restriction, he pulled her tightly against him.

It wasn't anything like she'd imagined. It was more than she'd ever dreamed. It was right. Perfect. "We fit."

Chuckling, he buried his face in her neck. "Yes, we fit."

His hands traced her sides, bold now. Every inch of her flesh burned with the blistering contact. Every stroke, every new exploration drew her nearer to an unknown precipice, one she gladly embraced. Laughter drifted through the open window; she could hear the town revelry. Laughing, dancing, celebrating this most perfect union.

"Don't stop," she cried against his lips when his hands momentarily strayed.

The heat of his body meshed with hers as

Her arms tightened around him. She would hold him forever.

"It feels so good, so right, to be loved by you."

Lifting his hand to her breast, she whispered, "Hold me."

His fingers touched the pulse at the base of her throat, gently cupping her breasts, then spread his hand across her stomach.

"Like this?"

She nodded, unable to speak now.

"Or like this." His hands grasped her hips and he kissed her temple, her neck. Dipping his head, he kissed between her breasts; then his mouth trailed lower and lower.

A wall of heat consumed her.

"Please make love to me," she whispered. "Or I think I shall die."

Meeting her eyes in the dim light, he smiled. "My pleasure, Mrs. McAllister."

Sighing, Ragan ran her fingers through the mat of hair on his chest, damp from lovemaking. She pressed her lips to it, kissing

He pulled her mouth back to meet his. "Don't be too tired."

"Don't worry." She smiled, circling her fingertip around his navel. "I think I'm going to take to married life quite nicely."

"You think so, do you?"

Yes, that's exactly what she thought.

Their mouths drifted back together, and Johnny whispered, "Thanks for waiting for me."

"Thanks for finally showing up."

His hands gently investigated her ribs, and she squirmed when he playfully tickled her. "I guess the judge was right," he said.

"About what?"

"About life. He says it's funny—"

"That if a person holds on long enough, his problems will work themselves out," she finished.

"Do you believe that?"

She wiggled up the length of his firm body, kissing his worries away. "It worked for you, didn't it?"

He met her eyes, and the love she saw reflected there made her weak again with desire. "I believe I'm the luckiest man in the world."

Dear Reader,

This month, two of your favorite series return! First, don't miss *A Rogue's Proposal* by rising star Stephanie Laurens. Her series about the scintillating Cynster clan continues with this, her first Avon Romance Superleader. Demon Cynster has seen love bring his brethren to their knees, and he's not about to fall into this trap—until he meets pert Felicity and falls under her spell.

And if you love Draycott Abbey, don't miss Christina Skye's latest, *The Perfect Gift*. A talented jewelry designer is invited to the abbey and discovers a connection to the past—and an exciting, passionate love in the present. It's a delightful love story, filled with sensuality and, of course, a touch of Christmas spirit.

Contemporary readers have been waiting for Michelle Jerrott's follow-up to her exciting debut, *Absolute Trouble*. Well, wait no longer, because here she is with *All Night Long*. A long, tall hero—a man of the land—finds unexpected romance with a woman who just can't settle down. Warning: this story sizzles!

Beverly Jenkins is historical romance's premiere writer of African-American historical romance, and her newest, *The Taming of Jessi Rose*, is an irresistible blend of western romance and historical tidbits that give her books that something special.

And if you love Eve Byron's unique heroines and fascinating look at Regency romance, you won't want to miss *My Lord Destiny*, the follow-up to *My Lord Stranger*. It's delectable!

Avon Romantic Treasures

*Unforgettable, enthralling love stories,
sparkling with passion and adventure
from Romance's bestselling authors*

❋❋❋❋❋❋❋❋❋❋❋❋❋❋❋❋❋❋❋❋❋❋❋❋

SO WILD A KISS	*by Nancy Richards-Akers* 78947-7/$5.99 US/$7.99 Can
UPON A WICKED TIME	*by Karen Ranney* 79583-3/$5.99 US/$7.99 Can
ON BENDED KNEE	*by Tanya Anne Crosby* 78573-0/$5.99 US/$7.99 Can
BECAUSE OF YOU	*by Cathy Maxwell* 79710-0/$5.99 US/$7.99 Can
SCANDAL'S BRIDE	*by Stephanie Laurens* 80568-5/$5.99 US/$7.99 Can
HOW TO MARRY A MARQUIS	*by Julia Quinn* 80081-0/$5.99 US/$7.99 Can
THE WEDDING NIGHT	*by Linda Needham* 79635-X/$5.99 US/$7.99 Can
THE LAST MAN IN TOWN	*by Susan Kay Law* 80496-4/$5.99 US/$7.99 Can